Gingko Season

Gingko Season

A Novel

Naomi Xu Elegant

W. W. NORTON & COMPANY

Independent Publishers Since 1923

Copyright © 2025 by Naomi Xu Elegant

All rights reserved
Printed in the United States of America
First Edition

For information about permission to reproduce selections from this book, write to Permissions, W. W. Norton & Company, Inc., 500 Fifth Avenue, New York, NY 10110

For information about special discounts for bulk purchases, please contact W. W. Norton Special Sales at specialsales@wwnorton.com or 800-233-4830

Manufacturing by Versa Press
Book design by Chris Welch
Production manager: Delaney Adams

ISBN 978-1-324-08614-7

W. W. Norton & Company, Inc., 500 Fifth Avenue, New York, NY 10110
www.wwnorton.com

W. W. Norton & Company Ltd., 15 Carlisle Street, London W1D 3BS

1 2 3 4 5 6 7 8 9 0

For my parents

The birth and the close of day, the course of the evening star as it cast its silvery light over copse and field, the changing seasons, the varying vistas, the concerts of birdsong, the murmuring waters—everything struck him as if he were seeing it for the first time.

—Napoleon Bonaparte, *Clisson and Eugénie*

One

ONE

That September I was spending more time than usual on the fire escape, climbing through the window of my bedroom when the weather was fine or just after it had rained. The fire escape overlooked an empty lot, and on clear nights the amalgamation of light from the streetlamps, the LEDs and the neon signs, the apartment windows, the lines of ceiling-strip fluorescence in empty office buildings, the cars and buses and trucks, and, farther afield, the detrital glow of Delawarean and New Jerseyan industry and manufacturing failed to entirely obscure the stars. On those evenings I leaned against the brick wall that separated my bedroom from the outside world and wondered if they were going to build something in that empty lot, and how it would affect my prospect of survival in the event of a conflagration.

There was a Buddhist monastery below the apartment, and because I was afraid of startling or upsetting the monks if I appeared suddenly at their window, I had never descended the emergency stairs. During the day, if I stayed home, I could hear the monks chanting sutras, their voices coming up through the floorboards to me as I lay in bed. When I went out to work in the mornings the smell of incense suffused the common hallway between the two sets of double-latched doors, where the mailboxes were located, and I would stop in the anteroom, pretending to check for letters and bills if someone else was passing through, turning the small key in the lock without opening the door. If I was alone in the vestibule I didn't need to perform the mail-checking pantomime and was able instead to stand in the quiet, inexplicably carpeted room, breathing in the scent of frankincense and cloves. Across the street was a kung-fu academy led by an imperious man with a walrus mustache, and every day after school, children in tracksuits would file up the stairs and reappear an hour or two later, chattering and pummeling each other, their cheeks flushed, sweat plastering locks of damp hair to their small foreheads.

I shared the apartment with a couple in their late thirties and a rotating selection of youngish men starting out jobs in management consulting or finance, many of whom were the first in their families to attend college and were renting the room next to mine while they waited for a few weeks of paychecks to accumulate, after which they possessed enough cash and the requisite proof of employment to move out of Chinatown and rent a studio in a building with a doorman off Rittenhouse Square, or perhaps in one of the newer developments with large windows that faced the Schuylkill River.

Although the young men replaced one another like seasons, the couple, whose names were Xinwei and Raymond, had already been living in the apartment before I arrived and, I assumed, would indefinitely remain one of its fixtures. They were not the landlords nor did they seem to have any special relationship with the landlord; they did not work in particularly low-paying fields; they were easy to live with, and they appeared sociable, friendly, and well adjusted. It seemed rude to ask why they had chosen to live for so long with an ever-changing cast of younger strangers in a cramped flat in Chinatown, and so their presence became, for me, mystifying but inoffensive. Xinwei was from Guang-dong, and I spoke with her in Mandarin; Raymond was from Philly, half-Vietnamese and half-Chinese, and I spoke with him in English; to one another they spoke in Cantonese. If we were all present at the same time and equal participants in the conver-sation we resorted to English, so that no one person would be excluded, but this was still not ideal, because Xinwei, though she understood everything, held herself to exacting standards and in English struggled to articulate her thoughts with a level of preci-sion that satisfied her, so it almost always ended up that Raymond and I spoke in English and she responded to us in both Mandarin and Cantonese, translating herself twice for our benefit. If Ray-mond or I tried to address her in the language we spoke with her when the other was not around, she would switch to English, a tacit signal of her displeasure, and, suitably chagrined, we would revert, and she would do the same.

Often Raymond had his relatives over. Other times he and Xinwei invited friends to play cards or dice, which I joined if I had nothing else to do, because it was more fun than staying in my room and listening to them laugh and yell into the early hours. The living room of the apartment was too small to fit much furniture. For the days they hosted family dinners, they had pur-chased three collapsible camping tables, which they arranged in a row in front of the sofa. To get to the bathroom or the kitchen or the front door I had to bypass this makeshift banquet, sidling past curious aunts and uncles, wary children, and blinking grand-relations, and, so as not to risk toppling the densely packed and precariously perched dishes of white rice, pork ribs, steamed fish, or water spinach—I had always thought it a shame that its Chinese name, "empty heart," had not migrated into the English translation—I was obliged to press myself against the wall and shuffle sideways, shouting greetings as I passed.

The occupant of the third room, six foot five with lugubrious basset-hound eyes and an oppressive hunched posture, had the habit of ordering McDonald's, and the strong smell of the fast food—either nauseating or tantalizing, depending on my own level of hunger—seeped through the thin wall separating his room from mine, raising in me a fury so potent I found it impossible to concentrate on anything else, and I had to climb out and sit for a while on the fire escape until the rage subsided or the scent disappeared. Apart from the McDonald's, his intrusive behaviors included talking in his sleep so loudly that it woke me up in the middle of the night, and practicing German on an app that had him repeat the robotic sentences in his low and dour tone. *Ich komme aus Amerika. Mein Hemd ist blau. Wo ist der Bahnhof?* One of the only times we spoke, we exchanged basic biographical details and friendly smiles, and I began to feel guilty for having silently seethed. I made a lighthearted reference to his somnolent chatter, and, familiar now, he told me that he also sleepwalked, and that earlier in the week he'd woken up in the morning to find that every single one of his socks had been removed from their drawer and stuffed under his mattress in an orderly row. After that I always locked the door before I went to bed.

When she was able to leave the office at a reasonable hour, my friend Apple would join me on the fire escape to drink and chat, I against the brick wall and she facing me, resting her elbows on the railing, her back to the empty lot, a position I could never manage because it induced in me a terrible sensation of vertigo, similar to the feeling I got when I traveled up very long escalators. On this particular evening, arranged just so, we were discussing her day at work. She had recently started a job at a large law firm, and had been assigned to a new team that was overseeing the takeover of a small electronic cigarette startup by a large tobacco company.

"Pee," she was saying—her affectionate rendering of my name, Penelope, an abbreviation that I hated but she loved—"it's all true. Lawyers are evil. Like, cartoon villain shit. I'm kind of into it."

"You're into it?"

"I feel like it's not immoral, because I myself vape," Apple said. "And I'm learning a lot about M&A. But everyone on my team kind of sucks. They all brag about how late they worked and how little they slept, which is very college, you know? And how much they hate their clients, and how much more they hate the losers who criticize them. And it's not like anyone even really criticizes them, I mean no one they've actually met, but they just bitch about these hypothetical people, who definitely do exist but who they've never talked to, and who they imagine would call them immoral, or amoral, they use the words interchangeably, I don't think they know the difference. But like it's all about the money for them. And the status. Which it is for me too, but they take the fun out of it. We get these free lunches every day, they send out an email on Sundays with the whole menu for that week, like taco Tuesdays, Wienerschnitzel Wednesdays, fish Fridays."

"Fish Fridays? Are they Catholic?"

"The food is really good too, like gourmet level, and there's dessert and starters and beverages and everything. Gluten-free options, vegetarian, vegan, kosher, Jain. But all the senior lawyers order salads or whatever from outside, like it's not cool to eat the provided lunch. Do you see what I mean?"

"You want to eat the lunch, but because of the social pressure you forgo it."

"No, I eat it, I just resent that I feel self-conscious about it."

"You should quit," I said, "and become a human rights lawyer."

Apple snorted. "And do what? Work for the UN?"

"What's wrong with the UN?"

"It's impotent. I want to wield power."

"Civil rights lawyer? That's different, right?"

"Yes, but I have loans to pay off, so no."

Apple sighed and extracted a silver vape pen from her pocket and took a long drag, as if to prove her earlier statement. I always wished I smoked cigarettes, because they looked really cool, but I never wished I vaped.

Apple and I met in college, in a half-credit samba ensemble class that she was taking to boost her grade point average for law school, and which I was taking because I was interested in cultivating a low-pressure hobby that couldn't be carried out alone or on a computer. Apple was assigned the caixa, a snare drum, which was by far the best instrument. The caixa made sexy sounds and came with a shoulder sling: it was the electric guitar of samba ensemble. I was given the tambourine. We were both terrible at our instruments, Apple because weekly attendance and participation in the end-of-semester performance were the only requirements for an A grade, I because I hated the tambourine. Secretly I coveted the surdo, a drum the size of my whole body, taut with goat hide and beaten with mallets, a drum whose sound made me feel like my bones were alive and humming inside my skin.

One day in samba class, early in our friendship, Apple revealed to me the genesis of her name. Her father, a software engineer, had christened his children according to his aspirations for them, which was to become software engineers. "He could have named me, like, Ada, after the woman who literally invented computers," she had complained, swiping absent-mindedly at the skin of the glorious caixa while I rattled my miserable tambourine. I asked her if she'd known that Ada was the daughter of Lord Byron, and she said that she hadn't, but that it made sense to her, and the math and computer stuff was probably a reaction against her philandering poet dad. "Anyway, guess what my brother's name is? Steve." Both children resisted their father's will and opted out of software engineering. Dentistry was Steve's compromise; corporate law would be Apple's. She had readied herself for it since high school with the grim diligence of a public executioner. Now, after years of mock trials, she was at the guillotine for the first time, watching tumbrels of American teenagers roll toward her.

"I don't think I know the difference between immoral and amoral," I admitted.

"I always thought of it as, people are immoral and non-people are amoral. Like markets, rocks, ants. Anything that doesn't possess a moral code."

"They always call psychopaths amoral in TV shows."

"They call a lot of people a lot of things in TV shows."

"What about scruples?"

"What about them?"

"I don't know," I said. "Can you make rings?"

She sucked at her pen and then made a funnel shape with her mouth and huffed little puffs of milky smoke, the circles growing wider and wider as they drifted into the night.

"How was your day?" she said, after she was done.

I told her that it had been good. After some hesitation I added, "I think I'm in love."

That morning, I had taken advantage of the bright and temperate early autumn weather and biked to work. After hauling my bicycle, a scuffed red-and-black hybrid with a top tube, which apparently classified it as a men's bike, but which I rode and loved anyway, down the stairs of the building, pausing as I usually did in the vestibule to bask in the Buddhist aromas, I walked through Chinatown, where the trucks carrying fresh choy sum, freeze-dried mushrooms, and other special foodstuffs were delivering their wares to the wet market. I passed the tattered Obamacare sign and my favorite douhua stall, and then underneath the arch, which proudly declared 埠華城費—"Philadelphia Chinatown." I mounted my bicycle and set off down Tenth Street and up Spruce and watched as the buildings became gradually more ornate and less run-down, the trees more manicured, the shopfront windows larger and more imposing until they began to fall away around Twenty-First Street, where the lanes narrowed and the cars thinned out and the rowhouses blinked with alternating colors: brick, cream, cerulean, pink. Acceleration and a gear change for the ramp up the South Street Bridge, past the AT&T fortress—brutal brutalism, a monument to corporate offense—and on the other side of the bridge the museum.

The museum's side entrance was closer to the side of the street I was on when I arrived from downtown, while the main entrance required me to continue biking for another two minutes then, once I was inside, to loop back through the exhibition halls in the direction I had come in order to reach my office. But it allowed me to pass the large pond where fat and boisterous koi fish lurked. The koi were so accustomed to humans that if you held your hand over the surface of the water they would come toward you, expecting a snack, and if you submerged your palm in the water they would let you touch their bodies and stroke their cool gelatinous skin. I had been yelled at by the museum security guard for doing this, but this had not stopped me from doing it again. In winter, when the pond froze over, the koi remained, sealed inside their murky green home by a thin film of ice, unmoving but somehow alive. I kept meaning to ask someone how they survived through the cold months, but I never knew who to ask, and I always forgot.

I locked my bicycle and walked on, past the koi, who were making their usual rounds in the water, and up the marble steps. Inside, I beeped my card at the front desk, where, if schoolchildren on field trips were awaiting registration, I would assume a beatific smile, sweep in, greet the man (Darren, MWFS or Sharif, SMTW) or woman (Carol, TWTFS, or Annalisa, MTF) on duty, touch my card to the machine, and glide through the corridors, imagining myself mysterious and authoritative in the schoolchildren's eyes. I remembered, at their age, being constantly impressed by such figures, people with access codes to private areas within public places that allowed them to enter and leave in different ways than the rest of us hoi polloi.

Once, on a family trip to Italy, I was especially struck by one such figure, in the Uffizi, late in the afternoon. I was ten, dazed with hunger and jet lag, and we had been in the museum for what seemed like hours as my father studied painting after painting, expressionless and motionless in front of Botticelli's *Venus*, in front of his *Primavera*, in front of innumerable saints and Madonnas, taking so long with each, immersed in his private experience, while my mother, behind him, sullen and sharp, chided me for my bad mood, hoping my father would register both mine and hers, which of course he didn't. My father remained rooted in place, as unmoving as David, noticing nothing except for Christ and his golden nimbus. I could see him looking at a painting, and my mother looking at him, and then, slowly, I began to perceive myself, gazing with longing and despair at my mother's slender shoulder, encased in gray wool, and her stony profile, aware of but unmoved by my suffering, waiting for my father to notice it so that she might point out that he had not. I turned to one of the paintings on the wall in an attempt to bring my soul back into my body. I tried to move toward it, but found myself, like my parents, fixed in place. The obese putti in the painting seemed to be beckoning me. The whole room was swaying, and the edges of my vision crinkled with black, like television static. Suddenly I was on the ground, and there was commotion around me, and sniping voices. My parents floated above, along with a third Asian person I did not recognize, wearing what looked to me like a ship captain's hat. My father asked me what had happened, and I said I didn't know. The person in the hat, hearing us speak Chinese, switched from Italian-accented English, which she was using with my mother, to Wenzhounese-toned Mandarin and informed my father that I had fainted, and said that if we followed her she would lead us through a shortcut that would take us to the exit much faster than the "official" way. She was the designated guard for the room we were in. My father made a gesture that indicated his reluctance to leave so soon, but the twin glares of my mother and the guard shut him up. We scurried after her as she led us away from Botticelli. She unlocked a door and then a second door that opened into a long unpeopled hallway. She held my hand as I walked, and told us about herself. She turned out to be a second-generation Italian whose parents had emigrated from China to work in a leather factory outside of Florence. As she relayed the story of her life, I gazed with wonder at the things past which she was shepherding us: Corinthian pedestals bearing bulky shapes shrouded in heavy brown cloth; suits of medieval armor in dusty vitrines; writhing Medusas on circular shields, leaning against the walls like cheap film props; many, many paintings ("Bronzino!" my father whispered at one); objects which, had I seen them outside, would have meant nothing to me, but because of the exclusive manner in which I was experiencing them, became founts of delight, meaning, and awe. At the end of the corridor the Wenzhounese-Tuscan unlocked another door and motioned for us to pass through it. "Arrivederci," she said, "zaijian, baibai," and slipped back into the secret passageway like it was nothing. That was the kind of impression I hoped I made on the Pennsylvanian sixth-graders when I passed them on my way into work.

That day it was Annalisa at the front desk, and I nodded gingerly at her. Unlike the other three front desk attendants, who commuted from Mount Airy or Kensington, and for some of whom the job was one of two or even three that they juggled, Annalisa was an undergraduate in art history who took shifts at the museum as part of an internship. She wore a gold septum piercing and black mock turtlenecks with no bra and smiled, but never laughed. None of us had seen her teeth, which was why the others referred to her as "Mona Lisa" when she was not around. Everyone had nicknames but she was the only one whose nickname was not spoken in front of her, signaling her separation. Darren was Dasher, because he walked with a limp due to an adolescent motorbike injury; Sharif was the Sheriff, for obvious homophonic reasons; Carol was the Water Goddess, which she resented because it spoke to her resemblance to a fertility statue in the Central American collection that she did not find attractive; and I was Antelope, not because my coworkers had identified in me any particular grace or agility, but because one of them, upon receiving the staff-wide email welcoming me to the museum, had read "Penelope" and thought the pronunciation rhymed with that of the ruminant. I had always admired the sleight of hand on the part of whoever had first mispronounced my name. Their deflection had been so quick, so skillful, that not only did no one remember whose mistake it had been, but, apart from me, no one could recall with certainty the origin of the nickname, and a few had begun to think that it was some characteristic of myself that had inspired it, and see in me traits that did not exist: that I had long legs and ran fast, when in fact my limbs were an average length and my gait unremarkable; or that I had the aura of a potential victim, of prey. Nevertheless, I had gotten off lightly compared to Darren or Sharif, who hated his nickname because he hated the police. Sometimes I felt bad for mirthless Annalisa, since she was the odd one out, and if not for her it would probably have been me.

After passing through the main hall I entered the Americas, dim hallways of spotlit displays: beaded gourd with horsehair, hickory wood lacrosse stick, buckskin bag, and a life-sized diorama that I always mistook for real people roasting brown objects over a false fire. In the next room, there was a small Aztec man made of volcanic rock, and a woman made of stone, and many clay cups. I took an emergency stairwell shortcut into the lower level of the museum, fluorescent-lit and security-padded, underground.

On the days I worked in the office, at the computer, I could do whatever I wanted, relatively speaking, but on days like that one, when I needed to spend time in the collections room, I followed strict procedure. If I had a cup of takeaway coffee from the museum café, I would have to finish it before I entered, because food and drink were banned, to protect the objects. Pens were not allowed, because of the ink; if you needed to write something you used a pencil. Water bottles were permitted, but only those with sports caps and nozzles. They were very specific that it had to be nozzles, not the foldable straws or the fun spouts. The bottles made of aluminum or insulated steel, with screw-top lids and bright matte coats, which were very trendy (Mona Lisa carried one, in austere black), had been explicitly banned. The water bottle rule did not concern me, because I preferred to quench my thirst at the cooler, with a paper cup, a system that also provided me with luxurious and illicit mini-breaks throughout the day. My hair was already tied back, so I swallowed the dregs of my coffee and entered the clean white room.

For several months I had been in charge of organizing a large number of items in the museum's archives: shoes for women with bound feet. The museum had, over the decades, amassed hundreds of slippers, boots, socks, and other paraphernalia, such as wood or plaster composite models of the small pointed foot with etchings to show the painfully crimped toes, crafted by "natural feet societies" to be flourished at rallies calling for the abolition of foot binding. Prior to my arrival these hundreds of items had languished in storage, untagged and uncataloged, piled on top of one another in cabinet drawers in the basement of the museum, collecting dust. Then the museum had appointed a Korean American anthropologist named Dr. Bartholomew Bae to "spearhead new programming." Dr. Bae's stated priority upon joining was a vigorous revamp of "underserved" (a word I never read without mistakenly seeing "undeserved") areas of the museum—in practice, everything aside from the Greek, Roman, Egyptian, and Americas exhibits, i.e., Asia and Africa—and more programming for these places. I had been hired to work on the Chinese section, rescued from the pleasant tedium of data analytics by a former professor who remembered my interest in the lives of women in the Qing Dynasty and my success in wheedling money from the department to attend a summer archaeology course at Peking University. My time at work was split between the white basement room where I dealt with the objects and the quiet beige office, one floor above, where I helped with administrative tasks involving membership records, accounting files, or events, depending on who needed a little extra help.

That September day, during whose evening I would have my fire escape conversation with Apple about her new job, I spent the morning in the white room, matching tiny eggshell-colored socks with their partners, introducing them to the small plastic cases that would become their permanent home, pressing sticker labels with brief penciled descriptions of the items onto the boxes, and taking pictures on my phone so I could enter the particulars into the database when I left. Sometimes the socks came with little tags, attached by an unknown museum employee years earlier, offering hand-scrawled clues to their histories:

1974 donation, Ms. Fang, says great-aunt's wedding shoes
1999 donation, Mr. Wong, claims late Ming (unlikely but verify)
came with one red slipper (pair lost)

Other times a sturdier shoe might have on its sole a faded stamp with a number and a few words in a European language, indicating that after leaving its original owners in China, it had lived a second life as a curio of Parisian or Berliner trade houses before embarking on its third life decomposing in an American museum basement:

2272 chaussures brodées chinoises pour pieds bandés
8963 Baumwollene Frauerschuhe für Faschfüsse aus Newchwang

But most of them were unadorned with information. One of my tasks was to note details like the style, material, and condition of the sock or shoe and make an educated guess of the item's provenance, age, geographical region, social class of origin, and anything else I might be able to surmise. Late that morning I spent nearly ten minutes studying a pair of longish white socks, relatively thick, probably meant for indoor winter wear. They were rimmed with dark red thread and embroidered with small yellow flowers. The leaves of the flowers were green and the red thread had been used again, very sparingly, to outline the midrib

and veins of the tiny leaves. Whoever had sewn and decorated the
sock had finished the threads in three clusters, one on the front,
one at the back heel, and one on the sole, so that tufts of soft
frayed cotton burst out into tassels of green, red, and yellow from
these points. After enough time it had become easy for me to
spend hours sifting through the shoes and socks, carrying out my
tasks with an indifferent concentration, unplagued by thoughts
of who the owners of these garments had been, what their lives
had been like, and what had become of them, but occasionally
some insignificant detail—a small stain or tear, a worn and tattered heel, or, conversely, a slipper so pristine it was obvious it had
never been worn—affected me so immensely that it derailed the
rest of my day. Today it was the punishing needlework evinced by
the careful veins stitched atop the green leaf, which to me made
perceptible the long-dead, anonymous maker's love of beauty.
Suddenly it was as if she was very nearby, and veiled from me by
only a very thin screen.

I left early for lunch and, on my way outside, accepted a request
to drop off a stack of posters for an upcoming Mummy Night
at the university's main administrative building. The morning's
coolness had worn off, and I was glad when I reached the office
and found the air conditioning on full blast.

After I passed the posters to the receptionist, she told me that
she had received some mail for the museum that had been deliv-
ered there by mistake, and asked me to wait while she fetched it.
I plucked a Polo mint from the tray on her desk and sat in one of
the waiting room chairs with a clear view of the front door. I was
the only person in the room when a tall Asian guy wearing glasses
and an Eagles hoodie walked in and sat down next to me, even
though all the other chairs were free. I looked at him, and he, perhaps sensing that I was confused, said, "I like to face the front, in
case people come in shooting. Not that it would make much of a

difference. But there's something about the idea of getting shot in the back that just doesn't sit right with me, you know?"

As he spoke, I was rolling the donut-shaped mint around in my mouth, allowing it to deposit its piquancy all over the inside of my cheeks, feeling the embossed letters dissolve, and poking into its hole with the tip of my tongue. I nodded along to what he was saying, agreeing with it precisely because he had admitted there was no logic motivating his behavior, only a feeling. But he spoke as if the feeling was sufficient, and did not need to be justified with reason, or even a caveat assuring me he was aware of his own irrationality. With my molars I bit down on the sweet, cracking the ring in half, and said, "Me too."

He leaned forward and pointed at the clock on the wall in front of us.

"Have you noticed all the clocks in here are tilted?" he said. He pointed at another clock, on the adjacent wall, above the receptionist's desk, and then he swiveled in his seat and pointed to a third clock, hanging above us. They all leaned to the left. "Weird, right?"

"It's weirder," I said, "that there are so many clocks at all."

"Maybe it's because—"

"Dinh?" the receptionist said. She had reemerged, without mail. "See you."

He disappeared down the hall leading to the offices. The receptionist apologized and told me she hadn't found the letters where she thought she'd left them, but had dispatched someone named Norm, whom she suspected of having moved the letters, to recover them. She added that if I had somewhere to be I could leave, and she would find another way to send them along to the museum. I thought of the yellow petals and the red stitching and said that I could wait. I tapped my feet on the ground and wondered whether "Dinh" was a student, and how old he might be, and what he was doing there. I tried not to look at the clocks.

"Hey, you don't study biology, do you? Or psych?"

He was back, and sitting down next to me again.

"No."

"Neuroscience? Pre-med?"

"I'm not a student. I'm a member of the workforce."

"Oh, great. Me too, kind of. Can I tell you a secret?"

I glanced at the receptionist. She was reaching for a Polo mint with one hand, thumbing her phone with the other. I looked back at "Dinh." The lenses of his glasses were smudged, and I, who did not wear glasses, felt a passing urge to remove them, gently, and wipe them for him with my shirt and then place the frames, just as gently, back on the bridge of his nose.

"A secret?"

"Yeah."

"What if I can't keep it?"

"I trust you."

"You don't even know me."

He paused to consider this.

"Well, I'm a trusting person. I just need to get this off my chest. I'm Hoang, also."

"Okay. What's the secret?"

"Wait, what's your name?"

"Penelope."

"Penelope. So," Hoang said, dropping into a low voice, "I work in the cancer research lab, right? And the labs have been reporting all these missing mice. The techs are supposed to euthanize the mice after experiments and put the bodies in the biowaste freezers. But a ton, like forty or fifty mice, have been disappearing from the freezers over the past year."

"How did they know they were missing?"

"The mice have numbered ear tags. So a bunch of numbers are gone, and they think someone has been releasing the mice instead of euthanizing them. So they've been calling us all in, to interrogate us. They thought it was one of the undergrads, but they're wrong."

"How do you know?"

There was a pause. He looked expectant.

"You're the culprit?"

"The culprit." Hoang smiled, and a dimple appeared on his cheek. "I like that."

"You gave them your confession just now?"

"My confession! You're making me sound like a criminal. But yes, yes, I confessed. They were pretty shocked, they didn't really know what to do. They just told me to go home and they'd contact me soon, I think it's all over."

A disheveled man who must have been Norm came ambling into the room, holding a sheaf of papers.

"What's all over? You'll get in more trouble?"

"Big trouble. I'm almost definitely losing my job."

"Then why did you admit it was you?"

Hoang shrugged. "I don't like lying."

"Weren't you lying when you took the mice? By omission?"

"Maybe. Is breaking the rules lying, if the rules are bad?"

"I don't know," I said. "Why did you release them?"

"I spend all day with these mice," Hoang said. "I hold them, I feed them, sometimes I talk to them. I play them music. I get to know their personalities—you know they have personalities? They're playful, they're really smart, and they have preferences, like dogs, or people. Favorite foods. After all that, how could I kill them?"

The receptionist was waving at me.

"I have to go," I said.

"See you later, Penelope."

"See you."

I walked up to the receptionist and she began to hand me the letters, one by one, insisting on reading aloud to me the intended recipients of each, even though their names were clearly written and I knew better than she where in the museum to find them. When I glanced back, Hoang was slipping out the door. He saw me looking, and waved, and then the door clicked shut.

"And both of these are for Bartholomew—"

I grabbed the rest of the letters from her and rushed out of the room.

"You heading this way too?" Hoang said, when I caught up with him on the sidewalk.

"Yes," I lied.

"I want to go to the park where I release the mice, since I probably won't be doing it anymore," he said. We walked on, in the opposite direction of the museum and the halal food truck where I had planned on purchasing my lunch. The sidewalk was pasted with brown leaves, some of which had been trampled so many times that they looked like they'd been painted onto the concrete. We reached Clark Park, where I had spent a lot of time as a student, watching people unclip the leashes from their dogs' collars to let the dogs bound across the grassy bowl.

"If you ever see a mouse with an ear tag running around here, now you know why," Hoang said.

I asked him how he got them out of the lab without people seeing, and he said he usually put them in his pockets; because they knew and trusted him, they were calm and did not wriggle too much, or make any noise. I asked him if he was this devoted to all animals, and he said that he liked animals, but he ate meat and had never seriously considered stopping, so he supposed that the answer would have to be no.

"It's more just because I know them personally," he said. He stopped walking and pointed to a tree.

"What? Is there a mouse?"

"No. Just saying. I love a good birch."

I looked at the tree again. It just looked like a tree to me. I didn't think there was a tree in the whole city that I'd be able to identify on sight, unless maybe there were willows somewhere.

"My last name means forest in Chinese," I said.

"Really? What is it?"

"Lin."

"That's crazy. Our last names kind of rhyme."

He stopped at a cracked curb, looking around, and I stopped too.

"The light's weird, isn't it?"

He was right. It was midday, but there was a flatness to everything, and a darkness that didn't correspond to storm cloud shade.

"Is it September fifth?" he said.

"It might be."

"Okay, don't look up, but I think there's an eclipse."

Immediately I looked up, and found the strange but still-bright sun. I looked at Hoang. He was squinting at it too.

"I thought you said don't look."

"I know, but then you did, and I didn't want to miss out."

I laughed, and he looked at me and grinned. "I didn't even see anything," I said.

"We're gonna go blind. I know what we can do, though."

He jogged over to the birch, scanning the ground like he was searching for something. Whatever it was, he didn't find it, and he moved to a different tree.

"Come here! Quick!"

He was pointing at the pavement.

"Look."

I looked, and found, wavering between the leaf shadows, hundreds of tiny crescent moons. Hoang crisscrossed one hand over the other, making a lattice with his fingers, and in the daubs of sunlight that passed through the gaps and shone onto the concrete were more false moons—hangnails of sun, lunar masqueraders. I tried to copy him, but the crescents were already blurring away.

"It's ending, I think," he said.

"So soon?"

"They only last like a minute, right?"

"I don't know," I said. "I've never really considered eclipses at all."

"So which way's your house?"

"I live in Chinatown."

"Didn't you say you were near the park?"

"Oh," I said, "I guess I lied."

He frowned, looking not annoyed but confused, which was worse, like he didn't understand why anyone would want to lie, and had not expected me to be the type of person who did. At least, that was what my conscience led me to infer. I cursed myself for telling the truth.

"I mean, I used to live around here. I wanted to see my old house again. But it was too weird to explain, so I just didn't."

"Okay," he said, "that's cool."

"Yeah, so. Yeah. I'll go look at it now. It was nice to meet you."

He nodded. "See you, Forest."

I waited until he turned the corner, and then began walking back to the museum. The sky was returning to its normal state. I decided when I got home I would start reading up on North American trees so that I could identify them too. I considered actually visiting my old house, and thus unmaking the lie I had told, but I didn't really see the point. The stray cat that used to sun itself on our porch and claw at the wooden banisters had died a few months before, according to a Facebook post from one of my former neighbors, and I suspected it would make me sad to see the scratch marks on the painted wood, and either the presence or the absence of the metal bowl that Paul used to fill up with water or milk for the cat to lap. Up ahead, a cable worker was sitting on a stoop, legs stretched out on the steps, smoking a cigarette. He wore a utility belt and a baseball cap embellished with the logo of the telecommunications conglomerate for which he worked, and he sat in the shade of an unidentifiable tree. He saw me staring and he nodded. I nodded back.

"Eclipse," he said, pointing up at the sky.

"Yeah," I said. "Eclipse."

T W O

That June I had turned twenty-five, a fact I welcomed without any particular emotion, perhaps because Apple's birthday had passed just a month before, and she had driven herself into such hysterics over what she termed her "descent into hagdom" that I resolved to indulge as little as possible in any self-pity that might arise. Twinges of disquiet occurred only when I compared my life thus far to my favorite historical figures. Cixi seized power at twenty-five; Einstein had completed the annus mirabilis papers in which he described the special theory of relativity for the first time. Then again, Napoleon Bonaparte at twenty-five was languishing unemployed in Paris, and only made his name on 13 Vendémiaire, a couple of months after turning twenty-six. So maybe I still had a little time. In general, though, I was sanguine about birthdays and new years' eves, which for Apple were essentially marked-off days in the calendar during which she would sink for hours into existential malaise, or toska, as we called it, after discovering the word in Nabokov. For me the changes in seasons were much more harrowing reminders of the passage of time, even the jollier ones, like the transition to summer from spring.

I was also happy to distance myself from the "early twenties" phase of life, when I had been beset by comments—they appeared triply as encouragement, reassurance, and warning—that I should binge drink and take as many drugs as I could, that I should lack a clear grasp of my personal finances, that people in general would not have very high expectations of me, morally or professionally, and that life would never be as good or as bad as it was then. I understood that such ideas must be helpful for some in their twenties, many of whom seemed to revel in the sanctioned adolescence, but they did nothing for me. Rather than consolation I felt an oblique pressure to perform incompetence, and had on some occasions murmured along as companions commiserated and bragged about their ignorance of the tax system and the stock market, when in fact I filed my taxes without incident, enjoyed researching ETFs in which to place my savings, and had always kind of liked filling out forms. I was looking forward to twenty-six as much as Apple dreaded it. Twenty-six felt like it was really out of the danger zone.

When it came to love, too, I had often been out of step, but found that as I aged, the distance between cultural expectations and my experience of reality began to close. The people who knew me, at least, grew used to my abstention from dating apps, my disinterest in casual sex, and my relative lack of a romantic history. I had the one "big ex," and that was something everyone could understand. Of course there had been missteps with Paul, but I had, I believed, learned from them. To be in love was to be destabilized, that was what I had learned, and, until the day I met Hoang, I had established a happy equilibrium of habit, solitude, and friendship.

On the evening of the mid-autumn festival, two weeks after my first encounter with Hoang, Raymond, Xinwei, and I were eating mooncakes. The fourth resident of the apartment returned just as we were unwrapping the pastries, and Xinwei asked him to join us, but he politely declined, explaining that he had sampled a mooncake once while vacationing in Hong Kong and found it disgusting. He didn't use the word "disgusting," but he mimed sticking his fingers in his mouth to induce vomiting. It was true that mooncakes were something of an acquired taste, but I was surprised he had such strong feelings, because their flavor was quite mild. They were stodgy and calorific, like most of the food he ate, and pretty to look at, which no one could find fault with, although they were not very sugary or very salty, and so perhaps failed to excite the vulgar American palate. People often said mooncakes looked better than they tasted, but I thought their taste was roughly commensurate with their appearance. I had, however, always believed their name to be superior. Mooncake, yue bing: in English as well as Mandarin it was a substantive word, one that filled and satisfied the mouth. Even better was the way Raymond said it, in Cantonese: yut beng, a bouncy, bountiful word, the snappy *yut* tumbling into the drawn-out *beng*, which twanged like the echo of a plucked bass string.

Xinwei had arranged the mooncakes in concentric circles on one of the collapsible tables in the living room, placing a classic lotus paste and salted egg yolk in the middle, with mini mooncakes of various flavors, some archetypal, some outlandish—red bean, green tea, snow skin, ham and nut, durian, lava custard, lavender, English rose, passionfruit cheese—encircling the central, larger one, like Ptolemy's model of the universe. We spent some minutes waiting for Xinwei to capture a photograph of the arrangement that satisfied her, and then we began to eat.

"When's the last time you were home for mid-autumn?" I asked Xinwei in Mandarin, thinking that perhaps she would grant a dispensation from our intricate language rules for the occasion. She shrugged and offered me a wedge of red bean, which always made me think of winters in Beijing: warm dessert soup in white bowls and the smell of coal in the frozen air. I expressed some of this to Xinwei, and she asked me if I planned to go home for the spring festival. I said I wasn't sure.

"I don't like going back on holidays either," she said.

I nodded sympathetically. "Too much pressure? Family can be tough."

She frowned. "No. Too expensive."

Apple showed up later in the evening, bearing mooncakes handmade by her mother, who had baked them at home in the suburbs and then driven fifty minutes to Apple's apartment to drop them off, along with two hundred frozen dumplings, a sixteen-pack of single-ply toilet paper, and a large leek. Apple burst through the front door, hurling the container of cakes in my direction. As I caught it, she withdrew the leek from her tote bag and lobbed it at Xinwei, who lacked a sportsman's reflexes and yelped as the vegetable bounced off her small frame.

"Sorry," Apple said, scooping up the leek and handing it to Xinwei. "I have no idea how to cook this, but I thought you might want it."

"Thank you," Xinwei said, rubbing her collarbone and looking displeased. She appraised the leek and perked up a little bit when she noticed its heft and its thick healthy leaves.

I popped open the lid of the mooncakes Apple had brought. They were plump and round, the color of ivory, and dotted with red.

"Taiwanese style," Apple said, "I think."

Apple dropped herself into a free chair, drew her legs up against her chest, rested her heels on the edge of the seat, and balanced the English rose mooncake on her left knee, pulling out her phone to take a picture. She was tall and gangly, with impressively foldable limbs. Sometimes she reminded me of a baby giraffe, sometimes a swan.

"Your mother made this?" Xinwei asked, nibbling a cake.

"Yeah, they're kinda gross, right?"

"No!" Xinwei looked horrified and turned to me for help. I shrugged and smiled in a manner I hoped would show that I understood she had not been implying the mooncake was gross, and had in fact been lining up a compliment, and that I agreed with her that Apple was being rude about her mother. I tried to do all this without Apple noticing. Interacting with them at the same time was a challenge. When Xinwei and I were alone, she thought me pitiably white-washed, but when Apple was around, I was a fellow Chinese to whom she looked for moral support, to interpret and shield her from Apple's blaring Americanness. I had to provide this without seeming to undermine my loyalty to Apple, even in cases where I was on Xinwei's side. I felt guilty, like I was betraying Apple, but at the same time I didn't want to cause strife by alienating Xinwei, who could be just as strident. By now I was versed in this balancing act, and neither of them saw me sending sympathetic signals to the other.

Apple began to tell us about her day at work. She said the HR department had discovered it was mid-autumn and distributed mooncakes to everyone in the office, but since they had only purchased a small amount, each person received a wafer-thin slice, resting on a paper napkin, and accompanied by a plastic fork. Then a paralegal asked Apple what other activities Chinese people did for the occasion, and Apple, sensing an opportunity, told him it was tradition to give red packets of money to your colleagues.

"And then he was like, isn't that Chinese New Year? And one of the HR ladies was like, actually it's called Lunar New Year, and I was like, *anyway*, with the new year it's married people giving them out, but for today, it's the younger ones giving money to the older ones, so for example, you, Justin, should be giving me money. And then somebody else started reading out from Wikipedia like, 'It doesn't say anything here about blablabla,' and I was like, my parents are Taiwanese, it's a local custom. Justin smelled a rat because I'm always picking on him but I honestly think I had the rest of them. Not that it mattered because they're all older than me, except for Justin. And they're so cheap. You guys would not believe how stingy lawyers are."

"But why do you lie to them?" Xinwei asked Apple in Mandarin. I thought it was funny that when it was just me and Xinwei alone, we spoke Chinese, but with Apple, whom she regarded as American, she spoke English, except when Apple did something of which Xinwei disapproved, in which case she moved to Chinese, assuming the role of disciplinarian mother.

"Why not?" Apple said, in English, consciously or unconsciously reprising her own role of defiant daughter, one of whose characteristics—she had told me—had been a refusal, growing up, to speak the mother tongue.

"You shouldn't lie," Xinwei said, and got up and began clearing plates and glasses while Apple continued her story. "We can cook this with the lap cheong," Xinwei said to Raymond, holding the leek. I couldn't speak Cantonese, but I understood all the food words. My phone buzzed on the table: a message from my father. An animated red lantern danced across the screen. The lantern smiled toothlessly and wished me a happy mid-autumn festival. I sent one back, along with a picture of Xinwei's mooncake formation. It was the next morning in Beijing. I wondered if he was alone, if he had eaten any mooncakes, and if he had plans for the day ahead. I checked his WeChat profile. The night before, he had posted a picture of himself smoking a cigarillo. He was outdoors, and the moon was a white glare above his head. Caption, in English, accompanied by a thumbs-up emoji: "moonlight sonata." As far back as I could remember, my father had been obsessed with Beethoven. The trips to art museums were Disneyland compared to my father's pilgrimages to Bonn: a city so boring it might have been designed by God as punishment for humanity's sins. I realized with some surprise that the last time we had talked on the phone had been my birthday, back in June—three months past. I'd asked him what Beethoven was doing at twenty-five, because I was collecting data points to compare with my own life. "I don't know," he'd said. "I think he was probably drunk somewhere. You should try it." Perhaps it had been too long since we spoke, but he was a hard man to pin down. I didn't mind; our relationship had improved considerably after I lowered my expectations of him and learned to meet him at his level.

Apple's story, which seemed to have no resolution, and might not even have happened, as sometimes she just liked to let off steam by making something up—she called them her "bits" if anyone questioned their veracity, but otherwise gave no indication whether what she was saying was true or false—petered out, and she and I headed to the fire escape so she could vape in the open air. The last time she had come over was the day of the eclipse, and she must have been thinking of it too, because when we were outside she asked me, "Still in love?"

I shrugged. I didn't feel like discussing Hoang with her anymore. Sometimes I hesitated to share things with Apple, because of how easily they became jokes, but usually I ended up telling her anyway. In general I was reluctant to describe my emotional experiences to other people. There was something about the journey from private interior to outside world that corrupted them. Vocalization diminished meaning: I grew conscious of how my words might sound to the person hearing them, and I was never satisfied with the impression. For example, for the whole day between saying goodbye to Hoang and telling Apple about him on the fire escape, the world felt open and alive, small moments were permeated with immensity, and I was alert to color and sound. I walked down the street buoyed by new and exciting feelings of boundlessness and potential, floated through the rest of the afternoon at work, and laughed out loud on the bike ride home, feeling the wind and the sun on my face and seeing many trees that could have been birches and parks that may have sheltered fugitive mice. When I tried to convey this to Apple, we just ended up arguing about whether we thought Hoang was Korean or Vietnamese. Apple said she knew a Korean guy named Hwang, I said I thought Hwang was a last name and anyway he hadn't looked Korean at all, Apple said it was racist to say that someone could look or not look Korean, I said it wasn't. I hadn't told her his full name, which might have settled the disagreement, because I knew she would immediately google him to look for pictures and other biographical information, and I wanted to spare him and myself that kind of scrutiny, which I knew would inflict further retroactive damage on my experience of the world that afternoon of the eclipse, which depended, I think, on its ineffability.

"Hello?" Apple said. I had been silent for a while.

"I was just trying to remember the last time I was home during mid-autumn."

"And?"

"I can't remember."

"You should come back with me for Thanksgiving. We'll have

hot pot, and then after dinner we can drive around and guess the market value of all the mansions."

"That sounds fun." I said. "How's your mom?"

"Annoying. She started talking about the midterms in the car, it was giving me hives. She's the one who brings it up but she won't even tell me who she's voting for."

"Why not?"

"She says I criticize her too much. I told you how she votes, right? Obama the first time, then Romney, because she liked his hair, then Trump, because taxes? I honestly don't know who's worse, her or my dad. He won't even register to vote because he thinks it'll increase his chances of getting jury duty. He got mad at me and Steve when we first voted because we ignored his advice, and literally made us promise not to complain if we ever got called up for jury duty. Meanwhile all I want in life is to be selected for a jury panel."

"What's your ideal case?"

"Celebrity attempted murder. It has to be attempted. I don't want anyone to die, because I want everybody involved to be present at the trial. And I want a Kardashian in the mix. Obviously I'd lie in the screening interview and say I'd never heard of them."

Clouds parted above us, revealing the round moon, dull and flat in the light-filled sky. Seeing it reminded me that there was a dark sky park somewhere in Pennsylvania, promising unobstructed views of the Milky Way.

"Do you think your roommates like me?" Apple said.

I nodded.

"Do you think it was okay that I gave Xinwei that leek?"

I nodded again. After another moment Apple started telling me about the toilet paper her mother had dropped off with the mooncakes, how she appreciated the gesture but resented that her mother refused to stop giving her toilet paper, because it would be a dereliction of maternal duty, but also refused to purchase double or triple ply, because she thought it indicated improvidence and houseguests would cast negative judgment on a person who stocked their bathroom with such luxuries. I was content to look out at the shadowy walls of the buildings on either side of the empty lot, swing my legs back and forth over the fire escape, and listen to Apple talk. Comfortable silences were a foreign concept to her, one I'd tried to accustom her to, but which she'd fiercely opposed. She, in turn, learned that sometimes I didn't feel like speaking; now, if I fell silent, she was happy to take over and talk.

When Apple left I googled Hoang's full name together with the name of the university. I couldn't find him on any social media, and unearthed just one reference to him in a database of scientific journals, where he was listed as a coauthor of a research paper titled "Excitatory synapse formation in juvenile Myoxidae." I looked up "Myoxidae." Images appeared of tiny, obscenely cute mice, huge-eyed, nibbling blackberries, the fruit like monstrous bowling balls in their small pink hands.

The next day I met Inno for breakfast at a new café in Chinatown that only sold food and drink containing matcha in some form. Inno was the only person in my life who asked to meet for breakfast, and probably the only one for whom I would entertain such a request. He carried out his days according to a strict schedule, and if you wanted access to him you had to work within its restrictions. Sometimes they were temporal, like our breakfast, which would end at ten thirty, when Inno had to return home for his three-hour chess session with a Russian man named Gleb, followed by a pre-workout protein shake, some weightlifting at home, a run along the river, a post-workout protein shake, and then half an hour of logic problems to refresh himself before his weekly reading group, which that month was focused on Spinoza. In the evening he had dinner at his favorite Ethiopian restaurant with one group of friends and then drinks at a new bar with different friends. Sometimes his requirements concerned the nature of the hang-out; for one six-month period he refused to meet indoors, and I could only see him if I took a walk with him around the city, the traffic lights dictating our conversation, because he would stop speaking whenever we stood still. His in-person demeanor belied his odd and exacting habits. He was cheerful and humorous, and he had a calming presence. He never made his companion feel rushed, even when they knew the minutes were ticking by until he would leave them to fulfill the next item on his schedule. He gave the impression that he understood you, so that you didn't feel you had to explain yourself to him, though naturally you would still be eager to impress him, given his accomplishments, personality, and manner of living. He was very good at appearing fascinated by whatever it was you were telling him. He was like this with everyone, but when you were with him you felt that his warmth and attention were especially for you, and had never been bestowed on anyone else in quite the same way. I considered him a close friend and I knew he considered me one too, but in the years I had known him I had never been able to shake a feeling of deprivation that stemmed from a desire, probably unfulfillable, to be closer. He was that kind of extrovert whose gregariousness can feel like a barrier to intimacy—like he was so close to everyone he met that it was impossible to differentiate your relationship with him from his relationship with everyone else.

We arrived outside the café at the same time, Inno in workout clothes, his typical daytime wear. I had reserved a table by the window, from which it was possible to see the fire station and its mural of a green Chinese dragon, bathed in yellow light from the morning sun. I was looking forward to the waffles, which I had seen in photographs but never tried: mossy golden-green slabs with square wells of syrup and scalloped edges like cartoon hearts. But as the door clicked softly behind us and the waitress descended, Inno, who had only recently come off his phase of wanting to meet exclusively outdoors, said he had changed his mind and asked if we could instead take a walk. I got a matcha latte but no waffles, and followed Inno, who had purchased nothing, back outside, but not before glancing longingly at the table I had reserved, which looked simple and inviting, with its sunny aspect and its view of the fire station's dragon. We walked east so that we would be able to sit on a bench by the water, with a view of the beautiful teal-colored Benjamin Franklin Bridge. The latest with Inno was that he had terminated a fling on account of cultural differences.

"He's so provincial that he didn't know what a margherita pizza was. He'd never heard the *term*. I explained it to him, and he said, 'Oh, you mean a cheese pizza!' As if I was the philistine," Inno sighed and took a sip of lemon water from the reusable liter bottle he carried everywhere.

"Why were you talking about pizza? You don't even eat pizza."

"I was telling him that tomato crops emit more greenhouse gas than pork or poultry. Did you know that?"

"That just doesn't sound true," I said.

"It is true. Also more than milk, cheese, and eggs. And farmed fish."

"So if you give up tomatoes, you can start eating sushi again?"

Inno shook his head, solemn. The loss of omakase from his life had tested his altruistic faith more than any of the other sacrifices he had made. For several months now he had been shaving what he called "the unnecessaries" from his life, by which he meant expenses one could live without. At first, given his

lavish spending, it made sense: he let go of his standing reserva-
tion for a table at the nightclub; he downgraded, and eventually canceled, his gym membership; he took the bus instead of
the Acela first class to New York. He donated the money he
saved to very specific charities, small organizations dedicated to
solving one issue, like iodine deficiency or rickets. He adjusted
to the habits of austerity and giving, and the habits deepened.
He stopped buying books and began to torrent online versions
instead. He gave up meat—he was unsentimental about animals,
but beans were cheaper than imported wagyu, and he was suspicious of American supermarket chicken. Plus, the environment.
He started bringing cans of bottom-shelf lager whenever we
went for drinks. He hated beer and chose it specifically because
it would take him a long time to finish. Most notoriously, he lob-
bied his parents to let him divert his trust fund to his pet charities; they refused, and instead purchased a one-bedroom for him
to live in, worried that he would otherwise relocate somewhere
ill-advised to save rent money for the rickets groups, and die of
asbestos poisoning.

"Isn't the point to calculate which actions will lead to maxi-
mally good outcomes?" I said.

"Yes."

"Do you really believe that the world will be a better place if
you stop eating tomatoes?"

"The evidence bears it out."

"I think you might be indulging your ascetic impulses and losing sight of the bigger picture."

He slurped his water and glared at me.

"If I stop eating these foods, maybe it won't make much of a
difference. But if you do, and the next person, then it might. And
someone needs to make up for your dairy guzzling."

"This is soy milk."

"Please. I've seen what happens when a grilled cheese sandwich has the misfortune of meeting you."

Inno and Apple were the only people from university I still saw on a regular basis. I never spent time with them together, only separately. They had never really gotten along, but their tenuous peace was completely demolished on the night of the U.S. presidential election in 2016, when we were at a bar watching the results come in on TV, and, when it became clear that Donald Trump was going to win, Apple started to cry at almost the exact moment that Inno burst out laughing. It might have been salvaged if Inno, when he saw that the prospect of a President Trump had brought Apple to tears, had not laughed even harder.

I met Inno during orientation week, when we were standing in line to register for American debit cards, sheltering from the sun under a series of blue marquees erected to form a temporary command center for international students who had flown in from their respective countries with foreign bank accounts and SIM cards. Inno, I learned, had landed that morning on a redeye from Abu Dhabi, because there were no direct flights from Lagos to Philadelphia, and left his earbuds on the plane. Just before I met him he was at the Apple store, perusing the phone cases and the chargers when he noticed, after a few minutes, that a polo-shirted employee was skulking in his peripheral. He moved to the next shelf, and the polo shirt moved with him. He crossed the store, experimentally now, and his shadow obeyed. He stopped in front of an iPad and tapped on its screen, which prompted the polo to ask, in a tone that did not imply a real willingness to provide assistance, "Can I help you?"

"I'm just having a look," Inno said, at which point the stony face lit up.

"Oh!" the man said, beaming. "You're from Africa!"

He said the interaction reminded him of a story often told by one of his father's friends, who was from India, of his family's first and only holiday in America, in the sixties, when the friend was just a child. They checked into their hotel at night and the next morning headed to the pool. They chose some lounge chairs in the shade and set down their towels. It was the biggest pool Inno's father's friend had ever seen. He watched people wade and backstroke, their pale swimcapped heads bobbing like buoys. He slipped into the water and kicked to the bottom, where he touched the seahorse mosaic tiled into the sun-dappled floor. When he resurfaced, he was alone. The other guests were crowded at the opposite end, clambering up the ladder. He wondered if they'd seen a snake. Later, the friend and his parents made their way to the hotel restaurant for dinner. His mother wore a sari. They were seated, and the friend recognized some of the swimmers at the adjacent table. "Oh, look!" a woman said, smiling at them in a way Inno now imagined must have been identical to the way the Apple store employee smiled at him, "It's fine, they're *Indian!*"

Inno described to me, as the line inched forward and we stepped out of the sweltering August heat and into the shade of a blue tent, under which were tables cluttered with brochures, laptops, and plastic cups of ballpoint pens, the peculiar sensation of déjà vu he had felt, and the tinge of unreality in the polo shirted employee's words, which came across, to Inno, like a conscious reference to the story he had heard so many times. Inno had looked at the floor, he said, expecting to find a seahorse spelled out in terra-cotta tiles. "Now I can tell my father's friend that the racism problem in this country against its own black citizens does not seem to have improved," Inno concluded just as we arrived at the front of the queue, startling the student volunteers at the booth.

We reached the beautified pier that jutted over the Delaware River in the shadow of the suspension bridge and chose a bench. I sipped my latte through a plastic straw and Inno drank his lemon water. He asked me if anything profound had happened to me at work that week, and I told him about the embroidered socks. Inno liked to hear stories about people being overwhelmed by their emotions, as long as there was an intellectual bent, while I only felt comfortable discussing my emotions if I intellectualized them, so it worked well for us both. He considered emotionally overwhelming experiences foreign and whimsical and claimed they never happened to him. He often asked me about the museum because when I started my job there, I described to him what happened the first time I picked up one of the shoes in my latex-gloved hand. Reading about bound feet, or looking at drawings and photographs, some of which are quite graphic, can give a vivid impression of what they are, and an effort to apply one's imagination to the words and pictures can render that impression more vivid still. But when you hold the shoe in your hands, everything else falls away. It is so much smaller than you imagined, much smaller than you could possibly expect, even when you have read the measurements beforehand and know what the numbers signify. Everything falls away: the three-inch golden lotus, the royal concubine and the besotted emperor, the feminist revisionist scholarship that rejects the word "mutilation" and recasts the bound-foot shoe as kinship, as accessory; it all falls away when the shoe is in your hand and all you manage to think is, how can this be? My father's mother ran away from home as a girl and joined the Communist Party to avoid getting her feet bound. My mother, we think, had Hakka origins, so probably none of the women in her lineage ever had bound feet. When I closed my eyes with the shoe in my open palm, it felt almost weightless. There might have been nothing there at all.

"I'm afraid that I need to run home before this settles in my stomach," Inno said.

"The water?"

"It will disrupt my whole day if I don't."

He was already jogging in place, warming himself up for the thirty-block sprint back to his apartment. He signaled apology as he receded, and texted me a few hours later, inviting me to join him for drinks that night at the bar of some swanky new hotel. Things like this were why, before the election night rupture, Apple and Inno had never been close. Each was uncompromising in their own way: Apple had a very low tolerance for people who flouted norms, and Inno, if he sensed that someone would not be amenable to his quirks, presented a cold and civil front that the lowest-EQ type could not fail to pick up on and that Apple, alert to the point of paranoia to the smallest ripples in social dynamic, detected the moment it occurred and reacted to in kind. I knew that if I told her how he had just behaved she would be infuriated, somewhat on my behalf but more so because I did not mind. The fruits of my friendship with Inno made up for such moments, so I accepted them without rancor; it also added richness to one's life to have a friend who acted eccentrically, and did so out of compulsion rather than affectation. I stayed on the bench while I finished my matcha latte, watching the cars cross the Benjamin Franklin Bridge, which I had once walked across with Inno to reach the Harleigh Cemetery in Camden, because he'd wanted to visit Walt Whitman's grave. The rate of violent crime in Camden was four times the national average, and twice that of Philadelphia; but Camden had an aquarium, and Philly did not.

I reconvened with Inno later that night, in the twenty-ninth-floor bar. The hotel was called the Rivebelle, and it had replaced an older hotel that had occupied the same building. The walls of the elevator were made of curved glass, and the floor of the bar was such a glossy black that I was scared to look at it for long. In its reflection, the dimensions of the room, the chairs, the tables, my own legs appeared in photographic clarity, the false depth of the obsidian combining with the mirrored image to summon an abyss into which I feared I was about to plunge. I found Inno stretched across a chaise longue, chatting with two of his friends, Louisa and Femi, whom he referred to as "Mother and Father," because Louisa was Filipina and Femi was Nigerian, like Inno's parents. There was a glass bowl of peanuts in the middle of the table, illuminated by a lamp with an oblong green shade, the kind you come across in libraries. In the shadow of the lamp, a bottle of champagne rested in a silver ice bucket.

"This doesn't look very frugal," I said as I sat down next to Inno. He kissed me on both cheeks and then flung an arm around my shoulders, squishing my face into his neck.

"Is that a jibe?" Inno whispered.

"Mm–hmm."

"In that case you can go get us another bottle, please. This one has been bled dry." He released me from his grip. "And Femi is treating us, I'll have you know. I've tried and failed to awaken the dormant effective altruist in him, so I may as well imbibe the drink he so stubbornly provides."

Again I crossed the glistening obsidian depths. The bar counter was studded with pinpricks of light, meant to resemble stars, and amber bottles of whiskey and rum glowed on the shelves, which stretched to the ceiling. The bartender had his back to me. Later I wasn't sure if I had recognized him before he turned around, or if all I felt was a premonition of recognition, apprehension and joy mingling in my heart like balsamic and oil, swirling and failing to integrate. When he saw me he looked surprised, and he smiled.

"Forest!" said Hoang.

"Hello!" I almost shouted. I couldn't believe it was him.

"Hi."

"You're here."

"I am, I am."

"You work here?"

He nodded. "Needed a job."

"Because of the mice?"

"Because of the mice."

Hoang told me, as he mixed whatever complicated drink I had ordered, not because I wanted it but because I wanted to prolong our interaction, that he had indeed been fired for freeing the mice, or tampering with biowaste, depending on your perspective, and had started this job earlier in the week. He'd previously worked as a bartender for a couple of years, and someone from his old restaurant had let him know about an opening at the Rivebelle. He did not seem particularly upset about losing his research position, which I presumed had not been easy to obtain, but I did not know if this was because he was stoic, or if he was actually not upset. I wanted to ask if he had purposely sabotaged himself, and if he was happier now that he had left the lab, but I didn't feel I knew him well enough to ask. I watched him rattle ice and alcohol in the gleaming shaker and admired his hands and the sinews of his forearms. His left shirtsleeve revealed the ends or beginnings of a tattoo, shaky black lines depicting something I could not discern. Later, walking home from the bar, I thought about how Hoang's time working in the lab would become a smaller and smaller fraction of the whole person he appeared to me to be, his past that I had not witnessed being equivalent, for me, to the oblivion that exists before one's birth; whereas for him, the moment in which I had come into his awareness was characterized by this huge change—the dishonorable discharge from one job and the start of a very different one, a rupture in the laid-out plan of his life, the beginning of a new, unplanned and uncertain path. It was interesting to think of the arbitrary points at which one person collides with another, of the expanse of potential experience that is opened up to you when you meet someone to whom, for whatever reason, you are drawn.

Hoang finished making my drink and I returned to the table, cocktail in hand.

"I do not believe the sturgeon survives the operation, so I cannot see how it counts as vegetarian," Femi was saying.

"Then why do they call it eggs?" Louisa said. I sat down.

"Are they bringing it over?" Inno asked me.

"Bringing what over?"

"The champagne?"

"Oh," I said, and stood up again. In giddy spirits I returned to Hoang.

"Forest," he said, "you're back. Did you like the drink?"

"Yeah," I said, although I had not tasted it yet. "I forgot I was supposed to get champagne."

"I can get you champagne."

"What do you usually drink?"

"Whatever's around, I guess. I don't really drink, though."

"Really?"

"Not like as a rule, I just tend not to drink that much, I don't know."

"This job must be pretty boring then."

"No, it's fun. I like talking to people."

This was incomprehensible to me, for whom the greatest pleasures of work were the paucity of human interaction, the long blissful days spent in quiet rooms alone, examining silent objects. My job at the museum would probably have been, for Hoang, a description of suffering.

"What do you like about it?" I asked.

"I just like hearing what people have to say, you know? People say all sorts of stuff, and it's fun to listen. Also, I've been wondering, are you named after the Penelope from the Odyssey? Or another Penelope? Or are you just named after yourself?"

"Hm?" I looked at him, too caught up in the wonderful implication that he had been thinking of me.

"Odysseus, his wife was Penelope, right?"

"Oh. Yeah. I don't think I was. I think it was random."

"Oh, okay. That's good, right? 'Cause she was pretty unhappy."

"I don't think I'm unhappy."

"I wouldn't want you to be."

From what seemed like a far-off distance, I could hear, "Penelope Lin!"

I turned around. Inno and Femi and Louisa were waving their empty flutes at me.

"I think they want this," Hoang smiled, and handed me the bottle.

When I returned to the table, Inno was telling a story about an ex-boyfriend of his, a concert pianist with a penchant for infidelity, the man for whom the cheese pizza guy had functioned as a rebound. Enough time had elapsed that Inno could describe his old pain with some detached irony, but I remembered the recent past when that hadn't been the case. He filled each of our glasses almost to the brim with champagne as he described how he believed he had fallen in love with the pianist solely because of the way he played the piano, or more precisely the way the playing transformed the pianist. He would take his seat at the piano bench, in a concert hall in a suit or naked in his living room (it did not matter to Inno, the effect was the same) and begin to play. When he touched the keys, he shed his slouch and his loopy gait and his other human tics and became graceful, powerful, beautiful. "I've thought about it a lot, and I've concluded that I was stupid—that we all are," Inno told us, shifting, for some reason, into the present tense to describe a man he no longer saw. "I watch

him play, I listen, and I fall in love. I mistake the beauty drawn
out by the mechanical movements of his hands, music written by
another man, as an expression of his own inner beauty, as proof of
it. I am falling in love with how Rachmaninoff's piano concerto
makes me feel and mistaking it for love for this mediocre man,
this cheat. I misplace the feeling. And physical beauty is the same
thing. A signifier of virtue where no virtue is to be found."

I did not look over at Hoang, but I imagined looking over at
the bar and finding him there, making someone a drink or talking to a customer, enjoying himself, smiling his dimpled smile.
Was I like Inno, so easily waylaid by beauty, by appearances, by
form? Beauty was something that Inno and I often discussed. His
pseudo-philosophical approach allowed him to bypass his usual
reservations about emoting. He might say things like "aesthetic"
and "ideal," and I might cover my face with my hands and say,
"Oh my god, look at his arms," but really we were talking about
the same thing. Both of us appreciated and were sometimes awed
by feminine beauty, which we responded to like art, but we were
paper crumpled in the hand of masculine beauty, powerless to
stop ourselves from being unformed by it. Apple was indiscrimi-
nate when it came to attraction, whether it was gender or physi-
cality, though she was something of a puritan about age. But she
found discussions of beauty sentimental. She should have been in
agreement with Inno on that, except that when it came to beauty,
he lapsed into the romanticism, cloaked in analytical terms, that
he was displaying so characteristically that night at the bar as he
spoke about the unfaithful pianist. It was another way in which
they—Apple and Inno—were incompatible.

THREE

W hen I told Apple that Hoang was now working as a bartender after being fired from the lab for rescuing all the
mice, she said he sounded "volatile" and asked to see his social
media so she could vet him, believing, not incorrectly, that an
intertextual reading of a person's online presentation could yield
information about who they were in private. I told her I didn't
think he had any social media.

"God, he's one of those," Apple said. "I bet he looks at sunsets
and doesn't take pictures and feels great about it."

Finally, I offered up his full name so she could scour the Internet.

"He barely even has Google results." Apple looked up from
her phone, her face a mask of horror. "What if he's some kind
of Unabomber?"

"Not everyone without Instagram is a potential Unabomber."

"But every potential Unabomber is someone without Instagram."

Her next campaign was to get me to text him, and, when I told her I didn't have his number, it morphed into a plan to return to the bar. Apple was in her element, harassing me into doing something I didn't really want to do until I relented, though I was a bit pleased that my resistance had proven futile. It was sometimes fun to be carried along by the force of Apple's personality into situations I wouldn't have otherwise dared to enter.

It was golden hour when we got there, and sunlight flooded the room, making the terrifying floors normal. By that point I had tried to back out of the plan and leave, but Apple marched me out of the elevator. The bartender was not Hoang, but a white guy with a buzzcut and silver studs in his ears. He was polishing glasses with a dishcloth.

"Do you know where Hoang is?" Apple demanded.

"It's his day off," the bartender said. "You friends of his?"

"Yes," Apple said, at the same time that I said, "Not really." We all looked at each other and then Apple smiled and asked for two lychee martinis. The guy's name turned out to be Gus, and he made very good lychee martinis. Apple gave him an abbreviated, slightly untrue version of the story—that Hoang and I had met here and meant to exchange numbers before he got called away by another customer—and asked if Gus could help me out.

"I don't think he has a phone right now," Gus said.

"How unusual," Apple murmured, flashing me a triumphant look.

"I think he lost it, but he hasn't gotten around to buying a new one. You know how he is," Gus said, as if we did. "I can pass a message on from you guys if you want?"

"Perfect!" Apple said. "Can you give him her number? Instagram? Email? LinkedIn?"

Gus said email would probably be best, since Hoang couldn't call anyone at the moment, and he didn't have social media. Apple gave me another gloating smile, and then they made me write my email address on a bar napkin. I handed the napkin to Gus, feeling nauseous.

As we sipped our martinis, Gus launched into a convoluted story about a dispute between the management of the hotel and the housekeepers, who had to use some kind of electronic system to log the rooms they cleaned, and who had been having trouble with the program since the hotel introduced a new "sustainable stay" feature where guests could choose not to have their rooms cleaned until they checked out, which would save water since there would be no daily change of the towels and the sheets. But this created havoc for the housekeepers, who needed more time to clean the "sustainable stay" rooms—"You can't imagine what a mess the average person makes," Gus told us ominously—but weren't able to request extra time, and so were racking up penalties in the points system that led to docked pay and other disincentives. Apple asked why they didn't just tell their manager about it, and Gus said they had, but the manager didn't want to relay the problem to her own boss, who had instituted the "sustainable stay" program, and so had done nothing. The new program made the hotel look good and it helped cut costs, and, Gus added, the housekeepers were afraid to kick up a bigger fuss because many of them were undocumented immigrants and feared, more than losing their jobs, the threat or actuality of deportation if they attracted too much attention. Then a pack of college girls deposited themselves at the other end of the bar and Gus left us to attend to them.

"Greenwashing is a huge issue these days," Apple said as we watched Gus pluck leaves from a sprig of mint for the girls' mojitos.

"What's greenwashing?"

"The thing he was describing, where they want the customer to think they're environmentally conscious, but it's pretty much just for show. Like how my law firm makes a big deal about giving us free SEPTA passes but the partners all drive to work and almost everyone else just takes Ubers and expenses them. I'm sure the museum does stuff like that too."

I told her I wasn't sure, that I had never really paid attention to that kind of thing, and she said that I should start paying attention. I asked her why, and she said because it was important.

"But why?"

"You know why."

"I really don't. And I don't think the greenwashing was even the point of his story. He seemed much more upset about how it was affecting the housekeepers."

"But part of the reason he's upset is because it's greenwashing. Like, you hear about a hotel trying to save the planet and you think they're great."

"It's crazy that not washing towels for a few days can be construed as 'saving the planet.'"

"The water, Penelope." Apple said "Penelope" instead of "Pee" when she wanted to jokingly signify that she was annoyed with me.

"But I thought greenwashing was bad because it was only for show. If not washing the towels actually does save the planet, then it's not greenwashing, right?"

"I mean I don't personally know how much of an impact it has, but I'm sure there's some impact. I don't know, ask *Inno*."

"You seemed a lot more sure about the water a second ago."

Apple told me I was being contrarian and our conversation was going nowhere, and then asked me if I thought Gus was hot. Every time I questioned her snippets of received wisdom, she accused me of being contrarian and started talking about something else. I think she perceived my questions as condemnations of her beliefs, when most of the time what sounded to her like rhetorical attacks were genuine inquiries. She often forgot that I didn't have the same frame of reference as she did. This wasn't a trait specific to her—I'd discovered in my years in America that Americans always assumed you understood what they were talking about, perhaps because their cultural and political hegemonies were so total that, most of the time, you did. Apple saw that Gus was standing idle and waved him over again.

"Greenwashing," she said, "that's the big problem, right? With the hotel?"

"Hey," I interrupted, "remember that piece of paper I gave you? Can I have it back?"

"Huh? The napkin?" Gus shrugged. "Sure. Greenwashing?"

Apple explained to him what she had told me.

"I guess so," Gus said. "But I think it's more of a labor issue. Here you go."

"Thank you." I excused myself to go to the bathroom, where I flushed the paper napkin down the toilet, feeling, at the same time, relief and regret.

I woke up the next morning to a text from Apple:

Good news! Gus says there's a party tonight and Hoang's prob gonna be there, and wants to know if we wanna go. Do we?

?? when did you even get his number

:) I told him we're coming!

I stayed late at work to help set up Mummy Night, where elementary school kids came in for an educational sleepover at the museum. It was the event whose posters I had been dropping off at the university the day I met Hoang. Annalisa and I arranged foam mattresses around the base of a ten-ton granite sphinx, the museum's pride and joy. The sphinx had a featureless, eroded face, but the hieroglyphs inscribed on its chest were still visible, deep etchings in the three-thousand-year-old stone. I pointed at the hieroglyphs and turned to Annalisa.

"'My name is Ozymandias, king of kings,'" I said, in the deepest voice I could manage.

"That's not what it says," Annalisa said.

"You can read it?"

She looked at me with pity. "It's on the plaque."

I walked around to the back of the sphinx and pretended to rearrange some sleeping bags. I had recited the only poetry I knew, and it had not warmed Annalisa's heart. I looked at the curved hind leg haunches, the clawed feet. How many people had chiseled away at this rock, and for how long, for it to assume the form it had now?

I decided to try making small talk.

"Annalisa?"

"Yeah?"

"Have you ever been in love?"

She didn't respond, and I presumed she was ignoring me. But then she said, "I'm in love right now."

"Really? With who?"

From the other side of the sphinx, she began to describe a party she had gone to just a few weeks before, a typical Thursday night frat gathering of the kind she preferred not to attend, except that one of her close friends had her sights set on one of the "brothers," so Annalisa had accompanied her. Annalisa stood in a corner for most of it, nursing a tepid beer and watching people lob table tennis balls into plastic cups. Then her friend reappeared, distraught:

she had been rebuffed by the brother. Annalisa set down her gross drink and prepared to leave. Then, she told me, at the threshold of the door, a guy with intense blue eyes grabbed her arm to stop her. He was arriving, she was departing. He looked into her eyes with his crazy blue ones, his expression imploring; then he collected himself, released her arm, and said, in a husky, sexy accent she later learned was Uruguayan, "I'm so sorry. You have my mother's perfume." The guy, whose name was Luis, walked Annalisa and her friend back to the dorm where her friend lived, and then Annalisa and Luis returned to the party, which no longer felt boring and contemptible to Annalisa, but at once familiar and profound. They sat on a damp brown couch and talked for hours, ignoring the people and sounds that fizzed around them, while Annalisa quietly filed the encounter away as the germination of their love story.

"We've spent every day together since," Annalisa said.

"That's really beautiful," I said. Her story was so similar to the way I met Paul that I wanted to shout, *I know! Me too!* But I understood it would be uncouth. I walked around to the front of the sphinx to smile at her, feeling that I had finally broken through some layer, and now we would be friendly confidants. When she saw me, she glowered.

"I'm going to get more pillows," she said, and left. I looked at the plaque to see what the hieroglyphs said, hoping for a mystical, anguished proclamation, like Shelley's in "Ozymandias" or Luis's to Annalisa, but all they recorded was the name of the king.

Philadelphia in late September was a lot like Beijing in late September. For the whole summer the weather was hot, muggy, inert; the noonday sun warmed the sidewalks and the top of one's head, and on the hottest afternoons, just as in the middle of winter it was difficult to recall the heat, it was impossible to remember, in fact barely possible to believe, that the temperature in the city at any point of the year could have dipped below eighty degrees. But then one day near the end of the month—and the point at which this happened postponed itself every year—the air cooled and the trees soughed in the breeze. When I cycled to work that morning, it was the first of those days, and when I left the museum in the evening, dusk was settling over the city, the streetlights were coming on, and everything was charged with possibility. As usual I had my pick of bridges over which to cross the Schuylkill River. Four were especially close to the museum. There was the South Street Bridge, built in the 1920s and reconstructed ninety years later after a period of several years in which huge chunks of its concrete flank would dislodge themselves, now and then, from the main structure and plunge into the waters below. There was the Walnut Street Bridge, held up by steel prongs, V-shaped like slingshots, wide and open but in my opinion more suited to cars than pedestrians. There was the Chestnut Street Bridge, on which construction began in 1861, during the onset of the American Civil War. The first horses trotted across it in 1866, by which time the war was over, Lincoln was dead, and the grand, ill-fated project of Reconstruction was living out its brief life. The bridge once had cast-iron arches that looked like Gothic church windows, but they were demolished for the sake of an expressway. The Market Street Bridge was the oldest of the four. It began as a series of pontoons: a chain of American boats, destroyed as the Redcoats advanced; then British boats, after their forces invaded and occupied Philadelphia; then it was a procession of floating logs that kept getting washed away. Finally they built a wooden bridge, much admired until it burned down in 1875. In 1932 the current version was completed, and so far neither water nor fire had managed to destroy it. Perched on each corner were large stone eagles salvaged from the old Penn Station in New York City, which used to have a waiting room that made Grand Central look like a subway station, until it was torn down and replaced by a grim, low-ceilinged, subterranean chamber. Once, returning to Philadelphia from a trip to New York, I missed my train and had to wait several hours for the next one, at two in the morning on a Sunday night. I sat on the floor, my backpack a cushion, and tried to doze off. I saw at least three fist fights; I saw strangers spit on each other and wail and pull one another's hair. I was convinced, at the time, that none of it would have happened if they hadn't destroyed the beautiful old station and sent everybody underground.

I biked across the Market Street Bridge, my favorite. The lampposts that I loved had switched on and the sky was a bioluminescent blue. The wind picked up and I felt alive, and then it ebbed and I started to worry about the immediate future. I was glad that Apple and I had agreed to meet before heading to the party. I didn't know what I would do when I saw Hoang, what I would say to him, or even what I wanted from him. Apple kept bringing up that I had said I might be "in love," and I regretted saying it. At the time, it hadn't mattered, but since seeing him again and now trying to insinuate myself into his life, the intensity of this early declaration seemed absurd. And I worried because the hyperbole contained an element of truth—not that I was in love with him, but that I recognized in him the possibility of falling in love. I had been in love once before, with Paul, and it did not seem like a state I could re-enter. When I was in it, I had reveled in the fixation on one other person, in the particular greedy joy: thinking of him as mine, as so known, holding the cutout of him in my hands and looking back at the shape of the world with its empty outline where I had rescued him from the blank monotonous dough of everyone else. When I stopped feeling like that, recalling the feeling scared me. Now that I thought it might not be impossible to feel that way again, I was recalling, too, the obverse of love: abjection. I braked at a stoplight and briefly, unaccountably, was awash with guilt—guilt that I was being disloyal to Paul by heading now to another party, hoping to talk to another guy. I thought of Annalisa and Luis and shivered in the seasonable air. The way her story echoed our first meeting had upset me, even though the details they shared were generic. It was a reminder that the past never loosened its grip. No matter everything that came afterward, no matter that we didn't speak anymore, the memory of the night we met lay unblemished in my mind, like a boxed jewel. I was the one who noticed him first. All he was doing was standing in a corner, talking to somebody, and holding a drink, but his presence seemed to drain the vitality of everyone in the room, as if beauty were a zero-sum game. He was one of those people you always notice first. Apple had seen me staring and identified him as a French exchange student named Paul and "the least annoying person in my bioethics seminar, but low bar." I said he looked like an actor who would play a heroic surgeon on a television show, and Apple made a face and said, "Natural blonds scare me," and I said, "Is that blond?" and she said, "What would you call it?" and I said, "Tawny? Ochre? Dusky gold?" and Apple said, "Jesus Christ, fine, I'll introduce you," and dragged me over to him, and then Paul and I argued about Napoleon's legal reforms until Apple got bored and strode off. A few months later I was in Charles de Gaulle Airport at the end of a summer spent with Paul, watching my flight to Philadelphia turn red on the departure board as the final boarding call went out. I hadn't been able to walk up to the check-in counter and hand over my passport. I let the flight take off, deciding that rather than be apart from him, I would drop out of college. It was the first time I had missed a plane in my life.

Apple and I had dinner near where she lived in Center City, and then I left my bike in her apartment and we walked to the address Gus had given her, somewhere in Spring Garden. On the way, I told her about the pontoons that the soldiers had used to cross the river at the site of the Market Street Bridge. From there we reached the topic of the Civil War and slavery, and Apple told me that when she was in elementary school in the Pennsylvania suburbs, her teacher, in an effort to make the text they were studying more "interactive," had organized a class activity where the students pretended to be slaves and slave owners. The teacher made the white children play the slave owners and the black children play the slaves, and then joked that she didn't know where to put Apple and the other Asians. First she made some of them slaves to round out the numbers, because there were more Asian kids than black kids. When there were an equal number of children in each group she turned to Apple, the last student standing in the odd-numbered class. The teacher told Apple she could choose which role she wanted to play: the slave owner or the slave.

"I was obviously mortified, and I was pissed that I was standing there alone after everyone else had their teams—not teams, you know what I mean—which, by the way, never happened to me in gym. No offense, I know it probably happened to you. Do they do that in China? Anyway, in high school somebody brought it up again and we all agreed that it was weird and racist, which it was, but I do find my specific dilemma interesting now. Like, what if Mrs. Healy, recognizing me as, like, the smartest kid in the class—and I'm not just saying that, you know I was valedicto-

rian, Pee—what if she was, like, versed in Asian American studies and was implicating me in this radical commentary on what it
means to be yellow in the black and white race politics of the US
of A? Do you know what I mean? Obviously that wasn't what she
was doing, but isn't it interesting to pretend that she was?"

I didn't think it was interesting, but I didn't want to hurt
Apple's feelings, so I just said, "Do you think there were any Chinese Americans in the Civil War?"

"On which side?"

"Either."

"There were probably like five Chinese guys in the Union
army. There had to have been. I don't think there would have
been any in the South. But who knows."

"Wait, what did you end up choosing? Were you a slave owner
or a slave?"

"I don't remember," Apple said, unconvincingly. "I wonder where Mrs. Healy is today. Still teaching? Maybe dead? She
seemed so old, but it was probably just because we were kids, and
she was actually, like, thirty."

We turned the corner, and I realized we were about to arrive. To
distract myself from my nerves, I fed Apple more historical trivia.

"Can you guess what the deadliest conflict of the nineteenth
century was?"

"Is it the Civil War?"

"It's *a* civil war."

Apple groaned. "Just tell me the answer, I know you're itching
to info-dump."

"The Taiping Rebellion. Twenty million people, and that's the
low estimate. It might have been like a hundred million. The
Civil War didn't even hit a million. What's crazy," I continued,
rushing to catch up with Apple, who had started to walk at a
faster pace, "is that they were coterminous."

We reached the designated house. A five-step stoop led to a green door, the paint peeling off the corners, showing the wood. I could hear music playing inside, filtering out to the street through the walls, muffled, softened at the edges, the bass pronounced and the human voice indistinct, an auditory experience that induced the intoxicating feelings of anticipation and restlessness that preceded one's entrance into a party.

There were more people inside than I was expecting, and nobody really looked up when we walked in. The living room was unremarkable, except for an unusual amount of koala-related objects: there were posters of koalas on the walls, koala figurines on the coffee table, a limp koala cushion on the sofa, and, balanced on the sill of an open window, surrounded by people lighting cigarettes and leaning out to blow smoke in cursory attempts to keep it from thickening the atmosphere of the room, a small koala bowl, the ceramic animal on its back, arms and legs outstretched, stomach hollowed into a depository for ash.

"So which one is he?" Apple said.

I said I didn't think he was there, and then watched her scan the room with narrowed eyes, as if she thought I might be lying and was searching herself for a face she had never seen, confident she would be able to recognize him by some other mechanism.

"Well," Apple said. "Drink?"

We found beers in the kitchen and lingered there, not quite sure what to do with ourselves. Apple started going through the cabinets and commenting on everything she found inside, ignoring me when I begged her to stop. There were koala magnets on the fridge.

Apple shook a box of Cap'n Crunch in my face.

"Do you think they'd be mad if I ate some of this?"

"Yes."

"Hm. Almond butter. What if he's a vegan?"

"He's not. And this isn't his house."

"Yes, it is."

"You said Gus lived here."

"I said Gus invited me." Apple tipped her head back and threw a handful of cereal kernels into her mouth. "This is Hoang's house."

I looked at the mother and child koala embracing on the fridge magnet. They had suddenly gained a sinister aspect.

"Maybe we should leave."

"Why would we do that?"

"You don't want to leave?"

"Who's leaving?"

It was Gus. He had switched his stud earrings for small gold hoops. Apple placed the cereal box on the kitchen counter and smiled. "No one. Hi."

I left them in the kitchen and returned to the people and the koalas, scanning the room to decide which conversation to crash. I could hear the man next to me telling a story about a fight he had started on the playground when he was a child. He laughed as he told the story, and spoke of his younger self in a tone of fondness, as if he were talking about his own son. Americans, I had noticed, loved telling stories about themselves as children. The stories often illustrated positive aspects of their personality—in this man's, he had started the fight after the other boy yanked some girl's ponytail—and the idea, I guessed, was that the actions of the younger self were evidence of the older self's positive qualities. I often wondered if I should be doing this too, telling stories of myself as a child, but these people seemed to remember much more about their childhoods than I did, and by inference thought much more about that period of their lives. It was like Apple and her incredibly detailed story about Mrs. Healy. How had she remembered all that? I had had what I considered a fine enough childhood, and I never felt the desire to bring up its happinesses in conversation. The parts of my early life that were not happy, for example certain episodes with my mother, lay similarly dormant in my mind, and of course I would never bring those up. I remembered images, people, events, but I had no arsenal of stories to tell, and I felt no kinship with the four- or six- or twelve-year-old versions of myself, as these people seemed to feel. If I thought about painful memories, I felt pity for the child who experienced them, but I no longer felt like that child was me. Was it that other people dwelled more on their early lives than I did, or did they integrate these stories into their present identities in a way I had never thought to do? Or was it that I was incapable of doing so? Either way, I had no interest in this guy's childhood. I could hear Apple in the kitchen, asking Gus if he knew how many people died in the Taiping Rebellion. I wandered over to the window, where a black guy and a white girl were smoking cigarettes over the ceramic koala.

"I don't see why I should do it," the guy was saying.

"But that's what they want you to think, that's what they want you to do," the girl said.

"Seems like they want me to think that, but they also want me to think I have to. No matter what I do I'm doing what they want me to do, so, might as well do what I want, no?"

I searched for the alcohol-by-volume number on the bottle of beer in my hand, wondering if I was already drunk, so confounding was the exchange into which I had just walked.

"Don't you think it's better to do the thing that might make a tiny difference than the one that might do harm?" the girl said.

"Harm?" He repeated the word, sounding incredulous. "Harm? Who am I harming?"

"*You* know what I'm talking about, right?"

I realized she meant me.

"Sorry, I think I missed the start of the argument."

"We're not arguing," the girl said. "Mohd thinks it's useless to vote and I'm trying to tell him that it's not. Are you registered yet?"

"For what?"

"The midterms."

"When are those?"

Mohd laughed. "See?" he said to the girl. I began to wish I had joined the conversation about the guy's childhood instead. There was a lull as they drew on their cigarettes and tapped ash into the stomach of the koala.

"Do you guys know what's up with all this koala stuff?"

"It's the guy I live with," Mohd said. "He loves koalas."

"The midterms are in November," said the girl. "It's not too late to register."

I was reminded of a conversation with Apple, years earlier, when we were in college and some kind of state or national election was coming up that Apple was getting into a frenzy about, stationing herself on the main thoroughfares of the campus, thrusting flyers at pedestrians and threatening them with public humiliation if they did not comply with her urgings, like the religious doomsdayers who sometimes lurked outside the university buildings, telling us we were going to go to hell for "onanism" and "homo sex." In Apple's head I was Chinese, so I was spared her assaults, but then she saw my navy blue American passport on my dresser one day and froze. "Wait, Pee. Are you a U.S. citizen?" With a growing sense of dread I mumbled, "Maybe?" Apple accused me of lying to her and reneging on my patriotic duty, but calmed down after whoever she was supporting won the election. She thought I had deceived her, but the truth was it had never occurred to me to vote, no matter her exhortations. I'd lived much longer in China than I had in the U.S.; back in college, I'd only just arrived, and participating in elections had seemed like something "real" Americans did. Over the years I started to feel more American, but it took time, like breaking in a new pair of shoes, clenching your teeth through the pinch of stiff and unfamiliar leather.

"But did you vote in 2016? Please tell me you voted in 2016," the girl was asking me. I was barely listening, because I was realizing that "the guy I live with" had to be Hoang. So Hoang was the author of the koala situation?

"Let her live," Mohd said. "Maybe she voted for somebody you didn't want. What are you gonna say then?"

"I'm . . . Chinese," I said, so they would stop trying to make me participate. I was pleased with this non-lie. It was a factual statement, after all, made no less so by the fact that I was also, technically, American.

"You're Chinese? From China?" the girl said.

"Yes. Chinese from China."

"And you live here?"

"Yes."

"You don't have an accent," she said. "How come?" It was one of my favorite Americanisms—they said "you don't have an accent" when they meant "you have an American accent," as if their country's mode of speech was the default setting of every English speaker in the world.

"Oh, you know," I said vaguely, "TV shows."

"I was a political science major in college. It must be crazy for you to live in America and experience democratic elections."

"Abby, you don't even experience democratic elections," Mohd said. "You know in China they got trains, and free healthcare. Nobody's dying because they took dog insulin."

"I'd rather have no trains than live under an authoritarian dictatorship," Abby said.

"I'd rather live in their authoritarian dictatorship than this one."

"You know we're entering a new phase of the Cold War. Capitalism versus communism."

"What's so bad about communism?"

"You don't think it's important to defend human rights? America needs to counter China, I mean, we have a democratic duty."

"So you want World War Three?"

"I think we should be prepared for it."

"Some people argue that the Seven Years' War was the real 'first world war,'" I said.

Abby glared at me. "So?"

"So in that case, the next one would actually be World War Four."

"It would only happen if America made it happen," Mohd said.

"But don't you value freedom?" Abby said.

"Who said I don't value freedom?"

"You, when you said communism isn't so bad."

"Maybe I just don't value the kind of freedom you're talking about."

"Freedom of speech? Freedom of religion?"

"Yeah, and the freedom to starve to death on the street. In the richest country in the world."

Abby whipped around to me. "Which do you like more? China or America?"

I could tell they both wanted me to back them up, because my approval would lend one argument a knockout blow of authenticity against the other. I agreed with aspects of what each had said, and yet I had the feeling they were both wrong in other, more fundamental ways. Which did I like more, China or America? It was the question a thousand Beijing taxi drivers had posed to me before, and I gave Abby and Mohd the same answer I gave them.

"They're different. There's good and bad parts to each," I said, reveling, as I always did, in the platitude. They looked dissatisfied.

"That's it?" Abby said.

I shrugged.

"I'm not really into politics."

Mohd laughed. "See? She knows."

"Listen," I said, "the koalas. Why does your roommate like koalas so much?"

"Ask her," Mohd said. "She's his girlfriend."

"I'd rather not say," Abby said. "It's very personal."

"Oh," I said. Surely, surely not—Hoang had a girlfriend? And it was this girl?

Mohd turned back to Abby. "If you can get my boss to give me the day off I'll go vote for whoever you want."

"Would you actually?"

"Nah."

"But why not?"

"Told you. Doesn't make a difference."

"You think Obama didn't make a difference?"

"Fuck Obama."

The conversation went on like this, so I walked outside, back to the empty street, and sat down on the stoop. The koalas had made me despondent. They were a baffling aesthetic choice, and not one I would have ever associated with Hoang. I worried that I had invented him, that the connection I felt and hoped might be mutual was a figment of my delusion, that our interactions had been meaningless and commonplace, that he lacked the alluring qualities with which I had endowed him, that he would forever be a stranger with an unintelligible passion for marsupial-themed interiors. That he had a girlfriend, and that it was Abby.

Just then, a door opened across the street, creating a bright rectangular panel in the dark line of houses, and a figure emerged, first in shadow, and then beginning to assume more features as the door closed and my eyes adjusted to the sudden change, until I could see his expression and the reflected glare of light that danced in his glasses, and realized it was Hoang.

I stood up to meet him, remembering as I did that I had no idea whether he'd known I was going to be there.

"Forest!"

"Hi! Where have you been?"

"In my house?"

"That's your house? The koalas aren't yours?"

Hoang laughed. "My friend Mohd lives with a guy who loves koalas. We're neighbors. Is it neighbors when you're across the street, or does it have to be side by side?"

I was elated. "I don't know. Apple said you lived there. I was so worried."

"Worried? Who's Apple?"

"Oh, my friend. She's in there. Do you want to go for a walk?"

We walked until we reached the river, and then followed its course southward. Because I had mentioned Apple, we talked about fruit. Hoang said his favorite apples were the tart green ones, Granny Smiths. I said I liked pears, but only the Asian variety, which were floral and crisp, and not even shaped like pears.

"That's so weird to think about, that there's a canonical pear, to the point where you can talk about a non-pear-shaped pear," Hoang said. I agreed that it was weird. Then we talked about which shapes we liked the best. I said I loved the word "trapezoid" but was always disappointed when I saw a picture of one, because I didn't think it lived up to its name. Hoang said he liked hexagons, because they fit together so well, and formed honeycombs. "And circles, we gotta include circles," he said. "That one doesn't even need an explanation." I asked him if he'd heard of *Flatland*, the Victorian social satire in which shapes are people and live in a two-dimensional world. He said he hadn't, and asked me if I read a lot of books, and I said yes, but mostly history. He said, "Tell me a history book I should read." I gave him the name of one I'd just finished, an account of horses in the nineteenth century and their subsequent disappearance from public life, and he repeated the title to himself. "I want to make sure I remember," he said.

We passed a huge construction lot, empty except for a series of concrete pillars like obelisks, each equidistant from the next. As we walked, the pillars seemed to move without moving, perhaps the effect of the construction site floodlights, which gave them long shifting shadows. Hoang pointed out a big banner that said luxury condominiums were being built on the site.

We reached the railway tracks. We could see a long freight train, sitting still and large in the dark. We walked to the front of the train, the noise of it getting louder as we approached. By the time we were close enough to see the cab lit up and the engineer inside, a man with a white beard and a dark coat and one arm draped over the open window, the noise had grown to a magnificent blare. He didn't seem surprised to see us.

"Where's this train going?" Hoang shouted over the sound.

"New York," the engineer shouted back.

"What are you hauling?"

"What?"

"What are you hauling?"

"Nothing, we're just bringing the cars up."

He said he was heading off soon: all that noise was the train getting ready to move. We said goodbye to him and walked up to the bridge so we could watch him set off.

"I love how the lights are all piled up like that," Hoang said, pointing at the lampposts. I realized we were on the Market Street Bridge. In the distance, the date and time ran across the top of the PECO building in red letters. It was September 30, 2018, and it was almost midnight. The numbers disappeared, replaced by an ad for the PECO Primate Pen at the Philadelphia Zoo. There was a strong breeze, heralding the change in weather. I hadn't realized until then that it would be October so soon. We leaned over the side of the bridge. We could see the boxcars of the train that was about to leave and the open-topped wagons of the train beside it, which were filled with curls of silver metal that sparkled in the darkness.

Hoang told me that in high school they used to converge under the bridge and drink beer or vodka in plastic bottles by the river and get into fights with kids from other schools. He said one night he climbed onto a train from the side of the tracks and waited for it to move. He waited for half an hour, but nothing happened, so he climbed off again.

"Do you think I could jump from here?" Hoang said suddenly.

"Onto the train?"

"Yeah."

I leaned over the bridge, trying to judge the distance.

"For sure."

"I'm gonna do it."

"Seriously?"

"Can you hold this?"

He handed me his keys, and I put them in my pocket. He vaulted over the side of the bridge, landing lightly, grinning boyishly, his fingers clasping the edge. I stepped closer to see his feet; they were perched on a thin outcrop of ledge, heels hanging off. He twisted around to look at the train. It was about a fifteen-foot drop.

"I think I can make it."

"Are you sure?"

I worried that he might slip, and injure himself, or somehow die. I would be alone in the middle of the night with the dead body of someone I did not know much about. His family would find out I existed at the same moment they found out that he was dead, and that he had died by doing something I could have stopped him from doing. It would not be a good first impression.

"What if we both jumped?" Hoang said. "Since we know he's leaving soon."

"And then what?"

"We could go to New York. We could lie in the car and watch the sunrise."

"He might get mad at us."

"I don't think he would. I think he'd be chill about it."

"Yeah?"

"Yeah. He was a good guy. I liked him."

"Me too," I said. I liked to think of the three of us sharing some strange experience that none of us had planned for. Hoang was too optimistic, the engineer would definitely be mad. But I wanted to do it. I wanted to jump on the train with him and ride out to New York. I looked at Hoang's hands, gripping the pale stone of the bridge. I wondered if what drew me in was that he was not afraid of life, not in the way I was, whether it was fear of the people who populated it, fear of departing from the script, or just fear of too much of it at once. Hoang did not seem to have such hang-ups. He seemed to understand instinctively that the world was, in fact, full of people waiting to be talked to, full of places to head toward, full of things to see.

I decided if he asked again I would say yes. I waited, pressing my palms against the cool stone, feeling its weight. Or maybe I would say it first, beat him to it, call his bluff. But he swung back over while I was still working myself up to speak. I gave him his keys, and he thanked me, and said he'd already forgotten about them.

The train cars started to move. They moved for a long time. There were so many of them. We stood there for five or ten minutes, and they were still passing underneath the bridge. The train seemed to go on forever, like if we stayed all night we would still not see the end. I looked over at the PECO Building. The clock said it was October now.

When I got home I lingered for a while on the fire escape, feeling the cool air on my face and arms and listening to the wind rustle the leaves, which had already begun to drop from the branches. I felt nervous. I was developing a crush, a real one. I realized I had embarked on the evening hoping, on some level, that Hoang would disappoint me, but I'd enjoyed the time so much that I'd forgotten my conversation with Annalisa, and the memories of Paul it had resurfaced. Now I was remembering again. I went back into the kitchen and filled a glass with water from the sink, and drank it slowly, leaning against the wall, churning over the day in my mind. There was a scratching noise, and then something darted out of the gas burner of the oven. I yelped. It was a small brown mouse.

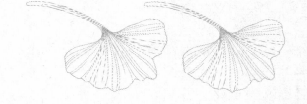

Two

FOUR

I came home from work one Friday in early November to find the apartment totally upended. The sofa had disappeared, and in its place was a long slim table with attached stools that folded out or tucked in, depending on one's requirements. Xinwei had read an article that said standing up during meals promoted longevity, while sitting caused cancer, and had adjusted our lives accordingly. When I walked in, she and Raymond were in the middle of dinner, wearing plastic gloves and breaking crab shells with tiny hammers. With one deft foot, Xinwei demonstrated the stool withdrawal mechanism, and explained the article's findings. She said I should feel free to use the seats whenever I wanted, though she and Raymond would refrain. Raymond, looking forlorn, gnawed a carpus and shifted his weight from one leg to the other.

The other occupant, the sleepwalker, had absconded to Munich for Oktoberfest, revealing the purpose of his late-night German lessons. But it was now November, and I wondered what our housemate was up to in Bavaria, and how he had secured such a long vacation.

"He moved there," said Raymond. "He's got a job at BMW."

"What? Really? How do you know?"

"LinkedIn."

"What about his room?"

"We should have made friends with him," Raymond said slyly.

"Free BMW, yeah?"

"Driving is more dangerous than flying," Xinwei said, spooning roe out of the carapace of the crab. She said this every time Raymond brought up driving, because he loved cars but had an as-yet-incurable fear of planes, meaning he had not once visited her family in China. The farthest they had traveled together outside of the continental United States was England, on the *Queen Mary II*. It took seven days, and when they arrived they didn't even go to London because there was a rail strike. They just stayed at the port in Southampton until it was time to return. Xinwei began to rattle off the statistical probabilities of driving deaths versus flying deaths as she stirred the soft orange roe into her rice. Sadly, Xinwei was a rational person, and would never understand that Raymond's issue had at its base irrationality, and was therefore immune to statistics.

I left them to their crab and retreated to my room, because my father was calling me on the phone. I was apprehensive. My father possessed that trait often ascribed to people my age, the proclivity for texting and the phobia of phone calls, so this was an aberration.

"Guess who's coming to *New York*!"

He was shouting over the scherzo of the Third Symphony,

and he was close to inaudible. It didn't help that he spoke to me in an unpredictable jumble of English and Chinese, peppering his Mandarin with English words for various reasons: to signal irony or sophistication, to mock an American pronunciation, to show off a new addition to his vocabulary, or sometimes just because he preferred one word over its translated other, as with the English *New York*.

"Can you turn that down?"

"Of course I can't!" he yelled.

"Why? I mean, when? When are you coming?"

"The *Whitney* Museum wants to do a *retrospective* of my work. My publicist says I should take it as a compliment, but it sounds like a death knell to me. What do you think? Death knell or compliment?"

"When is it?"

"May. You're coming back before then for your *Christmas break*, right?"

"I don't really have *Christmas break* anymore, I graduated three years ago."

"Ah," he said in his usual tone, inquisitive, almost abashed, but not really apologetic. "You know what?"

"What?"

"I told them I was working on a new piece, a *large-scale installation*, and I'm letting them premiere it. The second they heard me say '*large-scale installation*' they lost it. They couldn't say no. So we will bill it as a *retrospective with a twist*. Doesn't that sound great? They're fucking excited."

"That's good," I said. I was thinking about the sofa, trying to assess the implications of its departure. I didn't often sit on it, but I didn't like the idea of living in a house with no sofa, or, more specifically, in a house where the sofa could be there one day and be whisked away the next. Xinwei, of course, had made the decision unilaterally. Still, I couldn't lead myself to the conclusion that Xinwei might be lacking in certain interpersonal qualities, or that this behavior was something I should communicate with her about. I decided I didn't mind living without a sofa. Apple, I knew, would call me a pushover and send me a link to Joan Didion's essay about self-respect, even though I had repeatedly told Apple that according to the metrics laid out in the essay, I did have self-respect. Didion seemed to suggest that feeling like a doormat was a much greater indicator of being a doormat than appearing, on the outside, to be one. But Apple had a hard time grasping my perspective. She assessed other people's behavior through the prism of her own: she distrusted Hoang, for example, for what she saw as his affectation of "quirk" when he did things like not having a phone, freeing the lab mice, and getting fired for not lying about freeing the lab mice. She viewed these behaviors as "fake," as pretensions, because she could not imagine herself doing them, and therefore could not imagine that someone who did them was not being "fake." For the same reason, if I told her, as I surely would, what had happened to the sofa in my apartment, she would think I was being stubborn and only pretending—if not to Xinwei, then to her, or, most intractably, to myself—not to mind, because if Apple's roommate disposed of a large piece of common furniture one day and she shrugged it off, she would only be pretending not to mind.

"This Xinwei sounds like Napoleon," my father said, after I told him about the new table. He always found a way to mention Napoleon when the Third Symphony was playing, ever since I told him that Beethoven originally dedicated the piece to him, but ripped up the manuscript in a fury when Napoleon crowned himself emperor and betrayed the republican ideals that Beethoven so admired. I fought dual impulses to defend either Xinwei or Napoleon against the unfair comparison. My father returned to the subject of the retrospective, and mused about the weather in Manhattan, and after a few minutes I realized that he thought I lived in New York. By now it was too late to issue a correction—he might think I had deliberately misled him and become upset—so I said nothing. After a while, he said that Fei, his personal assistant slash girlfriend, was summoning him to breakfast, and ended the call.

I left my room and ate some crab with Xinwei and Raymond, who were somehow still discussing air travel. As I cracked open a pincer with the ridged inner thighs of Xinwei's steel crab tong, I realized I should have taken the rare opportunity of getting my father, for one, on the phone, and two, paying relative attention, to tell him that earlier in the week Dr. Bae, the head of new programming for the museum, had called me in to tell me that he wanted me to take the lead in curating a small exhibition on women and domestic life in the Qing Dynasty, which would of course feature the institution's heretofore undisplayed collection of shoes for bound feet. I sent my father a brief voice message on WeChat, summarizing the news, and a while later he sent back a picture of his own painting, a blue-toned, shadowy portrait of his mother from two decades earlier. He had depicted her as a girl, just before she ran off to join the Party, scaling a mountain rock with her flat and useful feet. The painting was titled 大脚儿 / *unbound*, and it had been a huge hit, one of my father's first break-through works, putting him on the map in the Western art world. A message popped up after the picture:

remember this? only sold for a million.

The next day I set out for the library, where I planned to spend the morning before meeting Apple and Gus at some kind of protest to which the latter was bringing the former, and to which she in turn was bringing me. After that, I had a meeting at the museum with Dr. Bae, who apparently worked on Saturdays. The air outside had a bone-dampening chill, and the sky was a sooty sheet. Leaves crunched under my shoes, and the weight of my steps transformed those freshly fallen, their edges curling up in the air as if still stretching toward the sunlight, into powdered debris, frosting the gum-spotted pavement with their copper hue.

I had always disliked November, which I regarded as a fallow month, full of shrinking days—the beginning of the smallening of the world that was winter, which did not let up until the first day of spring, whenever that happened to be. My distaste for November had eased when I moved to America, thanks to the warm balm of Thanksgiving, which I had spent in Apple's home many times, and also thanks to the Black Friday sales. This year I hoped to get my hands on an Instant Pot. But those events were at the end of the month, and long bleak weeks separated me from them.

The library was a nice place to spend a cold weekend morning reading about Napoleon. Of course I could read whatever I wanted at home, online, but the simple rituals of library-going—securing my favorite seat, consulting the stacks—made it an enjoyable outing. Because of my work at the museum, I now regarded the study of nineteenth-century Chinese history as my day job, which made the study of nineteenth-century European history feel like a fun hobby, and for me it was. Napoleonic history had been a pet subject of mine for years, and my conversation with my father had refreshed my interest.

The only people I ever saw in the library were the elderly, the odd, the homeless, and the student poor—not college students, whose campuses were amply furnished, but high school and middle school students whose schools might have had places designated as libraries, but were so in name only, lacking comput-ers and most books.

I took my favorite seat and spent some time going over what I planned to say to Dr. Bae in our meeting later that afternoon. In my notebook, I doodled bicornes and tricolor cockades with my six-in-one multi pen. The detail that endeared me most to Napo-leon when I first started reading about him was that he never lost his Corsican accent, and French people made fun of him for it his entire life, from his schoolmates in dreary Aube to the aristo-crats who surrounded him when he was emperor. From time to time I glanced up to see what the people at the computers were doing with their screens: playing solitaire, writing an essay about the cotton gin, scrolling down the WHYY homepage on a font setting so large I could make out the subheadings of the articles. Although I loved the library, I could never quite get used to the whiff of the carceral, especially the entry and exit point, with its metal detector and turnstile and its security guard who sat behind bulletproof glass plating and never spoke, only glumly motioned for you to open your bag as you left so she could see if you had stolen any books. According to the kids who sometimes chatted with me across the shared tables, their schools had a similar setup.

I found Apple and Gus in a coffee shop, nestled in a corner table, their heads close together. I was still adjusting to their acquain-tance. As I moved closer, I could hear Gus talking about the house-keepers. One of them, a woman named Mariama, was friendly with one of the line cooks in the hotel restaurant, Dorothea, because they lived in the same neighborhood, and they some-times commuted together when their shifts coincided. Mariama had lately learned from Dorothea, Gus said, waving to me when I pulled up a chair but not pausing his narration, that a couple of the kitchen employees, frustrated about various issues, including that their wages had not gone up by more than a dollar and a few cents in a decade of work, not even after the hotel renovation, had been in contact with representatives of a nationwide hospitality workers' union, just to get a sense of what their deal was, to hear what they had to say.

"Now a bunch of us are getting into the idea, most of the kitchen folks, a couple in housekeeping, and a lot of the bar staff. Hoang too," Gus added, nodding, I feared, specifically to me, before turning back to Apple.

"You're forming a union?" I said.

"We're forming a committee."

"You're forming a committee to form a union?"

"Exactly. But we haven't gone public. We're exploring our options."

"How easy would that be to do?"

"Unionize? Hard," Gus said. He made brief mention of the National Labor Relations Board and the Trump administration's anti-worker policies. But, he added, there was no point worrying about that now; it was early days, and they were focused on talking to everyone who worked at the hotel, trying to see how open they were to the idea of some kind of collective action, to which many people, for various reasons, some practical, some ideological, some arbitrary, were averse. Gus began talking about the difficulties of getting his coworkers alone to talk, and how some of them didn't even want to be seen with the employees who supported unionization, because they worried their bosses might see and think they supported it too, which could jeopardize their jobs. To avoid this, the committee was making house calls, but most people slammed the doors in their faces. The more Gus talked, the more I realized I didn't really know what "unionizing" entailed. I knew about Reagan and the air traffic controllers, and Thatcher and the coal miners, but those episodes had involved preexisting unions, things fully formed. I had no idea what was involved in trying to make one from scratch. Apple and Gus finished their coffees and we started walking.

"Is anyone else coming?" I asked Gus.

"Yeah, a few people. It'll be good."

"Anyone we'd know?" Apple said, trying to catch my eye.

"Don't think so."

The police had blocked off the section of Market Street that ran past Independence Hall, and forty or fifty cops were standing in a line in front of the crowd among which we numbered. The gathering, Gus explained, was a semi-spontaneous counter-protest of a preapproved rally organized by a far-right group not local to the city. The right-wing group said they were gathering in support of the president, ahead of the midterm election on Tuesday; Gus said they were white nationalists. They had bused in members and supporters, some from several states away, and a few people had even flown in from the other side of the country for the occasion, according to the group's Twitter announcements, which Gus and his friends were monitoring. Apparently a lot more members had planned to come but were scared off when they heard how many people were showing up to oppose them. The police had propped their bikes up tire-to-tire to make a barrier separating the counterprotesters from the sanctioned rally. The officers faced us with folded arms. They wore conical silver bicycle helmets, and some of them had bottles of blue Gatorade tucked into their big black belts.

On the grass, behind the cops, the men milled about. Most of them wore sunglasses and baseball caps, and many held up American flags larger than their own bodies. One man had a Gadsden flag, a bright yellow pop in a sea of red and blue. The flags billowed hugely in the wind and made a pleasing visual symmetry with the even larger American flag above Independence Hall that wafted above them, big as a car. The men were outnumbered by the counterprotesters, who were a funny mix of old people in tie-dye, young people with cardboard signs that said Sharpied things like NO SAFE SPACE FOR HATE, and a loose gaggle of figures garbed head to toe in black, bandannas obscuring their faces, lingering at the edges of the crowd. Gus said hi to a few of them. Apple had briefed me beforehand: they were anarchists, like Gus.

I looked at the flag-bearing men again, the men whose right to assembly the cops were making sure was respected. A couple of them were setting up an amplifier and microphone, which brought to my mind the squads of women in Beijing with blue-rinse perms and tattooed eyebrows who square-danced in the public parks at night. The rest of the men watched as their companions fussed with the electronic equipment. I was too far away to make out the expressions on their faces, but it didn't look like they were talking, and I wondered how many of them knew each other, if they were mostly strangers or friends.

We stood around for a while, observing the people on either side of the police line shift around and sometimes shout insults across the cordon of cops. Gus occasionally threw one out, or else turned to Apple and me and made mysterious references to "comrades." I thought maybe he was in normal clothes, rather than masked and wearing black, in order to chaperone and reassure us, which, if true, was very nice of him. He suggested we walk around to the far side of the park to get a different view.

"So are you still avoiding him?" Apple said to me. Gus was a few paces ahead, but she said it in Chinese, which she rarely ever used with me, claiming that I would mock her Taiwanese accent and childish syntax. She made exceptions when she wanted to gossip.

"Who?"

"You know who."

"I'm not avoiding anyone. What do you think of all this?"

"This? Gus says it's more important than—how do you say *voting* in Chinese?"

"Is it?"

"More important? Of course it isn't," Apple said. She switched to English and added, "But I'm investigating the claim."

The grassy slope was cut up by metal barricades between which we zigzagged to reach a second line of bicycles higher up on the field. We were farther away now, and we could see everything spread out below like Napoleonic army formations before a battle. I still couldn't make out anybody's expressions. A reporter from a local newspaper hovered a few feet away, wearing one of the biggest backpacks I'd ever seen, tagged with the word PRESS. He extracted a camera from the bag and began to fiddle with it.

A woman and a toddler walked by on the grass, and the woman hoisted the child onto her shoulders. "See the big group on the other side of the street? Those are the good people."

A group of Cub Scouts walked past, right as the counterprotesters chanted in unison, "NAZI SCUM OFF OUR STREETS!"

"Those are the people that disagree with the president, right?" one of the boys asked the adult that was leading them.

"Those are the people that disagree, period," the man replied.

Gus perked up when he heard this, and as the Cub Scouts trailed off, he shouted, "That's a facile reduction!" A few of the boys turned their heads, but the man leading them did not.

"Were you talking to the guy or the kid?" I said. I was jesting but I was also unsure.

Gus paused. "Both," he said.

There was a shuffling behind us, and we turned to see six blinkered police horses trotting over the grass. They passed us and moved nearer to the road, and their riders arranged them in a neat brown row. A Buick trundled by, windows down, and the driver slowed the car and leaned out. "Thank you!" he shouted to the horses.

Gus shook his head. "This country is full of bootlickers."

The horses snuffled and pawed the dirt. The men with the flags started to recite the Pledge of Allegiance. Two of the cops in front of me were splitting a mini packet of Cool Ranch Doritos. My hands were getting colder and colder, and I was quite hungry. Apple said we could eat later. I said that I would be right back, and left to get a breakfast sandwich from Dunkin' Donuts. I ordered a hot coffee to warm my hands, but the cup was Styrofoam and no heat came through. I listened to my favorite podcast, *The Age of Napoleon*, and checked my phone as I ate. There was an email from Dr. Bae, confirming our meeting. On WeChat, my father had posted a picture of some ugly purplish shoes, captioned with the crocodile emoji. By the time I returned to the demonstration, maybe twenty-five minutes later, everyone was dispersing. One of the anarchists had gotten too close to the police line, and a cop had grabbed him by the collar and hurled him to the ground. The guy's friends had jumped in to try and drag him away before he was arrested, and more cops swarmed in, and so more protesters followed. The men with the flags had paused their rendition of the national anthem to watch the drama unfold.

"Pigs," Gus spat. He pointed to the road at our feet. Blood speckled the asphalt.

"So what now?" I said.

"Not everyone got away. There's jail support later if you want to help out."

"She has a meeting. But I'll be there," Apple said, and touched his shoulder. I wasn't used to seeing her express physical affection, or, for that matter, sincere investment in political causes beyond electioneering, and I found the novelties both unsettling and sweet.

I left, calculating that if I walked to the museum via a slightly meandering route, I would reach it just in time for my appointment with Dr. Bae. I walked up Race Street so I could take a topical route past the Roundhouse, the pleasingly globular building where the police were headquartered. The architects who created it had come in second place in the competition to design the Sydney Opera House. Had they won, Sydney Harbour would feature a lopsided concrete accordion instead of those lovely expressionist shark fins. The Roundhouse had soft curves and wide stairs leading to its entryway, and I watched it undulate as I walked. Thin black windows were set in the concrete like sprocket holes on a roll of film. It wasn't far from my apartment, and I sometimes walked over to see it, because I liked the way it looked, but now, recalling the blood on the road, admiring it felt strange. I'd read somewhere that the architects gave the building features that embodied certain positive ideals, believing it was possible for the design to transmit these ideals, somehow, to the Philadelphia police. I also knew that the Philadelphia police were world-famous for decades for being one of the most brutal police forces in the country, so the design of the Roundhouse had evidently had no effect. But I thought I did believe that buildings influenced people's moods and even their behavior, like the old and new Penn Stations. Was this the same, or was it different? Surely it was different. But how?

On Eighth Street, I spotted some of the men from the rally, holding their rolled-up flags and trying to hail taxis. I wondered where their buses had gone. The anarchists were there too, jeering from the other side of the road. A few cops stood near the men with the flags. They had swapped their bicycle helmets for black patrol caps; their arms remained crossed. Taxis kept passing, sometimes slowing down, but every time the drivers saw the two groups on each side of the road, they drove away. One taxi driver slowed his car to a crawl, rolled down his window, and flipped off the cops. The anarchists cheered.

I continued walking, turning onto Vine Street so I could see the cars speeding along the expressway and the Mormon temple, which always reminded me of a bank building, though no bank had spires like those. The street signs on that section of the road were my favorite. In Chinatown, all the streets had two names: Vine Street wasn't just Vine Street, it was 萬安街 in red underneath the green, a secret second geography. Ahead of me there was a massive gingko tree, curry-powder yellow, its shedded leaves making an aureole on the ground. When I stepped over the leaves, they were soft, nothing like treading on the crackly sloughed fronds of oak, maple, or ash. And that woodsy musk, another of those maligned scents, like durian, like stinky tofu, like certain French cheeses, that was nothing nearly as bad as people made it out to be; that was, in its own way, enticing. I reached the river. Sparrows were hopping around in front of me, bouncing from the pavement to the railing and back, over and over, like they were playing a game. A man wearing layered sweatshirts and pushing a shopping trolley came past, singing. *I got a voodoo princess, her dark beauty can't be beat.* He wore an Eagles beanie, and his trolley was full of empty Sprite bottles.

I realized, belatedly, the difference between what I thought about Penn Station and what the architects thought about the Roundhouse. You could believe a beautiful building made people happy and a depressing one made them sad without thinking it was possible to design your way out of social problems. The architects who came up with the Roundhouse created a building with no edges or sharp corners, so that people would look at it and associate its gentle benevolence with the police, and think that cops must be gentle and benevolent too. The wide stairs were supposed to be welcoming to the public. Every feature was cast as a manifestation of progressive ideals. The architects didn't just want to make a beautiful building; they wanted the building to be modern, open, and progressive, in the belief that the cops might absorb these qualities and the public would associate them with the police. But what had happened to the Round-house was the opposite of what its creators intended. The design had not influenced the course of events; it had been influenced. Now the building was a visual shorthand for violence, brutality, and pain. For a while I watched the sparrows playing their game, and then I walked along the river so I could cross it by the Market Street Bridge.

Dr. Bartholomew Bae had a beautiful high-ceilinged office with arched windows that overlooked the pond of koi, which I petted as I made my way into the museum. It was too early in the winter for ice to have sheeted over them, but the fish were sluggish, nothing like their peppy summer selves. I hazarded a nonstandard topic for our preliminary small talk, telling Dr. Bae about my encounters with the koi and the trouble I had gotten into in the past. I didn't know him well enough to predict his response, but he smiled, and told me he had once spent several weeks conduct-ing a research project at the National Archives outside of London, where he formed the habit of leaving the archives building several times a day to sit on a bench and observe the waterfowl—swans and ducks, mostly—that wandered the grounds. He always liked, he said, how comfortably they mingled with one another, even allowing pigeons to join their ranks; he also liked that they did not scatter when humans came near.

"Every day I ate my Tesco sandwich and watched them," he

said. "Do you know about those sandwiches? They cut them into triangles. That's what everyone eats for lunch over there."

Dr. Bae had a handsome crinkling smile, broad cheekbones, and brief, dense brows, like expressive ink splashes. I couldn't confidently estimate his age. Because of his good looks and his last name, he made me think of Juwon Bae, the boy all the girls had been in love with in high school. Part of Juwon's charm had been his aloof friendliness, and the fact that he never spoke at length. A hot boy who didn't talk much was like catnip for teenage girls, because it meant we could project onto him whatever we wanted, draw thought bubbles over his head and fill them, in our girlish script, with hidden longings, enlightened beliefs, and sensitive, poetic thoughts. On the weekends we would congregate in Wangjing, the zone of Beijing where all the Koreans lived, and spend hours singing in a strobe-lit KTV chamber at the top of a labyrinthine mall, and then we would go for dinner at our favorite fried chicken restaurant in the basement of a dingy building called Korea World Food City and order a tower of beer. Juwon only came sometimes, which added to his allure, even though we all knew that if he wasn't there, it was because he had tutoring.

"Some of the leadership were a little skeptical about putting you in charge of the exhibition, given your relative inexperience, but I've been struck by the work you've done cataloging the shoes, and I advocated for you," Dr. Bae was saying. "I also thought it would be a great way to expand on our underserved campaign. We'd be remiss not to give these objects a public showcase, just as we'd be remiss to deny someone with such a personal family connection the opportunity to helm it."

"Family connection?"

"You were telling me before about your poor grandmother and her bound feet?"

"No, no, I was saying she didn't have bound feet."

Dr. Bae faltered. "She didn't?"

"She ran away to escape from it happening."

"Ah, yes! So it was definitely going to happen?"

"Definitely."

"That's perfect. You must make a note of it in the exhibition. You can mention your father's work at the same time if you'd like."

"My father's work?"

"Your father is Yukon Zhang, correct?"

"Correct."

"I wondered, if I may ask, why your surname is different from his?"

"It's my mother's name. They were trying to be progressive or something."

In fact, my mother's last name was Williams, the name of my grandparents, the people who adopted and raised her. Lin was aspirational, a name she said might have been hers in her pre-adoptee life in rural Guangxi, and insisted her daughter bear. But I wasn't about to explain any of this to my boss.

Instead, I told Dr. Bae how I felt the first time I held a pair of the shoes in my hands, and how it had transformed the objects, whisking them out of musty history and instilling in them a startling, physical immediacy. I told him I didn't think it was enough for museum visitors to see the shoes on display; they needed to be able to hold them, to experience what I had experienced. Dr. Bae said he liked my unconventional thinking but that it would not be possible, given the necessities of preservation, for the public to touch any of the artifacts.

"Are you ready to take this on, Penelope?" he said. "Do you understand this means that you will be the one with whom the buck stops?"

"Yes," I said, "I'm ready."

After the meeting, I dawdled at the front desk, talking to Carol, who had finally strong-armed everyone into calling her Carol, not the Water Goddess, which did not affect me since I had never referred to her as such, in part because anything related to the maternal made me uncomfortable. Carol was in a bad mood because her son had come home the day before with a timber rattlesnake in a plastic container.

"He tells me some kid in his class is moving to Maryland, and they don't allow rattlesnakes as pets there, so this boy's parents say he's gotta give it away to one of his friends. He brings it into school and guess who volunteers to take it? My son." Carol sighed, and the stream of air whistled through the gap in her teeth. "Now. Would you let him keep the snake?"

"No," I said, sensing that this was the answer she sought. "Never."

"Exactly! What kind of parents does this boy have? Who is letting their twelve-year-old play around with a *serpent*? You know they shoot venom? And eat other snakes? I'm sitting here talking to you and back home a cannibal snake is slithering around my house, probably biting the hell out of my dog."

Carol shuddered. I had the Wikipedia page for the timber rattlesnake open on my phone, and I started reading out the highlights. "One of the most dangerous snakes in North America. Three types of venom. 'Neurotoxic,' that doesn't sound very good."

"I know, I read all that too. Look at the Latin name. Read that out to me and tell me that isn't a warning."

"*Crotalus horridus?*"

"Horridus! Hor-rid-us!"

I commiserated with her. My father had a brief snake phase, and I had watched many a mouse swallowed by his scaly pets. I never grew to love or even tolerate the snakes, and worried at my father's insouciance, at his total lack of what I experienced as a bone-deep, species-memory revulsion to the things he brought into our home. I told Carol this, and added that he once dropped a snake onto my head as I slept, as a joke.

"He did what?"

"It wasn't venomous," I assured her. "He thought it would be funny."

"Did you think it was funny?"

"No, no, I was very upset." I was smiling, but Carol looked like she was wavering between disapproval and concern. I added, "But I was very young, so. I got upset easily."

Apparently this made it sound worse, not better. She stared. "How young?"

"Where's the Sheriff?" I said, to change the subject.

Carol sighed and rolled her eyes. "World's longest smoke break."

Soon after, I was on my way to meet Apple and Inno at Apple's favorite margarita place. I was the cause of their rare détente: they wanted to celebrate my appointment to the exhibition. It was sunset, and the gloom of earlier in the day had been swept off by the wind, replaced by a patchwork of soft cloud that pulsated pinkly in the sky. My head was full of the Army of Italy and Juwon's diffident smile and the Pantheon-esque rotunda where the exhibition would be set, and I charged alone through the cold streets. The present, the future, the Napoleonic past and my own felt interlaced with a significance that was hard to define, though it seemed to hinge on the very fact that I could think of them all at once—that the past was made alive by my remembering it, and the present enriched by the deliberate invocation of history.

At the back of my mind was an insecure thought: Dr. Bae had only chosen me because he hoped my father might stop by and shower fame on the museum. But it didn't add up; anthropologists didn't care about contemporary art.

Apple was already at the table when I walked into the restaurant. I was brimming with everything I had been thinking about on the walk over, but outwardly this just manifested as a good mood, since these were not impressions I could share without spoiling them in some way. I asked her how her day had been, and she said it had been stressful. She said that after I left, they had gone to the jail to wait for the people who had been arrested. I'd completely forgotten about the protest, forgotten I'd even been there. They'd purchased food and water and cigarettes and some first aid supplies, and waited for several hours. Apple, on unfamiliar ground, had felt uncharacteristically shy, and wanted to ask if anyone knew how long they might be there, because she knew she was meeting me for drinks in the evening. But everyone had seemed kind of hostile, and even though she was sure they were all perfectly nice, and just preoccupied, she hated the idea, which she had put into her own mind, that they saw her as some spoiled hanger-on girl-friend, and were they wrong? I made a mental note of her use of the word "girlfriend" to revisit at a more appropriate time.

"But wasn't Gus there?"

"He was, but he had to go to work. You know they separate the men and the women? They take them to different jails. All the women go to the Roundhouse, that's where I ended up. We were ordering pizzas for when they got out, and the cops were arguing with us about it, saying we couldn't collect the pizzas?"

"I was at the Roundhouse too," I said. "Well, I walked past. I was thinking that architecture is kind of stupid. And I saw those guys outside, from the rally, they couldn't get any taxis to stop for them."

"You missed everything. Even at the protest, when you went to get food, you missed all the violence."

"Why didn't you just leave when Gus left?"

Apple ignored me and kept talking, first at her usual clip, then rapidly, each sentence coming out shakier than the last and slathered with her sarcastic overtone, which increased in proportion to her distress, so that even though its purpose was to mask her feeling, its effect was the opposite.

"Everything was fine when you left, and we walked back because the protesters were all returning to the rally, and then suddenly there was all this pushing and shouting. I literally saw one of the cops shove a girl to the ground, like an eleven-year-old girl. And this old woman went to go help her and they started hitting her too, like, beating her up. Doesn't this sound insane to you? It sounds so crazy to me, it sounds fake, doesn't it? A little kid and a grandma? Oh yeah, it was her actual grandmother. They were both at the jail later, they were the women we were waiting for. Everybody else they arrested went to the other jail. They had really weird names. The girl and the old lady. Like Hawthorn and Rosehip or something, I have no idea. Are those flowers? Now that I'm saying it out loud, do you think those were even their real names? But it was so fucked up. The cops were the worst. Like apart from everything I've been telling you. I tried to go find a bathroom, I don't know if that was dumb, and I ended up going outside for some fresh air, and this cop was out there, and he gave me the scariest look I've ever seen in my life. Like I've never been more certain that someone wanted to kill me, wanted me dead. And this will sound so stupid but I just kind of smiled? I didn't know what to do, it was instinctive. And he was like, 'Fuck you, bitch.' And then he walked back inside. But anyway, they finally came out and the old woman had dried blood on her head, and the girl was crying, but her face wasn't moving, it was just blank, with tears running down her face, and they were holding hands, and the woman looked so out of it, it was literally like the blind leading the blind, like you couldn't tell who was taking care of who. I don't know if it was worse to see a child getting hit or an old woman getting hit. They were kind of differently bad. But both so bad. Do you know what I mean? Oh, Innocent is here."

She sank into her chair, staring ahead for a moment. Then she sat up and began scrabbling in her bag.

"Hello, hello, hello," Inno said, taking a seat. "How is everyone? How is our star curator? Did you get a raise? You didn't even ask for one, did you? Oh, no, what are you up to, Miss Apple?"

Apple was unwrapping a single-serving packet of frosted blueberry Pop-Tarts.

"What?" she said in a low warning tone that Inno failed to pick up on.

"I am alarmed."

"I thought you loved it when people brought their own food to restaurants."

"Don't you worry about all the chemicals you're shoveling into your body?"

"You mean the chemicals they designed specifically for me to ingest and enjoy?"

Inno snatched the Pop-Tart wrapping and began to read aloud the list of ingredients.

"Xanthan gum, dextrose, baking soda, mm, blue one *and* blue two! Corn syrup, corn starch, high fructose corn syrup—"

"Corn" was the trigger word. I flailed at the waitress and started calling out for alcohol before Inno could begin his corn tirade; Apple was in a delicate state, and even if she had not been, it would not be a prudent conversational route to travel. She loved to complain about America, but if a non-American did it she flipped, becoming defensive and acquiring a knee-jerk patriotism. She also had an aversion to snobbery, and Inno, after all, was an international snob. They had already sparred about corn once, many years earlier, in Inno's pre-frugal days, when he returned from a trip to San Sebastián and Apple had interrupted his extolling of the Txuleton steak at a Michelin-starred bistro to say that she had been to France once with her family and the steak had tasted "weird" and that Europe in general was overrated. Inno had immediately replied that Apple was accustomed to "chowing down" on corn-fed cattle, whose flesh yielded sickeningly sweet meat, as if doused in caramel, and so of course she had not enjoyed her first taste of "the authentic." He had added that Apple's sampling and dismissal of "real" beef made her, spiritually speaking, like a person who lived their whole life in a cave and one day was released from the cave and let outside, like in Plato's allegory, only to return soon afterward of their own accord, complaining that the sun up there was too bright, the breeze too caressing, and the grass too green.

The waitress did not notice me. I asked Inno to fetch us a pitcher of water and he obliged, since this was the only thing he was going to be drinking.

"I can't stand him," Apple said.

"I know," I said. "Are you okay?"

Apple tossed the last corner of pastry into her mouth and crushed the plastic packet in her fist. "I'm good. Let's order."

On the walk home I tried to bring up our earlier conversation, but Apple dismissed me.

"I was just a little freaked out. I'm fine now. By the way, I met Hoang today."

I forced myself to keep walking.

"You did?"

"Yeah, I went to the Rivebelle after jail support, I wanted to tell Gus everything that happened after he left. And Hoang was there. In the flesh. It was like a celebrity sighting."

"You didn't—"

"Come on, of course not. But he asked about you."

"He did?"

"I mean, Gus introduced me to him, and I guess he already knew I'd met Gus at the bar with you. He still has no idea we were there to stalk him, by the way, you're welcome. I would praise Gus for being discreet, but I think he was just too stoned to remember that you wrote your email on a napkin and gave it to him and then insanely demanded it back. But yeah, Hoang was like, 'Oh you're friends with Penelope, she's really cool.' And I very innocently asked when he last saw you, and he said like a month ago, and asked me how you were, and I said she's doing great."

We walked on. I maintained a deliberate silence, laying it out for Apple like bait.

"I liked him," she said. "And he's cute."

"But?" I said. I sensed demurral.

"I don't know, he just seems very nice and normal. Which was actually a relief, because all that stuff you told me about the lab rats was so disturbing. But he's nice!"

"You already said nice. Isn't nice good?"

"I guess I was just expecting someone crazier. Not crazier, but someone, I don't know, more intense? Given that, you know."

"What?"

"He just seems very different from your previous paramour," Apple said, giving a derisive inflection to the last phrase, which she did whenever she employed an unusual or formal word in conversation, because she didn't want people to think her pretentious, and wanted to indicate that she was aware of the register in which she sometimes spoke. "Don't you think?"

"Yes," I said, "very." Internally, I was gaming out a way to respond without acknowledging her allusion to Paul. It had taken a long time for Apple to get past the way I behaved when I was with him. When I followed Paul back to France and very nearly dropped out of university in order to stay with him, Apple was the one who flew over to talk to me, and convinced me that I needed to come back. I had squandered the reputation I'd constructed of being a reliable, risk-averse person, a reputation I believed was an accurate reflection of my inner self.

"Is that why you lost interest?" Apple said. "In Hoang? Because he's different from him?"

I shook my head, knowing that she would be able to register it in her peripheral.

"I haven't lost interest."

"Then what?"

I remembered sitting with Apple in a café in the Latin Quarter as she told me how many thousands of dollars less I would earn than my degreed counterparts if I did not return to university, how I would regret it for the rest of my life, that if it was meant to be, then long-distance would work, and if it wasn't, then staying wouldn't help; and the way she looked at me when I told her I didn't care. *You're scaring me*, she had said, and I could see that I really was. It was that look on her face, not any of her arguments, that made me start to waver.

These days I agreed with everything Apple had been trying to tell me. Everything was good now because I had convinced Apple, and myself, that Paul had been an anomaly, a blip. I saw how stupid it would have been to drop out, and how inconsequential. But I knew then, too, how much I might lose, the things I'd miss. At the time they'd just seemed worthless. I'd been willing to do anything to avoid losing him, even something unnecessary, something that would have damaged me more than it helped. That was my experience of love: a warped risk calculus, a distorted perception.

"It started to feel real," I said. "With Hoang. It was scary. I'm not sure I would know how to act. Like, what to do."

"It's easy!"

"I don't want to push too hard."

"You won't."

"I might," I said. "I always do."

I sensed that Apple was putting in a great amount of effort not to immediately speak, and I felt a warm rush of gratitude.

"I meant different in a good way, you know," she said. I didn't respond to this last comment, and we kept walking, without hostility, until our paths separated.

In the downstairs vestibule of my building, I withdrew the small key to the mailbox and fitted it into the lock. There was no incense burning, no passing neighbor for whom I felt compelled to put on a show; I was checking the mail. The door swung open. Inside was a single postcard, message-side down in the dull silver box, and a sheet of coupons for a kitchen appliance emporium in South Philadelphia. The postcard showed two swans in green water, one with its long neck held aloft, the other with its head submerged, seeking fish. I turned it over.

Penelope,

They were selling these at the arboretum, have you been? I don't know why I thought everything would be green, most of the trees are already bare. Still beautiful though.

Hoang

After the night of the koalas, I had entered the address of the party on Google Maps and dropped into Street View to see the number of the house out of which Hoang had appeared. I wrote a short letter giving him the details of the book we had discussed on our walk, and which, unable to recall the name of the author, I had promised to share later on. Two weeks passed before I received a reply. He had tried to read the book, he wrote—it was *Farewell to the Horse*, by Ulrich Raulff—but found it hard to focus, and gave up. I was dejected, because in the same conversation that night by the train tracks he had told me how much he loved Frank O'Hara, and the next day I bought Frank O'Hara's collected works and stayed up all night to finish the volume. Inno was horrified when I described the manner in which I had consumed the poems, telling me it was like listening to a sonata on double speed and thinking you would "get the gist," though he grudgingly retracted the analogy when I brought up Glenn Gould's two recordings of Bach's *Goldberg Variations*. Hoang's casual admission of defeat worried me. The obvious unconcern that what he was saying might impact what I thought of him signaled to me that he was not approaching our relationship in the same way. With Paul I had been the pursuer: I was the one who had gone up to him at the party, I was the one who followed him back to France, who decided to stay there with him, at least for a while. When we broke up the first time—he called it a pause, he said the distance was too much to bear—I took it upon myself to make sure it was temporary and flew back to him again the day after graduation, betting on a grand gesture. It worked, we started dating again, he even came back to Philadelphia and lived with me for a time, but I never knew for sure if it was what he really wanted, or if he had only agreed because there I was outside the door, pleading. This time around, I had to enforce my passivity, and make sure I wasn't pursuing someone disinclined to be with me, even if I wanted them very much; I was afraid, in the first place, of wanting them too much. After receiving Hoang's reply, I became fearful of misinterpretation, and decided to relegate our interactions to the epistolary realm. So now we were pen pals.

I found an old postcard in the office to send to Hoang. It showed the original design for the museum, drawn up in the 1880s, in the form of a watercolor sketch. There had been plans for three rotundas with Romanesque façades, stacked roofs like Buddhist pavilions, and pencil pines standing sentry at each gate. Instead of the sprawling hospital, the multistory parking garages, and the clots of construction cranes, round-canopied trees stretched to the horizon. I flipped it over and affixed a stamp adorned with a yellow flower, from a roll I found in the office. They were nonprofit stamps, because of the museum; I hoped I was not committing mail fraud. In blue ballpoint ink I wrote his name, added the comma, and paused while I thought of what to say. After the stamp and his address there was not much space left for the message itself. If I omitted his name and my own, there would be room for a longer message, but I liked that we had adopted the letter-writing convention of naming the recipient and ourselves, which had mostly vanished from digital correspondence, being superfluous and quaint.

Hoang,
I've never been to the arboretum. This morning I found a possum sleeping in the garbage can outside my house. It was so cute. Did you know they're marsupials? How are you?
Penelope

As I walked to the mailbox, I flapped the postcard against my palm, wishing I'd thought of something better to write. It was one of my weakest efforts yet. I always made sure to include a question, to increase the chances of a reply, but the two questions I'd included were, in the first case, rhetorical, and in the second, so generic it might be interpreted as rhetorical. Often, since Hoang and I had started corresponding, I caught myself talking to him in my head, telling him about interesting things I came across at work or in a book, describing my feelings about something and soliciting his. I slipped the card into the post box. It was eleven in the morning, and I had nothing to do, because the museum had given us the day off to vote in the midterm election. Dr. Bae sent a staff-wide email encouraging us to "go vote" in order to "make our voices heard, no matter who you're choosing." The CR-V he drove to work had, on its rear, a HILLARY 2016 bumper sticker and a decal of the word TRUMP in black lettering overlaid with a red circle and diagonal slash, the universal sign for no. I thought that if I supported one political party I wouldn't encourage a random sampling of people to "go vote" when there was a chance that group would include at least one person who would vote for my opponent rather than my chosen candidate. I told this to Apple and she said I should be commending Dr. Bae for encouraging civic participation instead of mocking him, especially when I myself hadn't bothered to register. I didn't think I'd been mocking him, and I was curious why it was only Democrats who so strenuously encouraged the general population to vote. You never heard a Republican talking like that, those guys played to win. But Apple always got a little fragile in the run-up to an election, so I didn't press her. I checked Instagram, and she had already posted a story of herself, sporting an *I VOTED!* sticker on her jacket lapel. I wondered if Hoang was voting, but I wasn't worried, because he didn't seem like the type of person to think less of someone for not doing something he did, even if it was something he thought other people should do. I clicked to the next item in Apple's story, and it was a video of Bloody Marys on a bar top, captioned: "toasting to democracy!!" followed by a string of emojis: a ballot box, a rainbow flag, a blue heart.

Apple was zooming wildly in and out on the drinks, and I could hear Gus saying, "It's a distraction, it's performative, but I do like going in that little booth with the curtain." Apple started to make an exclamation of protest as the video cut off. I loved that she never muted the sound before posting, because people usually didn't realize she was filming, and so did not alter or cease their speech for presentation on social media, which meant she recorded snippets of conversation much more evocative than the usual staged photos and front-camera monologues. And then there was the voyeur's thrill of knowing the speaker had been captured unaware, the squirmy tension of whether they might say something personal or incriminating. Of course, I hated to be documented in this way, and remained vigilant when I saw Apple wielding her phone, but it was fun to be a member of the audience.

I decided to treat myself to an early lunch and headed for my favorite Lanzhou hand-pulled noodle restaurant, just down the street from my apartment, next to a little shop that sold Chinese bric-a-brac: embroidered peony wall hangings, rainbow-jeweled KTV microphones, paper calendars, chopsticks in lacquer cases, zodiac animal charms dangling from lengths of red string. There was a new holographic portrait of Communist Party leaders in the glass display of the store. First you saw an old Deng against a crimson backdrop with the five yellow stars winking behind him. Quickly he morphed into a middle-aged Mao, the chairman in the prime of his life, flanked by stone lions, both male, and, half-faded into his right shoulder, Tiananmen, the gate where his portrait now hung. Finally, Mao became Xi, oil-slick hair and Annalisa smile, fireworks exploding in the red sky above his head. I stepped back and forth in front of the shop, watching the faces change. Next to the triplicate was a holographic picture of Zhou Enlai, but he didn't turn into anyone else.

I ordered noodles with brisket, tendon, and extra tripe, and a can of Jia Duo Bao, a drink that had the double effect of making me feel homesick and at home. Since I was alone, I sat at a round communal table beside an old couple eating their noodles in silence, a spiky-haired guy in a Temple T-shirt who propped his phone against a bottle of Sriracha to watch basketball, and a young mother cooing to her toddler as she directed spoonfuls of braised radish into the child's mouth. We poured free tea for ourselves into small white cups from the metal teapot at the center of the table.

When I first moved to Philadelphia, I felt out of place in

Chinatown, initially dismissing it as poky and inauthentic, and then later, during my brief phase of trying to identify as Asian American, worrying that I didn't fit in with any of its dominant groups—the teenagers who huddled together in the matcha café and held fervent discussions about manga and anime, the grumpy octogenarians who spoke Chinese dialects I could barely identify, the entire Vietnamese population. Finally I discovered a third, happy state, the one in which I currently resided and from which I hopefully would not stray, a mode of existence made peaceful by my abandonment of both motherland superiority and diasporic insecurity.

I checked Instagram again as I bit into the chewy noodles. Another story from Apple, who was still at the bar. How did she not have to be at work? There was no way her law firm operated by the same liberal instincts as the museum. It was a picture of Gus, and in the background, I realized, was Hoang. I almost dropped my phone into my beef soup. It hit the table with a clang. The spoons and chopsticks clattered in their separate compartments, and the baby froze midway through a bite of mashed radish, gaping at me. I gave him a reassuring grin and picked up my phone. In the picture, Hoang was smiling in a disarmed manner, as if Apple had yelled his name and snapped the photo as he looked up. Susan Sontag was right, photography was soft murder, except in this case, I was the one being murdered. I wished I could jam my arm into the mailbox and retrieve the postcard I had addressed to him, with its ridiculous message saying nothing. I tortured myself with minuscule but excruciating scenarios, like Apple showing Hoang that I had seen the picture of him just seconds after she shared it. There was something about posting a picture of someone who didn't have social media that felt exploitative, as if you were exposing them to dark forces with which they had declined to engage, and violating the conditions they had set for themselves. I felt ill. How was it that Apple was in the same room as Hoang, talking to him, learning what he was like, and I was alone, watching it happen? What was I doing? I bought envelopes at the holographic portrait store and went home and deactivated my Instagram account on my computer and then, on the back of a sheet of Chinese writing exercises from the Saturday class Xinwei taught in the neighborhood, wrote a brief, declarative message, sealed and stamped it, and walked again to the mailbox where my wretched postcard most likely still lay. I would ask Hoang to go for a drink with me, like a normal person.

By the time I reached the mailbox, though, I had lost my nerve. I coaxed myself off the ledge of decisive action, taking slow steps away from the squat blue receptacle like it was an armed bomb. There was no need, I told myself, to be rash, to expose one's vulnerabilities. If he wanted to see me, he would try. I found a trash can and stood over it while I tore the enveloped letter into squares, and then released the shreds into the maw of the bin, watching the scraps flutter like snow.

After the morning's excitement I was restless and preoccupied, so I joined Inno and Louisa on a stroll through Fairmount Park. They were both graduate students, so they were always free on weekdays, and neither was American, so the events of that particular Tuesday meant nothing to them. We discussed our favorite parks as we made our way to the Japanese garden. I said Zizhuyuan in Beijing, Inno said Hyde Park in London, and Louisa said Gardens by the Bay in Singapore, "because of the electric trees." I told Inno and Louisa that Fairmount was Philadelphia's first public park, which meant it was probably the first public park in the whole country. Inno said I was wrong, it was in Boston. I didn't respond. Boston annoyed me because it was always competing with Philadelphia when it came to matters of historical significance, and I always wanted Philadelphia to win.

The grass on the slopes was still green, but fading. Inno asked me how my father was doing, and I told him about the retrospective at the Whitney, and the new large-scale installation.

"I'll probably go to New York to see him when it opens," I said.

"BTS performed in New York last month. They're the first Korean artists in the history of the world to headline an American stadium show, did you guys know that?" Louisa said. Louisa was in the third year of her PhD, studying the global proliferation of Korean popular culture, and she found a way to bring K-pop into every conversation.

We reached Shofuso, the traditional Japanese house and garden located within the larger park. The house was built in the 1950s and exhibited in New York, a postwar gift from the Japanese people to the American people now that they were friends again. When the exhibition was over, they disassembled the house and moved it to Philadelphia, which for some reason already had a Japanese garden.

"Wouldn't it have been nice," Louisa said, after I told her and Inno about the origin of Shofuso, "if they'd given all of us peace houses too? Or maybe apology houses?"

"That would have been a lot of houses," I said.

Louisa walked around the pond while Inno and I moved through the rooms of the house, admiring the woven mats, the sliding wooden doors with mulberry paper screens, and the tidy columns of bamboo that lined the outside walls. Inno stayed in the tearoom and I moved on to the kitchen, where there was a traditional stove with pots and pans, inside one of which lay a large silvery fish that for a moment I mistook for a live specimen. Inno walked up beside me.

"Look," I said, pointing at the fish, "a fake fish. Isn't it so realistic?"

Inno looked at the fish. "I'm quitting my program."

"What?"

"I've become concerned that I'm leading a small life," he said. "I've been drifting without rhyme or reason in the inland sea of academia like, like . . . driftwood."

Inno paused to usher me into the garden. He looked around at the trees, and then down at the koi pond, and then back at the trees. "You should come back here in the spring, for the cherry blossoms. I'll be gone by then. But where was I?"

"Drifting like driftwood."

"Yes. The parameters of my life have shrunk. My routine is set, my path is unchallenging, the stakes are low, the rewards are guaranteed. I am rejecting it all. The world does not need another doctorate traipsing around, attending conferences, flinging little research papers into the abyss of academic publishing. I've gazed into it, it's gazed back, and I've decreed I want no part of it."

"You love what you do," I said cheerily. Inno made such pronouncements every few months, and there was a reliable script to defuse the situation.

"Yes, I do, but what I am doing with the majority of my waking hours contributes nothing to the world. Do you know how many people read the last paper I wrote, which I worked very hard on and believed—still believe—contains valuable insight into the cultural role of ornamental crops in rural Nigeria? Whatever number you want to guess, it's lower than that. Two people read it, and one of them was contractually obligated to, and the other one was me."

"But you know that won't always be the case."

"I'm flying to Peru at the end of the month."

"Wait, what?"

"I booked my ticket last night."

From the green gloom of the pond, a koi materialized, its bulbous lips agape, begging for snacks. I was so disoriented I didn't even point it out as Inno, in a wild deviation from the reliable script, told me that he was going to a place called the Parque de la Papa in the Cusco Valley to work with indigenous farmers and learn about agrobiodiversity and traditional subsistence farming. He said that at the Potato Park, which was the English name, he could remain immersed in his core intellectual passion, crop yields, while also doing something meaningful and learning things that he would be able to apply elsewhere when his time in Peru came to an end. The Potato Park had agreed to take him on as a kind of hybrid research-assistant-farmhand. He would learn about the 2,300 varieties of potato they grew there, and, in order to experience the complete cycle, would stay for at least a year. He would improve his Spanish, which was already decent, and pick up as much Quechua as he could.

"I don't want to live a small life," he kept saying. I nodded and tried to look supportive, but Louisa returned before I could adjust to the new script.

The walk back was quiet, though not literally so, since Louisa, animated by our visit, provided us with a steady stream of information about the royal gardens of Gyeongbokgung, which had been destroyed by the Japanese in 1592 and then again in 1910. Rather, it was a quiet that existed between Inno and me, the kind of quiet that forms when, although there might be more to say, and it will probably be said when the obstacle preventing further conversation (in this case, Louisa, since she was in the dark about Inno's imminent departure; he preferred to tell her later when Femi was there) has removed itself, a matter has been settled, and each person is adjusting to the implications of that settlement. I was imagining my life without Inno, imagining receiving pictures of him squinting in the sunlight of the Cusco Valley, brawny and fulfilled; I was preemptively missing having him around, and, latterly, pondering the machinations behind such a decision, whether it was something he had been mulling over for a long time or something that had arrived without warning, and whether I might have predicted it. At the same time as I was having these thoughts, Inno, or so I guessed, was thinking about the way I had reacted and comparing it to how he had imagined I would react (I was the first person he'd told), but, I imagined, was thinking mostly of his trip, of what he had to pack, the phone plan to cancel and the acetazolamide to purchase. He was thinking of what awaited him: the people he hadn't met who within months would become those he knew best, the fresh landscapes, the texture of the soil, the smell of unfamiliar earth, the upside down constellations. He was thinking of the knowledge that would present itself to him once and only once as something glittering and alive, composed entirely of newness, and thereafter would just be something he knew. He was thinking also of everything he was leaving behind, because he knew dimly that he was not coming back to live in the one-bedroom in Philadelphia. It was, after all, his life as he knew it, his happy constructed life, that he was abandoning, that he would lose and not be able to recover in its current form, but this thought filled him with exhilaration, not sadness: it was the whole reason he was going away.

At home in my room, I lay on my bed and watched the enervated sunset leak in through the window. The light was weak, like the grass in the park, like it always seemed to be after the end of daylight savings, a temporal practice I had not grown up with, did not adjust to for years, and of which I remained suspicious. I was thinking of my old house in West Philly, with the porch and the stray cat and the squirrelly eaves; in particular I was thinking of the small panel of stained glass above the two casement windows of my bedroom. No other room in the house had such a panel, and no one knew why it was there. I spent a large portion of the days back then lying on my bed and looking at the stained-glass pattern, watching hexagons of light forming and unforming on the walls in synchrony with the movement of the sun and the strength of the wind, which dictated the motion of the shadows of the trees outside. Every morning I sat against the pillows and drank a coffee that Paul carried up for me, which he made using the espresso machine that he installed in the kitchen soon after moving in. That was the second of our two attempts at being in a relationship, and, while it had been better than the first in important ways—less volatile, more mature—it contained a certain quality that proved impossible to be rid of: the quiet melancholy of the doomed second chance, or, when I wanted to be harsh to myself, the stench of failure. Paul always woke up before me, and he always drank his own coffee first, alone, downstairs, while making mine. I did not feel sad when I recalled these memories. I found a soft but visceral pleasure in the specific textures of the days of that time as if they were surfaces I could touch—a period during which I went to sleep every night excited for the morning, excited precisely because I knew exactly what was going to happen, knew it would be a perfect repetition of the morning before and the hundred mornings before that. Had that been a small life? Was I living a small life now?

I was yanked from my reverie by a soft knock on my bedroom door. Xinwei was asking me if I wanted some pu'er tea. Xinwei was very particular about her tea consumption, and would not consume this kind of tea until after a certain date in the Chinese agricultural calendar. We had just come upon the start of winter, which for Xinwei meant it was time to brew warming beverages like pu'er, incidentally one of my favorite types of tea, but one that I could not have in the summer if Xinwei was around unless I

was ready for a world of reproach. She was bemused by my enthusiasm for pu'er, because, she said, it was a very masculine tea, and
I was not a very masculine person. I crept outside and joined her
at the standing table, taking sips from a tiny porcelain cup and
listening as she gave me a breakdown of the lunisolar phases of
the calendar. There was a feng shui master she insisted I follow on
Instagram, so I reactivated my account and followed him. She was
appalled that I'd never consulted one. I enjoyed Xinwei's good-
natured incredulousness whenever I revealed some knowledge
gap in something Chinese, which at first she had not understood
but, after I told her my mother was an American adoptee and my
father was an artist, had comprehended more. I knew the important dates, like Qingming and the solstices and equinoxes, and by
now I knew all the rest, but I let her run through them anyway,
because I liked the way she rattled off the names, which brought
to mind an age when people marked time by the weather, having nothing else to go by, and because the weather was the most
important thing in their lives: small snow, big snow, small cold,
big cold, small heat, big heat, white dew, frost.

Apple was unfazed when I FaceTimed her and recounted my
conversation with Inno in the Japanese garden. All she said was,
"It's like he says. He's a dilettante."

"What should I do?"

"Just tell him it sounds fun and say goodbye, it's not that hard."

"No, like, myself, in life. What if I joined the Peace Corps?"

Apple frowned. "That still exists?"

We checked. It did.

"I can't actually join the Peace Corps," I said, after we read the
website. "Two and a half years is way too long. I just want someone to send me to a remote island for a while."

"You're only saying this because of Innocent. This is a copycat crime."

"I'm not. It's not."

"I can see it in your eyes."

"What if we did it together?"

"Did what?"

"We could save up over the next few months and then we could leave, travel, dig some wells somewhere."

"You really think you have the upper body strength for that?"

"We could go to Beijing, how fun would that be? And then we could go to Mongolia!"

"I can't go to Mongolia, Pee. I have a ten-year plan."

"But imagine you didn't, and we just went to Mongolia instead. Wouldn't that be so cool? You know Genghis Khan and his soldiers used to cut their horses' veins and drink their blood when they were on the march, if they were running low on food and water?"

"Ew."

"You don't think it's cool? I think it's kind of beautiful. It's so intimate."

Apple sighed through her nose, and said she didn't know if she was in the "headspace"—a word she had injected into her vocabulary of late—for this conversation. At moments like these, I worried that one day she would tire of me on a permanent, rather than temporary, basis, would no longer find me amusing, and would begin to lengthen the intervals between replies to my texts until we barely spoke.

"You scare me sometimes," she said. "On the outside you're like, chill, and eat the same thing for lunch every day, but then you're like, oh, what if I moved to Mongolia."

"I don't eat the same thing for lunch every day. Just like, a lot of the time."

"And don't tell me it was just a joke because I remember very clearly talking to you, like I am now, to convince you not to drop out of college. This better not be like that."

"It's not," I said. I avoided making eye contact with myself in the little rectangle contained within the larger rectangle that displayed Apple's face on the screen of my phone.

"You should take this energy you're feeling and channel it into something you can do here, in Philly," Apple said. "I was talking to Gus and he was telling me how frustrated he felt that so many people put so much effort into voting, and then the moment the election ends they go back to doing nothing, when it's not like the issues they voted for stop needing attention."

"Isn't that what you do?" I said. She ignored me.

"Remember when he was telling us about the union? They need volunteers to hand out flyers and stuff. We should do it together. I think it would be healthy for us to redirect our neuroses."

"You want to hand out flyers? Like on the street?" I felt slightly put off by the "us" and the "our," because I didn't think of myself as a neurotic person; maybe in relation to Hoang I was neurotic, but certainly nothing like Apple, who raced through thoughts and hypotheses at terrifying, incomprehensible speeds, and who was constantly introducing problems that had literally never occurred to me before, like the research showing that women with gender-neutral names received more job offers because hiring managers assumed they were men, or the concept of "elbow fat"—things I felt infected by after she shared them, little glimpses into her mind, a haunted, hyperactive space full of objects both ghastly and admirable.

"Yes, seriously, we should volunteer. I think it'll be good for combating your toska. I can see Peru for Innocent, but not for you. You might be a dilettante too, but he's a free agent, you're just unmoored. Do you know what I mean? There's a difference."

"I'm not unmoored."

"Sure, but wouldn't you like to be *more* moored? Volunteering for the union could moor you."

"They're already a union?"

"They're like, preparing to start trying to do it. It's kind of complicated. Hoang could explain it to you. He's involved as well."

"Are you trying to bait me?" I said, trying to sound affronted. In fact, the moment she mentioned him, I had decided I would do it, whatever it was she was saying I should do.

"Of course I am. This is the closest you've gotten to having sex in like five thousand years."

"Please don't feel that you have to be invested in my—" I had to pause to compose myself to be able to say the phrase—"sex life."

" 'Life'? I'm trying to encourage a resurrection!"

Apple and I, perhaps unsurprisingly, had different attitudes toward sex. After I broke up with Paul, she advised me to download dating apps and pursue one-night stands, which she said would accelerate the process of "getting over it." She said if she were in my position, she would have been scheduling several dates a week and setting up a "roster." "Don't you want to get him out of your system?" I recoiled at the premise itself—that by having sex with people who did not matter to me, I could expel my feelings for someone who had. I had no moral objection, it just did not seem plausible. I said I would rather forgo the elusive reward that Apple claimed could only be accessed through anonymous sex than risk searching for it and finding nothing. When you had sex with people you were in love with, at least so it seemed to me, the experience had to be meaningful. It was when I said things like this that Apple joked there was no way I wasn't still a virgin. But I couldn't see why my preferences should be considered repressive and hers not. Didn't mine indicate an aversion to pretense, while Apple shied away from vulnerability? Apple said she didn't have sex to be vulnerable, she had sex for the orgasms.

Sometimes I imagined telling Paul about these discussions. I loved to hear him talk. I used to ask him questions I already knew the answers to, because I knew he would put my ideas into language better than I could myself. I got so used to it that when it was over, it was like I had lost a part of my own brain, and thinking felt a little lonelier than it had before.

Inno loved talking to him too. The three of us would sit for hours in conversation, and I was often content just to listen while they argued about Ortega y Gasset or econometrics or foreign aid. If the topic was the French Revolution or where to eat for lunch, then we all had something to say. But it was almost irrelevant what we discussed; the garrulousness, and the pleasure we found in conversing with one another, was the point. I was moved when I discovered that Inno, so particular about the nature of his interactions and the people he allowed into his personal life, had invited Paul to dinner at his house. Apple was never as enamored of Paul and his intellect as Inno and I were; though she allowed that he was the smartest person in their bioethics class (besides her), she held a grudge against him because he once dismissed her favorite place in the world, King of Prussia mall, as a "petit bourgeois playground for the dead souls of America." I was there when he said it; she had simply turned to me and said, "This is why I hate Europeans."

I was happy with Paul a lot of the time, but my happiness was entirely dependent on him. I still remembered the furtive and almost overwhelming thrill of domesticity the first time I saw him toss his shirt into my laundry basket. But I could also recall the occasions he interrupted me in the middle of a sentence to say that he needed to be alone, that I was a distraction, that I was being too "manic" (a word that made me wince, because of its associations with my mother, and that he had to have selected on purpose to wound me), and how I complied with his requests, and left the room so he could "think." Sometimes he seemed to just shut down, and when he was like that, I could try as much as I wanted to get him to react in some way—with affection, or interest, or jealous shock—to something I said or did, but nothing worked. He closed the door on me and I just had to wait until it opened again. But the bad days had made me more loyal, and made the good days sweeter, like they were a surfeit I had earned. When I thought of this, the image that came to mind was of objects falling into a black hole. If Paul was a black hole, then it made sense that Apple's "get him out of your system" approach was never going to work for me, because black holes weren't objects that you could move. Satellites, asteroids, even planets you could shift if you really wanted to. Black holes stayed where they were, and everything else moved around them. But why had I been so devoted to a black hole?

SIX

For most of the rest of the month I was ensconced in a happy busy period at work. I had to come up with a detailed plan for the exhibition, and I was still intent on getting approval for my idea to let visitors hold the shoes in their hands. Replicas were an option, but even a flawless re-creation was too removed from the experience of the real. Apart from that, I had other ideas I was pretty sure would not be implemented but that I would propose anyway, because there was nothing to lose in the attempt and everything to lose in its absence. I wanted color projections of the women who might have worn the shoes, imposed in such a way that it looked as though they were wearing the objects on display; then, I thought, rather than seeing the shoes as pretty artifacts, the viewer would be confronted with the horrific proportions of the deformed feet and really understand the function of the shoes, which was to mask manmade deformity with prettiness. I wanted to stage a show with the Chinese shadow puppets in the museum collection—the female figures had bound feet—or let visitors manipulate the rods and move the puppets around themselves. I wanted to bring people into the white room where pens and coffees were banned. But the bulk of my work revolved around researching the history of the period and writing material that would be used for the program brochures, the wall placards, the press releases, the script for the audio guides, and the website. On top of that I still had to carry out my usual tasks, cataloging the mass of loose and unlabeled Qing-era objects that lived in the basement storage units. Time would pass and I would look up and find that it was hours later in the day than I would have guessed, and I had missed lunch or dinner. I think my unconscious might have been egging me on, training me to be alone, in anticipation of the number of close friends who lived near me decreasing by fifty percent. But I enjoyed the feeling of productivity.

Since Inno's announcement, we had taken up our old habit of long city walks, which were not as enjoyable in the winter but which now had a valedictory quality to them that made them more precious. It was like we were rejuvenated by his leaving, removed from the torpor of habit by the awareness that we would soon have to accustom ourselves to new ones. I tried not to mention Hoang, except in relation to other things I wanted to talk about, like the book of poetry Inno accused me of reading incorrectly, or when we passed a tree I thought I could identify. I asked Inno if there was an appropriate rate at which to read a collection of poems. Was a few in one setting acceptable, or did it have to be one at a time? It was so much easier to memorize the names of cavalry regiments or pictures of cedars and dogwoods. Inno said I had to trust my instincts because no rule existed, and it would actually be odd for such a rule to exist. I found it funny that in all other areas of life—or, more specifically, in the living realm of life, i.e., when it came to romantic relationships, the observation of the physical world, and the feeling of feelings—he would never have cited instinct as a sufficient source of knowledge, and would probably accuse me of doing so to a fault, whereas in the realm of the arts—music, poetry, literature, philosophy—he was, to my mind at least, pretty woo-woo, while I longed for the non-existent instruction manual. I conceded that I might have been a little facetious in asking for an optimal rate, that I wasn't really so literal-minded, but I did want to address a deeper concern that I was reading poetry wrong. I took the example of the famous Frank O'Hara poem about having a Coke and going to the Frick and seeing *The Polish Rider*. All the lines that struck me were lines that made me think of Hoang (and sometimes of Paul, though this I did not share with Inno). Even if Hoang hadn't been the one to recommend the poet to me, this probably would have happened, but because he had, not only was I inserting myself into the poem's "I" and Hoang into the poem's "you," but I was also reading the poem *as* him, trying to deduce what he liked about it, fantasizing that he had read it once where I was the "you" and he was the "I." Surely, I said to Inno, as we walked past the Italian Market, where, that early in the morning, the wood-plank tables with rusty metal wheels stood bare, and men unloaded crates of canned tomatoes from unmarked white vans, surely this was not the right way to be reading poetry. My suspicion that I was not even really "reading" it was reinforced by my complete mental shutdown when I came across lines like the one about the "tree breathing through its spectacles." This phrase made so little sense to me that it made me angry, and proved to me that I was not "reading" the poem as much as I was skimming it for something that applied to my own life. Inno said it was a sublime image, and that part of the beauty of the blithe surrealism of the New York School, of which O'Hara was a prominent member, and of poetry in general, was that you could let the combinations of words, sounds, and rhythms wash over you, but it was necessary to liberate yourself with the realization that, when it came to lines like the one I mentioned, any "meaning" was secondary if not irrelevant; Inno rejoiced in the demonstration that it was possible to combine such words at all. Regarding my worry that projecting my own emotions onto the poem wasn't a true reading of the poem, Inno continued, as we passed a gated park inside which small dogs raced in circles around what looked to be fake grass, everyone did that and it was fine. Not just fine—it was remarkable, wasn't it, that a gay American man could pen an ode to his lover and, sixty years later, a Chinese woman lusting after a busboy could read what he had written and share his precise feeling? Ha ha, very funny, he's a bartender, not a busboy, but anyway, was the point to share O'Hara's precise feeling? Or was it something else?

Inno warned me that I was in danger of becoming deliberately convoluted, i.e., it wasn't that deep. "But I can appreciate that my answers are unsatisfactory," he continued. "I myself am unsatisfied with them. We may be missing things that someone with formal training in poetical analysis learns very early on, but I don't really care about that, unless we do know someone who fits that description. And even then, they'd probably be a bore. What I mean is I don't think we should resort to experts or search engines. It's more fun this way, no? And I like your questions, they put me on my back foot. It's like when a child asks you something so simple it's impossible to answer, and you realize you've been trained to take certain fundamentals so much for granted that it's difficult to explain them in a straightforward manner, which is all the child needs. I mean that as a compliment, obviously. Let's turn left here? I like this street."

"No, it's the wrong way," I said. I asked Inno why, since he loved poetry so much, he never tried to write a poem. He responded that he wished he could, but it was impossible for him, because it would "expose" him. He didn't mean that the content of his poems would reveal too much about his inner life, or that he was shy; he meant the attempt itself would humiliate him, because it showed that he cared enough to try, and was careless enough to try, even though the greatest poems in the world had already been written. I told him this mindset itself was very revealing, and he laughed.

"I only reveal what I want to reveal."

"Can anyone really claim that?"

"I can."

As we walked down Morris Street, toward the Delaware River, I elaborated on my theory that I'd never had the emotional response to poetry that I was convinced Inno and Hoang and other poetry readers were having. I gave another example. In school I was taken by certain verses of classical Chinese poetry, lines in which I recognized something of myself in the experiences described, but I was conscious that what moved me was the knowledge that these lines had been written more than one thousand years before I was born, rather than the words themselves, shorn of context. Inno said he didn't see what was objectionable about that, and wasn't it the same point he had just made about me and Frank O'Hara and our mutual yearning? I said it wasn't the same, because O'Hara's world was recent, comprehensible to me, indeed O'Hara might have been alive today had he not died so young in a car accident, whereas the world of, for example, Su Shi was unintelligibly distant, which made the fact that he and I both once admired a mountain and got drunk and felt homesick, to me, quite arresting. After I said this I realized I was not satisfied with it; it was not quite what I meant, and, as Inno said, it did not bear a significant difference to what he said. I tried again. Su Shi's world, and his psyche—not to mention that of the Tang poets, who lived and died three centuries before him—was inaccessible in a way that the modern poet's was not. The ancient poet, as an individual, is a black box, an unknown, I told Inno, deciding I would drop the subject after this. I was running out of steam as I spoke, reaching that point of speech when you lose faith in your ability to express yourself and begin to falter. I suspected that women experienced this more than men. The ancient poet is an unknown, I said, until I read what he writes about seeing the imprint of geese feet in the slushy snow, which makes him think that life is short—life ends as quickly as those impressions in the snow—and then he thinks, even as he is mourning his friend, that no one really remembers the dead, not in the total, undiminishing way that one would like to be remembered when one dies. He's also tired, and he has a long journey home. After I read that, I said, the poet was no longer an unknown, and the distance between us, for a moment, collapsed.

"I'm not sure I follow," Inno said.

"I'm just trying to say that what I'm responding to is the weight of the historical, not the aesthetic, or literary, whichever one it is."

"That's an interesting distinction," Inno said, and I knew he was going to ask me to elaborate, so before he could, I asked what plans he had for the weekend. He told me (workout, chess with Gleb, Spinoza reading group, Spanish lesson, dinner party) and then asked me about mine. I told him Apple and I were going flyering with someone from the hospitality union the Rivebelle workers hoped to join. I explained that Apple had diagnosed me with toska, and believed I should be doing something purposeful with my time. I left out that she thought the cause of my toska was Inno's departure to greener, potato-sown pastures.

"There's like a regional conference of dentists taking place at the hotel over the weekend, so more people than usual, so we're going to stand at the entrance and hand flyers out."

Inno found this image very amusing.

"Those poor dentists. That girl's going to be terrorizing them all within minutes," he said, meaning Apple. "And you? On the soapbox? Can I come watch?"

By the time we reached the riverfront, he had more or less stopped laughing. I tried to distract him by pointing out the SS *United States*, which we had come to see. It sat dormant in the gray water of the Delaware. It was sheathed in rust, which always made me sad, but its size was so impressive that in spite of its terrible state it retained an aura of dignity.

"It amazes me that you question poetry, yet find beauty in this," Inno said.

"It's the fastest ocean liner ever built. It crossed the Atlantic in like three days in 1952, and no one's broken the record since."

"It's ugly."

I shook my head. "One day a cruise company will restore it to its former glory, and you'll see how wrong you are."

"Don't you get bored?"

"I'm not even a real ship fan. A real ship fan would have taken you to see the USS *New Jersey*. You know, the battleship?"

"Of course I know the battleship. They do brunch there. But I didn't mean boats, I meant all of it. This morning you demand we meet on a particular street so that you can look at a plaque you've already read that says Napoleon's brother—"

"Joseph."

"—lived in one of the houses there for, what was it, a single year? And then, I'm sorry to say, we bypassed several picturesque alleys in favor of your historical tour. Don't you get bored?"

"Don't you get bored of poems?" I snapped.

"Poetry refreshes itself each time you read it, and oftentimes you come away with something new. But with this, I mean, there's nothing there."

"Why can't a place be like a poem?"

"It can be, but—alright, perhaps this doesn't apply as much to the big ship, although I would argue it's boring to look at the first time around. But take the street where we met. That was just a street. There was nothing there, not really. The house he lived in was probably demolished years ago. And he isn't even the one that you like."

"I like Joseph. He went to law school. Like Apple."

"There are just so many degrees of separation. And you've been before. Why on earth would you want to go again?"

I shrugged and said nothing, because I knew, since he hated sentimentality, I would make him uncomfortable with my answer, which was that I'd wanted to show it to him.

The monks were burning incense when I got home, and the vestibule was redolent. I peered into the mailbox, because I didn't have the key with me. Inside I could see a slim white envelope with my name and address written in handwriting I recognized. I jammed my hand into the slot. My fingers brushed the paper. If I could get hold of one corner of the envelope, I would be able to extract it from the shallow compartment. My hand was about halfway inside; I had range but no rotating power. I pushed at the envelope with the tips of my fingers. It was moving in tiny, infuriating increments, not enough for me to grasp it but just enough to make me feel that my actions were resulting in movement, which stopped me from giving up. I twisted my trapped limb, pawing at the paper.

"Gan sha ya?"

I jumped. Xinwei was behind me, asking me what I was doing

in a mimicry of Beijing dialect, her impression of me speaking Chinese. She held up the tiny key. I extracted my hand, rubbing the bone of my thumb, which was red from where it had scraped against the sharp metal sides of the mail slot. Xinwei opened the door, handed me the letter, and then took out a small mass wrapped in cellophane and tape.

"Hua jiao," she explained as we trooped up the stairs.

I relished our moments without Raymond, when we could chat in Mandarin with what I experienced, in my capacity as an only child, as a sisterly affection, a jiejie–meimei kind of dynamic. When we reached our apartment, Xinwei swapped her rubber slippers, which she used to roam the building, for her fluffy indoor ones, and padded to the kitchen to open her packet of peppercorns. When she was done with the scissors, I used them to slit open the envelope on its short side, in order to preserve its form, and not alter the parts of it that Hoang had constructed.

Penelope,
My friend Mohd set up traps around his house to catch mice. He ordered a bunch of them on Amazon, they look like the ones in Tom and Jerry. The trip that sets it off even looks like cheese, yellow with little holes.

Below this, he had included a sketch of the mouse trap, charming in its ineptitude.

He's been leaving them all over & the mice try to eat the peanut butter on the trip, which sets off the spring then this metal bar whacks them & locks them in. Some die right away because their skulls or spinal cords shatter, but sometimes the angle isn't right and they stay alive. I was hanging out with him and then I heard this screaming sound, and he told me it was probably one of the mice dying inside the trap. He's thinking of buying a more expensive one that's supposed to work better (as in it's better at killing them). He showed me a picture, it's plastic and it looks like dentures, if the teeth were really sharp. Mohd is one of my best friends and I've known him since we were in middle school so I kind of went off on him. As you know from when we met I have a soft spot for mice, and there are no-kill traps (not the glue ones though, they're torture chambers), although in my opinion you don't need traps in the first place. We live in these big houses with all this space, what's so bad about sharing some of it? Mohd said they kept shitting on the koala cushions & he woke up one morning to a mouse on his pillow, staring at him. He said that was the LAST STRAW! I didn't want to get into an argument so I left. I don't think I have a good reason why I was so against it, except that it's cruel.

This made me think about the mice at the lab, which made me think of the day I got found out (the day I met you). I guess it's obvious but it only occurred to me today how few people I've met like that. Most people in my life = family, school, or work. After I left Mohd's I biked up to the Wissahickon. I wanted to follow the thought I had about meeting you & how unusual it is to keep talking to a stranger without anything bringing you together. Maybe you do it all the time. I think I want to do it more. I started writing this in my head when I got to the creek. On the ride up I was thinking about the buses with the overhead wires, the ones that stick to the routes that the wires make, and how everybody kind of lives life like that, with these invisible wires holding them in place, making them take the exact same path to work/home/everywhere else. That was part of why I didn't want to go straight home. I wanted to get off my usual track, even though biking to the Wissahickon is another pretty frequent track (I took some detours to shake the feeling off). I think meeting you and now writing to each other is kind of a way we're diverging from the track, and don't you think this would be possible all the time, for everybody, it's just that nobody thinks of it or they're too lazy to get around to it, like I could be striking up conversations with

*way more strangers in my day to day? And then on my way home there
was a rainbow! Did you see it?*

Hoang

The morning we were supposed to flyer outside the Rivebelle,
Apple canceled, claiming she had a sore throat and didn't want
to get me sick. I knew she'd been out drinking, and saw through
her false concern. Now I wanted to go even less, but someone
from the hospitality union was on their way to meet us, and it
seemed unsporting to flake just because Apple had. It was the
coldest day of the year so far, and as usual I was underdressed,
having been duped once again by a brief blue sky that clouded
over the moment I left the apartment.

It was easy to spot Chris because he wore a bright red hoodie
with the name of the hospitality union inscribed in large capital
letters across the front. He said he had a meeting to get to, but he
would stick around to help me get the hang of things. In three
hours, someone else would come to take over. Chris said they'd
been short on volunteers lately, and he appreciated my coming
out. He didn't mention Apple's absence, which made me think
that people canceled quite often, and that he probably believed in
her alleged illness as much as I did. He brought my attention to
a hand cart, similar to the kind that retirees in Chinatown used
for their shopping, and which in this case held a stack of flyers. I
scanned the top sheet.

THIS HOTEL IS OWNED BY BONAVENTURE
BONAVENTURE WORKERS ARE ON STRIKE ACROSS
THE COUNTRY DEMANDING BETTER PAY
SHOW YOUR SUPPORT FOR THE WORKERS!

Chris explained that although the Rivebelle was marketed as a stand-alone boutique hotel, it was actually just a sub-brand of Bonaventure, a much larger hospitality company with properties all over the country. Several branches of one of the company's mid-market hotel brands had unionized. The workers at those hotels were currently on strike, which was why we were flyering outside the Rivebelle—so more people would know that the company running this hotel owned many others where the employees were so dissatisfied with their working conditions that they were striking. I asked why we didn't just hand out flyers asking people to support the Rivebelle staff who wanted to unionize.

"They're not ready to go public yet," Chris said.

"Of course," I said, resolving to look into this later. "So you're helping them to form a union, and then their union will be part of the bigger union?"

Chris laughed, though not unkindly. "So I work for the labor union. We represent about half a million workers across the country in the hospitality industry—hotels, restaurants, casinos, sports stadiums, airports. We're part of the AFL-CIO, you know what that is, right? Now the guys at the Rivebelle reached out because they want to unionize. We're guiding them through that process, like how to talk to your colleagues, how to deal with management harassing you, how to evade their traps. Strategy. How to win. Make sense?"

I nodded. Very quickly I realized I should have brought gloves. When you are handing out flyers it is impossible to place your hands in your pockets to warm them up, and they get cold almost right away. Chris, noticing my red ears, took pity on me and fished a union beanie from his backpack, which seemed to be filled with merch of all kinds, though no gloves. I was invigorated by the hat, which warmed me and had the added benefit of making me feel like I was in uniform, increasing my sense of duty and purpose, which was nebulous at best. No one was really walking past us or coming out of the hotel, so I started asking Chris about his job. He said he'd been with the union for five years. I asked if he knew Gus.

"Saw him yesterday. Him, Crystal, Mariama, Danny. I know everybody pretty well now."

"Do you know Hoang?"

"'Course. He was there too. You friends?"

I said yes, and, sated—the excitement of hearing a new person acknowledge Hoang's existence being enough for me—I asked him more about his own life. Before he was an organizer, he said, he worked in one of the concession booths of the football stadium. All the concession booths in all the stadiums in the city were run by one company, and when Chris was there they had decided to organize a union. He said what had really pissed people off at his old job and convinced them to unionize was when a new senior manager came in who centered his introductory speech around wanting to support "employees of color" and "hear their voices," but who, when Chris and some of his coworkers told him that only white employees were assigned to work in the VIP lounge—which was where you got the most tips—refused to listen to their complaints, even though what they were claiming was pretty obviously true—you only had to look—and reprimanded them for suggesting that management was racist. The new manager had said he was offended at the suggestion, pointing out that he himself was black. "It was the same line as all the others before him, but he was the first one to pretend like he cared," Chris said. "It was the hypocrisy that got to us." At that point, Chris had worked at the stadium for ten years, not once missing a day of work, and during that time had had a total wage increase of one dollar and fifty cents. A few months after they unionized, he quit and became a full-time organizer.

Just then, two women emerged from the revolving doors of the hotel, wrapping shawls around themselves. Chris moved toward them, and I remembered what we were meant to be doing. The women smiled politely and took the flyers and said yes when Chris asked if they were in town for the conference of dentists. I could hear him start to explain how Bonaventure mistreated its workers, and that thousands of hotel workers were on strike across the country. Many people, he said, had to juggle two or three jobs to make ends meet, because the company paid so badly. The dentists were nodding along and they laughed when he made some joke about needing to go for a checkup because he drank too much soda. I took mental notes.

He was still in conversation with the women when a man with gelled gray hair, wearing a black pea coat, walked out of the hotel. I lunged at him. He stopped walking, but he did not take the flyer I proffered.

"Good morning, sir, did you know that Bonaventure hotel workers across the country are on strike for better pay?"

There was a silence, and then he said, "Well, I hope they get it."

"Me too!" It seemed that there was more I should say. I pointed at the building in front of us. "Bonaventure actually owns the Rivebelle."

The man's expression moved from wary to hostile. I think he thought I was about to criticize him for staying at the hotel, because he said, "I'm just here for the conference, I'm not trying to sign any petition."

I didn't respond at first, because I had become distracted by his teeth, which were very white and very even. Of course, these were dentists. I wondered if the teeth were real or if they were those fake teeth that people got by filing down their own into tiny pointy nubs and then installing beautiful false porcelain versions on top. Apple sometimes forced me to watch videos of this procedure, because she was thinking of getting it done.

"I don't have anything for you to sign," I said.

"Okay," said the man.

"But, uh——" I was remembering my lines. "Will you stand with the striking Bonaventure workers who are demanding more from hotel management?"

"No," the man said, and walked off.

I turned around. Incredibly, Chris was still in conversation with the two women. Now it seemed they were asking him questions, and he was listening and answering. I was dispirited. He had made it look so easy, and I had tried to mimic him, but I had failed. Another man exited the hotel, and I thrust a flyer at him. He swerved with impressive agility and strode away. I felt that this must be payback for all the times I had avoided eye contact with people passing out flyers on the street, karmic retribution for all the church services I failed to attend, the gym memberships I eschewed, the meat I continued to eat. The third man to come out of the hotel didn't slow down to hear my entreaties but he did take a flyer. Chris's conversation ended just in time for him to see this, and I thanked the universe for its gift of serendipity.

"All good?" Chris asked, walking over.

"Yeah, great."

"You think you're gonna stick around?"

"Couple more hours, right?"

"I mean after today."

"Yes. Definitely."

He nodded. "You should come to the rally too. The more the merrier."

I asked him what he meant. I'd given up pretending to know things. Apparently there was going to be a big rally, probably in Boston, sometime in the new year, maybe early spring. All the unionized hotel workers were going to be there, and everyone working on the campaign in Philly was going too, provided they could get the day off work.

After Chris saw that I had a meager handle on things, he left, and I settled into a rhythm. I estimated the flyer acceptance rate to be around fifteen percent, and had yet to discern any trends based on gender, race, age, or another such distinguishing factor. The only pattern I noticed was that people entering and leaving the hotel were much more likely to give me a wide berth than passersby, but since I was strategically positioned it was harder for them to avoid me. Most people shrank from me and averted their eyes, or else tried to communicate a nonverbal apology with the wringing of a hand or a downturned smile and a cramped little shrug. Of the fifteen percent who did take a flyer, I watched several crumple their gifts and lob them in the trash can before they turned the corner. I didn't begrudge them, but it was interesting to note my own reaction to those who ignored me, who didn't shake their heads or hold up their palms in gestures of defense, but strode past without even a flinch to betray their awareness that I was there. It elicited a spike of anger in me, me who never got angry and who had ignored many a street solicitor in the past. I kept repeating the same couple of lines, similar to the ones on the flyer, with some minor improvised variation.

About an hour in, one of the dentists took the flyer, scanned it, asked me, "What do you expect me to do about this?," and then handed it back to me. I started to question the purpose of the exercise. What *did* I expect him to do about this? I understood that it was important that more people know about the strike and Bonaventure but I found it difficult to extrapolate what we wanted them to do after they became aware of the issue. Probably I should have asked Chris before he left. I checked my phone. Apple had texted, how's it going Cesar Chavez?

I didn't reply. I considered it an inappropriate tone for someone who had cajoled me into doing an activity with her and then not bothered to show up to the activity. I also had a WeChat message from my father, who had been in a dour mood for weeks, since finding out the Whitney was not, as he first believed, putting on a retrospective of his work but instead was staging an exhibition of several Chinese artists of his milieu, in which two paintings of his would be featured, alongside a new large-scale installation by an art school classmate with whom he had long feuded and who he believed to be an artistically inferior charlatan, and to make space for whose work the Whitney told my father that they would not be able to exhibit his own new large-scale installation after all. He was no longer coming to the U.S. for the opening. I was a little hurt that he'd canceled the whole trip when he could have kept his tickets and visited me, but I tried not to show it. His message said:

GUESS WHO'S A POTTER?

I had no idea what it meant. Normally he texted or voice-messaged me in Chinese; communicating in English, like calling, was suspect. I wondered if he was high. My father no longer drank, but he loved to take psychedelics, and kept a glass jar of mushrooms on a black lacquer sideboard in his living room, alongside his chrysanthemum teas, his ginseng root, and his Cuban cigars.

After a red-shirted union representative relieved me of my duties, I walked home, replying to my father's message with a single question mark and reacting to Apple's with a downturned thumb, feeling that this was the quality of response they both deserved. Part of me had hoped Hoang would appear while I was outside the Rivebelle, but I was also relieved he had not. The frisson of possibly being in his vicinity hadn't been as powerful as I had hoped. The letter had made him real again; I feared it might be time to end my self-enforced isolation, to try and see him in person. At home I put on the rice cooker and made tomato and egg and reread Hoang's letter, that perfect object, trying to make out words he had crossed out here and there. Shortly after we started writing to each other, I began dreaming correspondence-themed dreams. I dreamed of checking the mail, I dreamed of pages and pages of handwritten recollection, addressed to me. Once I dreamed I was walking by the banks of the Schuylkill when two lions walked past in single file, and in the dream I thought, *I have to write to Hoang about this.* I didn't want to lose this dreamlike quality, and I worried it would not survive if we graduated to more conventional forms of interaction. While I washed the dishes, my father messaged me again. It was four in the morning in Beijing. I dried my hands and unlocked my phone: an address for a pottery studio in Queens, New York. And then a second message came in.

Your mother works here. Pay her a visit?

SEVEN

Inno chose to have his farewell party at the Rivebelle, renting out the whole bar for the occasion, which meant, of course, that everyone who worked there would be present. He was expecting a hundred people, a number he described as "intimate," even though he had invited Apple, which indicated to me that he had been generous with his guest list. I didn't ask how this extravagance factored into his effective altruism calculations. Maybe his parents were giving him one last send-off. Apple declined the invitation, accusing Inno of scabbing, even though no one was on strike. By the evening of the party I believed I had reconciled myself to his departure. I still wished he wasn't leaving, but I decided to be inspired by his example and resolved to emulate in my own life the verve with which he was pursuing an unconventional path. I was ready to tell him so when I found him at the party, swilling champagne, but before I could say anything, Inno said, "It's over."

"What's over?"

"Peru, the Potato Park, and so on."

"You're staying?"

No, he was not staying; he was moving back to Nigeria, to work as a management consultant in McKinsey's Lagos office. His parents, after the threats to cut him off if he went to Peru proved ineffectual, switched the stick for the carrot, pulling strings with their fellow elites to secure their son a very well remunerated job at the firm.

"They realized how to defeat me. They finally read the books I've been giving them, and they argued I could improve many more lives if I took the McKinsey offer and donated a portion of my salary to my causes, rather than toiling in the hinterlands of Peru, which indeed may have benefited me more than anyone else. I couldn't argue with it because I would be arguing with myself. It is exponentially higher impact."

"But what about living a small life?" I said. I was floundering. I felt like the false fish in the pan in the Japanese garden. One of my worst housemates had worked at McKinsey. He once told me, unprompted, that he was trying a new regimen which demanded that he abstain from ejaculation in order to retain his qi, like a Tang dynasty court official, to improve his productivity at work; he hadn't spoken to his girlfriend in a week, he said, because he had come while having sex with her and blamed her for the slipup. It was unclear what she should have done to prevent this.

"Life will be big in Lagos," Inno said, but he didn't sound convinced.

"Why are you even throwing this party?" I said.

He frowned. "I'm still leaving."

"Did you tell anyone else yet?"

"Most of them know," he said. "You are in fact the only one to whom I disclosed my Andean adventure."

We were on the balcony of the bar. I leaned over the glass barrier, watching a woman in a black one-piece swimming laps in the hotel pool. She was thrashing around, trying to do the butterfly, which I thought must be one of the most ungraceful movements in the world, relative to its name. I didn't feel like I had the right to be mad at Inno, but I felt obscurely betrayed. Even more obscurely, I felt guilty, as if I was the one letting the potato farmers down, even though I had no idea how they felt about the situation, and in all probability they didn't care. The swimmer touched the edge of the pool and then kicked off again. She had switched to the backstroke, and for one sickening moment, I thought I recognized my mother, but it was just an Asian woman with a pixie cut. I turned back to Inno.

"Are you excited?" I asked.

Instead of answering, he told me how many children would be dewormed because of his contributions. I was sad about the Potato Park, but I agreed that deworming was good. We talked for a while longer. I told him about a recent meeting with Dr. Bae that had not gone well. Bae had asked me how my weekend had been and I'd mentioned the flyering, thinking it an innocuous remark. Immediately his demeanor had changed, the ink-splash brows furrowing, the handsome smile gone. He made allusive references to the failed graduate student unionization at the university, which had nothing to do with me, and to "grievances" at the museum, insinuating that people there, at some point in the recent past, had also tried to unionize, which I knew nothing about. What had begun as a friendly meeting ended with barbed pleasantries, and I'd left his office with a dull feeling in my chest. Inno said Bae probably thought I'd mentioned the flyering to spook him and that I was raising the specter of syndicalism, threatening his rule. I wanted to talk about it more, but other party guests began to peck at Inno for attention. I promised I would visit him in Lagos, and pretty soon, as always, he was swept up by the social needs of the numerous others, leaving me on the balcony to think.

Because I was staying clear of the bar, I had not yet had a drink. I had seen, or rather sensed, Hoang there upon my arrival. Now, discomposed by Inno's revelations, I went to look for him, but found only Gus, who made me a lychee martini and told me Hoang was in the kitchen, looking for limes.

"Everyone wants daiquiris for some reason," Gus said.

I asked him if he supported Apple's reason for skipping the party, and he said he hadn't even known she was invited.

"We're kind of taking a break. She didn't tell you?"

"Oh, yeah, sorry, I forgot," I lied. I downed the rest of the martini. "Can I have another?"

"He's paying, you should have as many as you want."

"He's going to work for McKinsey. You know, the consultants?"

"Your friends have some interesting careers."

"Who else? Apple?"

Gus stabbed a fleshy lychee with a garnish pick using what I perceived to be unnecessary force.

"You don't approve of her career?"

"You know what she does for work, right?"

"Yeah."

"I didn't. She told me she was a civil rights lawyer. Turns out she helps corporations circumvent antitrust law."

"That's why you broke up," I said, trying to place my tone somewhere between a question and a statement.

"Not broke up. Taking a break."

"Maybe she thought you would judge her if she told you the

truth," I said, raising my voice so he could hear me over the sound of the cocktail he was violently shaking.

"She was right. I do. But I judge her more for lying to me. It doesn't feel good when somebody you love deceives you."

"Wow," I said. "Love."

He handed me my drink. "I gotta go deal with those people. I'll see you later."

I wandered around until I found Femi and Louisa, who were in the middle of a discussion about whether K-pop stars should be exempted from military service. Louisa, obviously, believed they should. "Ballet dancers. Pianists. Athletes. How come they get out of it? It's not fair to Jin. It's not fair to the boys."

"Success in sports does wonders for national morale," said Femi.

"What about economic success? BTS contributes billions of dollars to Korea's GDP. And the soft power they've generated for the government is priceless."

"Patriotism is more important. Winning gold medals at the Olympics makes the average citizen much prouder of their country than knowing American teenage girls are teaching themselves Korean for a boy band."

"I disagree," Louisa said. She was speaking normally, but tears were streaming down her face and slicing into her foundation, like rivulets of water on beach sand. "It's not fair to Jin," she kept repeating. "It's not fair to the boys."

"Anyway, I'll see you guys in a bit," I said.

I stood next to a bowl of popcorn and ate mouthfuls at a time. For a while I played a game where I held a single kernel in my palm to see how long I could go without eating it, which never exceeded a few seconds. Later, I caught sight of Hoang, when I was back at the bar trying to commandeer more champagne from Gus to take back to Inno. He was at the far end, uncorking a bottle of wine with fluidity and poise. He smiled at me, and I smiled back.

Now that I had seen him in person, I knew that I would speak to him before the night was over, and everything felt resolved in a curious way. I was able to converse with people, to think of the work I had to do at the museum on Monday, and to swipe tiny food—blinis with shavings of carrot made to resemble smoked salmon, mini mushroom tarts, finger-sized vegan pistachio eclairs—from the waiters who circulated the room with trays. The anticipation of seeing Hoang powered me through these tasks like a battery.

I got into a conversation with Gleb, Inno's chess instructor. I knew from Inno that Gleb had been a child chess champion, and I tried asking him about it, because prodigies interested me, but he refused to go into detail, claiming that he had forgotten that era of his life, and he wouldn't be able to tell me anything that I couldn't read in a newspaper article. I let it go, because I'd probably have said the same thing. Instead he told me stories about his childhood in Russia. When he wasn't practicing or studying for chess, he said, he and his friends would go into the woods and play games. The games they played were: beating each other up, beating one specific kid up (sometimes the kid was Gleb), and, Gleb's favorite, stuffing a tin can with acorns, lighting the acorns on fire, and then swinging the can around on a piece of string. In the summer the can helped to ward off mosquitos.

"The sparks jumped like fireflies in the dark forest," he said. "That was so fun."

I asked Gleb what his favorite food had been as a child, because I had no idea what Russians ate. He said it was porridge: milk, oatmeal, sugar, and salt, boiled and then stirred continuously at a very low heat to make sure it cooked all the way through without burning. It was his father's recipe, and now he cooked it whenever he was feeling homesick.

"I know it sounds disgusting," Gleb said sadly. I reassured him it didn't, and said my favorite food when I was a child had also been porridge, but made of rice, and I also cooked it for myself when I felt homesick. Gleb smiled and, encouraged, told me his second favorite food from home was a dish I would know as "Russian salad," and his wife cooked it very well. I said I wasn't familiar with Russian salad, and he listed the ingredients for me, and this time I had to lie when I said it didn't sound disgusting.

I asked Gleb what he thought of Inno's career move.

"Innocent is a very intelligent man, but I do not subscribe to his philosophy of moral calculus," Gleb said, meaning, I think, calculation.

"Exactly!" I was enthused. "Like the ban on tomatoes. What's going on there?"

"The lodestones must be God and family," said Gleb, meaning lodestars.

"And country?"

"No," said Gleb. "Not country. In these days when people say country they mean government, and I do not support my country's government. Do you?"

"I guess not," I said. There was a pause.

"Hey, Gleb?"

"Yes."

"Do you get along with your mother?"

"My mother?"

"Yeah."

"Get along?"

"Like, do you like her? Do you talk? Does she like you?"

Gleb said, "She is my mother." His tone said, the answer is so self-evident that it obviates the need for an explanation, for any statement other than the most circular of all: she is my mother. My mother is my mother. What more, his tone implied, could possibly be said?

After that, Gleb spent so long guiding me through the streets of his hometown on Google Maps, showing me the route he had walked to school, pointing out his favorite churches, and complaining about the outdated details, that my phone ran out of battery, at which point he said he had to go home to his wife and baby. The timing of it made me feel like he had only talked to me in order to access my phone and look at images of Novosibirsk.

Almost immediately after he left, someone else sat down in his place. It was Xinwei.

"Hey," I said in Mandarin. "What are you doing here?"

"Your friend invited me."

"Inno? Have you met?"

"Yes, at your birthday karaoke. I remember he brought his own sandwich to dinner, he said he was saving money. He must have saved a lot of money to afford this party."

"Where's Raymond?"

Xinwei took a big sip of her piña colada. I watched the white liquid move slowly upward through the green curly straw and into her mouth.

"We broke up."

"What? Seriously? Why?"

"He doesn't want to get married."

"I thought you were married."

"We just said we were. It's easier."

I asked her when it had happened. She said it had been a week. I told her I was sorry, and asked why she hadn't mentioned it to me at home.

"I didn't want to bother you," she said. She drained her piña colada, moving the straw around the bottom of the glass like a vacuum cleaner nozzle. "I'm leaving now, I just wanted to say hello to you first."

"Xinwei, wait," I said.

"Don't worry, nothing will change," she said. "I will stay in the apartment."

"No, but, are you okay?"

She shrugged and stood up. In English she said, "That's life."

I wandered back to Louisa and Femi, who were on the balcony now and who said we should go visit Inno in the summer. Femi said we could stay at his family's "extra mansion," and Louisa said she would go if our trip didn't clash with the BTS Love Yourself World Tour dates. It felt like the party would never end, but eventually it did, with just a few stragglers sprawled on the couches, the bartenders refusing to serve anything but tap water, Gus warning that his shift ended at two A.M. and he was not going to stay a minute later for anyone. At one minute past the hour, I veered toward the bar, from which I had been keeping a respectful distance. Hoang was loosening his collar.

"Forest!"

"Hey."

"You good?"

I nodded. After so long interacting with him in my head, it was interesting to have him in front of me. Underwhelming was the wrong word; humanizing sounded too grandiose. Most of all there was the sense that I'd never had anything to worry about.

"How was the party?" he asked.

"I don't know," I said. "Everyone was acting strange. How was it for you?"

"It was okay. We kept running out of limes, we had to start using clementines for the garnishes."

"Are you tired?"

"I'm alright. Are you tired?"

"No, I'm not tired."

"Are you hungry?"

"A little. Are you?"

"I haven't eaten since like before my shift." He cocked his head at me. "Do you want to get some food?"

We took the service elevator to the restaurant on the third floor. He led me through the darkness of the dining room, where upturned chairs rested on tables, and our feet were silent on the carpeted floor. He pushed open the heavy double doors to the kitchen, flicking lights on as he walked. "You can just sit here," he said, drumming the steel countertop with his fingers. He filled a large and intricate pot with water and set it on the stove to heat.

"They have these great steamers, and Japanese knives." He disappeared for a moment and returned with two large artichokes, one in each hand. "And these! From Italy."

I watched as he sliced the stems and tops off the artichokes with a long delicate blade, and then picked away the errant leaves. When the water reached a boil, he placed the artichokes in the mesh net steamer of the pot and covered them. He asked me for the time and I went to check my phone, forgetting it was dead.

"It's alright, we can guess," he said. He extracted a lemon from his pocket and cut it into quarters. He set a white plate on the counter, and a bottle of olive oil.

While the artichokes steamed, I asked him about Mohd and the mice. He said that they hadn't spoken about it since that initial confrontation, and he didn't know if he was going to mention it again because he still hadn't worked out an argument that satisfied him.

"I just don't like the idea of telling somebody else what to do," he said. "Plus, it's not like I'm vegetarian or anything, so it would be pretty easy for him to call me a hypocrite, and he wouldn't be wrong."

"My friend Inno is the opposite. He doesn't eat meat, but he would be perfectly happy killing mice. And he loves telling people what to do."

"That's the guy who threw the party?"

"Yeah, we're close," I said. I described Inno's emissions-based reasoning about his diet—how he didn't eat meat but didn't have an ethical objection to killing animals, viewing cows and tomatoes as interchangeable units of sustenance with different nutrition-to-emission ratios. He also knew exactly how many dogs and chimps he was willing to kill to save one human life. His was a minority view among his effective altruist friends, who were vegan for ethical as well as environmental reasons, and one of whom once told me it was morally unjustifiable to ride a horse or keep a dog or cat. Hoang wasn't familiar with effective altruism, but he said he thought it was interesting that one concept had enough philosophical bandwidth to include "stone cold" types like Inno as well as the anti-pet guy.

"Sorry, I don't want you to think I'm ripping on your friend, calling him cold."

"He can be frosty."

Hoang laughed, and the laugh revealed the dimple in his cheek. I told him I was going to miss Inno because I could talk to him about things that other people didn't want to discuss, or got tired of after a few minutes, whereas Inno was always happy to delve; at the same time, there was an unbridgeable gap. I still had not figured out if this was due to his popularity—I gestured to the ceiling to indicate the party that had just ended—or because of something more specific to him, like an aversion to intimacy rooted in his upbringing (that was Apple's theory). Inno and I often discussed personal issues and dissected their causes and effects, but the tone during these discussions had to be jokey and unruffled and the mode of analysis objective. I couldn't say he had ever confided in me.

"What?" I said. Hoang looked like he was thinking of some private joke.

"No, it's just funny. I actually thought he might have been your boyfriend."

"What? He's gay!" I said. I was smiling too, hoping I came across as bemused in a relaxed and humorous way, even though hearing Hoang say the word "boyfriend" made my stomach flip.

"That time you came to the bar, I thought you were on a double date or something."

He got up to check on the artichokes. I could see his shoulder blades through his shirt, and a deeper tan on his neck that stopped at his collar. He removed the lid, and steam gushed from the pot.

I had eaten artichokes before, but only the insides, soft and stripped of leaves. I had no idea how to approach the imposing flowers Hoang placed in front of me. He said he'd never eaten them either until he started working at the hotel and befriended Danny, one of the line cooks, who had cooked them for him once.

Hoang squeezed lemon over the artichokes and then hopped up on the counter beside me. We sat with the plate between us, tearing off the steaming petals one by one, dipping them in the olive oil, and then raking them through our teeth to get at the slivers of flesh. Oil and juice snaked down our hands and wrists, making liquid bangles on our forearms.

As we worked our way through this task, we talked. Hoang told me about his cousin who had recently become obsessed with old issues of magazines like *Playboy* and *Penthouse* that had published serious investigative pieces about CIA operations and crimes committed against civilians by American soldiers in the Vietnam War. His cousin, who lived next door to Hoang's grandmother in North Philly, was going around vintage stores and scouring eBay for copies of these magazines, trying to get a collection going. The cousin was convinced it had been a deliberate tactic of the U.S. government to allow only those kinds of publications to write such stories, because it limited the audience, and because the pornography diluted the credibility of the reporting. "I don't know if anything he's saying checks out, but he's fun to talk to," Hoang said.

Circuitously, I learned sparse and shocking facts about his family. I made some offhand remark that the happiest I'd ever been was the first time I experienced a snow day, and he asked me if I did have an actual happiest day, one I remembered as such. I couldn't think of anything, so I said I would stick with the snow day. He said his was the Super Bowl, earlier that year, when the Eagles won for the first time.

"It feels pretty good when you've been waiting for something your entire life and it actually happens," he said.

I remembered the night. Apple and I had wandered around the city after the game ended, drinking and screaming with what felt like the entire population of Philadelphia streaming down carless streets, watching people joust with traffic cones and cops laugh as men tried to clamber greased utility poles. It was thrilling to think of Hoang somewhere in that crowd, not yet known to me.

"It was so great because it wasn't just me that was happy, it was everybody I knew, and everybody else. You could look at somebody you never met and know they felt the same way as you, and know they were looking at you and seeing it too."

I asked the next question without thinking; it seemed a natural progression from the earlier one. As I asked it I realized it was a question I would have refused to answer.

"What about unhappiest? Do you have an unhappiest day?"

"You know," he said, "I do."

His parents were boat people. They had known each other as children in Vietnam, fled the country months apart and by different routes, and then ended up in Philadelphia and met again as adults. "They were the best," he said, and my heart dropped, hearing the past tense. Both of his parents, and his younger sister, his only sibling, had died in a car crash that Hoang had survived. "I didn't even break a bone," he said.

I asked him when it had happened.

"When I was eleven. That's why I lived with my grandma growing up. And then the Eagles lost the championship to the Panthers." He'd been looking at the floor, but he looked up at me then, and laughed a little, to reassure me or maybe himself. "So it was a really bad year."

He took off his glasses, and rubbed them on his shirt, and then put them back on.

"Come on, we have to get to the hearts," he said. He tore off an artichoke leaf. I wanted to say something more, but I wasn't sure what. I tore off a leaf too. When they were all gone, he used the knife to carve away the prickly tendrils, which would choke you if you consumed them, and we poured the last of the oil over the sweet bulbs of flesh. Our fingers were pruned, as if we'd been swimming in the sea. Hoang got up to clear the dishes we'd used, somehow balancing everything in his arms with what looked like no effort at all. He seemed so agile.

"How are you carrying all that?"

"This?" He grinned. "Child's play."

He turned, and again I stared at his shoulder blades and his neck.

"Did you fall asleep in the sun or something?"

"What makes you say that?"

"Your neck looks a little toasted."

He laughed. "I was reading on the roof and smoking a joint and I dozed off."

"Wasn't it cold?"

He shook his head. "Remember how warm it was last weekend?"

"Right. Climate change is crazy."

"Nice sometimes though, right?"

"What were you reading?"

"Something Gus gave me about the history of unions in America. It's really good, but my attention span is terrible. Probably shouldn't have smoked at the same time. I think you'd like it, though. I can lend it to you."

"How's the union stuff going?"

"It's been amazing. More people are getting into it, I think we're gonna go public soon. Then we can start wearing the pins on our shirts at work. My manager's reaction is gonna be so funny. Chris told me you started volunteering, that's really cool."

"He told you?"

"He said there was a new volunteer called Penelope, who knew me and Gus, that's gotta be you, right? You still doing it?"

"Yes, definitely," I said, deciding then that I would.

"When I was still at the lab, a couple of the grad students there were trying to unionize too," Hoang said. "It doesn't look like they're gonna succeed, at least not right now, but I think we might. We can't afford not to, I would say. It's just wild, like, you've talked to Gus, right? He's got his theories, and I like hearing what he has to say, but I think it's even more simple than how he makes it out. Like I come into work, I'm here talking to Danny while he's cutting onions, or I'm upstairs with Gus and everybody else who works at the bar, or trying to speak Spanish with Hector, or hearing the gossip from Crystal and Mariama, they're like the vanguard of the housekeepers, without them there's no chance. Crystal read my palm the other day and she said she saw victory on my horizon. That has to mean the union, right? And it's like, I babysit their kids, we go to each other's houses for dinner, we already are something, you know? Which makes it feel inevitable. I just think we're gonna win, I have a really good feeling about it."

Outside it was snowing, almost imperceptibly, the snowflakes making leisurely revolutions in the air and then touching down on the pavement, where they vanished. I loved the feeling of the frost on my skin. We walked our bikes through the quiet streets, talking at first, and then silent. It was past three in the morning. I was in an internal struggle with my consciousness, between "being" in the present, privileging its sensations and blurring its passing seconds into one continuous moment, and "seeing" it, aware of its rarity and its finitude and irritated that I was already perceiving it the way I would when it would end. I faced ahead, watching the dark street reveal itself to us. The furrowed rubber of our bicycle tires made soft scudding sounds as they cut through the thin filigree of snow.

"Did you know," I said, "that the Mongols, like Genghis Khan and his soldiers, when they were on a campaign and ran low on food and water, would cut their horses and drink their blood? They didn't kill them, they took just enough to survive."

"That's so cool."

"Right?" Encouraged, I added, "The Mongols also had the world's first postal service."

"Like a Pony Express?"

"But way bigger. And earlier."

The snow continued to fall. It felt like the city had emptied out, and we were the only ones left. We walked over a sidewalk grate just as a cloud of sweet-smelling steam erupted from it, and we were briefly warmed by the strange dew. From my experience, the more detail you amassed about someone and the more time you spent with them, the harder it was to idealize them. This hadn't yet happened with Hoang. Maybe it was because we only saw each other in a limited set of situations. We had never spent time together in any way except alone with each other, and seeing someone interact with people who weren't you was an easy way to realize they were a normal person, a person who also succumbed to social pressure or said stupid things, and then they lost their sheen. Hoang still had a sheen. He was all promise, no disappointment. Was there a way to keep it like that forever?

"Hey, stop for a second," he said. We were in front of the First Presbyterian Church. On the other side of the street was a sex shop and the psychic that Apple once forced me to pay ten dollars to consult, because she was embarrassed to go in alone. The psychic told Apple that a life of prosperity and happiness awaited her, and then told me I had enemies who wanted to harm me across distant seas, and that I should avoid elevators. Next to the church was a beautiful townhouse, Jacobean revival. The stairs and the railings of the church were coated with snow, almost an inch thick.

"I don't think it's open, you know," I said, looking at the church.

Hoang didn't say anything. He scooped a small portion of snow from the railing into his hand and held it up for me to inspect. Then he took a bite of it. He laughed when he saw my expression. "It's like bingsu." He chewed, and reflected. "Or maybe more like water ice."

I was transfixed.

"You've never done this before?"

I shook my head.

"Try. It's nice."

It was, as he said, like bingsu, fresh and springy. We started walking again.

"Have you ever been to the zoo?" he said.

"Like, in general?"

"No, like the Philadelphia Zoo."

"Never."

"Do you want to go sometime?"

"To the zoo?"

"There's a new giraffe. A baby."

"Let's do it."

"Okay. Like next week? Sunday?"

"Yeah, okay," I was laughing at his enthusiasm for this simple thing. "Sunday."

"Awesome. I have Sunday off, and I never have Sunday off, so it has to be Sunday."

"Okay, Sunday!"

When we got to his house, I rested my bike against his in the hallway and waited on the sofa while he went to change out of his work clothes. He took my dead phone with him upstairs; he said he still had his old charger. I had forgotten he lived in the house across the street from the koala house, and not the koala house itself. He came back down wearing a white T-shirt and gray sweatpants, and I remembered the tattoo on his arm, which was visible now that he was in short sleeves. I asked to see it. He sat beside me and stretched out his arm. What I thought was just a jumble of lines looked now like the penciled outlines of trees, no leaves, just thin trunks and branches, the way they looked in the winter. I reached out to touch it, brushing my fingers against his skin.

"So cool," I said. I was overwhelmed by my own action. Had I touched him before?

It turned out I was mistaken, and the lines did not depict trees. Mohd was an aspiring tattoo artist, apprenticing somewhere in North Philly, and Hoang let him practice with the tattoo gun on his skin. Maybe some were trees, Hoang said, but mostly Mohd just wanted to be able to draw lines and curves without his hand shaking from the effort, which, as Hoang's skin proved, it still sometimes did. We talked more about the union campaign. I told him about my work at the museum, and he promised to come see the exhibit when it opened. He asked me again about Inno, because he said he felt like our conversation had been interrupted and he was interested in hearing more. The delay had given me time to think about it, and I admitted I was disturbed by Inno's sudden change of plans. Out of everyone I knew, he was the one I thought might go on to do something special with his life.

Hoang and I discovered that neither of us had a driver's license.

"We gotta learn to drive," he said.

"How come you can't?" I said. I liked that he'd said "we."

"I think maybe I was scared to for a while. Because of what happened with my family. I didn't want to go into cars for a few years. I walked, I took the train, the bus. Then one day I was on the bus and I was like, wait, this is just a car. It's bigger, but, you know, it's on the road, somebody's driving it. Stupid, right? And then Mohd got his license and the stuff I would miss out on if I kept avoiding cars multiplied by like a thousand. So I got in the car, and it was fine. Sitting in the backseat still creeps me out though, I won't do it. Which is maybe stupid too."

"It's not stupid," I said. "So you always call shotgun."

"Exactly. I'll override everybody else too, I'm ruthless. It's fine now, but when I was still sort of spooked, we would do these test drives, where Mohd drove me around the empty parking lot at school at like ten, fifteen an hour. He's a really good guy, that's why I was so bummed about the mouse traps, you know? But nobody's perfect. I'm talking too much, aren't I? What about you, why can't you drive, what's your excuse?"

I picked at a thread of sofa fabric. "I didn't grow up in the U.S., and I guess I've just been lazy since I got here."

"Where'd you grow up?"

"China."

"Whoa."

"Yeah."

"But you're American?"

"Yeah, I was born here," I said. It wasn't true, I was born in Beijing. I was American because my mother was American.

"It's cool you grew up there. I've never been to Vietnam."

"Do you want to go?"

"For sure. I've never been outside the U.S. I actually just applied for my first passport, because I'm trying to get this job as a cook in Antarctica, you know how they always need people to staff the research stations?"

"Antarctica," I repeated.

"Yeah, how cool would it be if the first time I left the U.S., it was to go to Antarctica? And if I get the job, I was thinking I could stop by Vietnam, hang out with some distant relatives, see how good my Vietnamese is compared to everybody there."

"When would you be going?"

"Not till next year."

I had to admit that it would be cool. Then I said, "This is weird, but just now I told you I was born in the U.S. I wasn't. I was born in Beijing."

"So you lied?"

"I guess. I don't know why."

"It's okay. You're telling me now."

"Yeah," I said. In fact, it wasn't okay, because I had lied again, when I said I didn't know why I'd lied the first time: because of an irrational worry that he might have asked how I was American if I was born in China and my father was Chinese, and I would have had to say because my mother is American, which would have meant mentioning my mother.

Possibly my father's text, or the phantasm of the woman doing laps in the pool below Inno's party, had dislodged some of my resistance to talking about the past. It wasn't as if there was much to tell when it came down to it. I hated to drag things on, and I was also paranoid, in light of Hoang's own familial circumstances, of mak-

ing too much of my own, a soap opera subplot in comparison. But I
didn't like the feeling that I was keeping something from him, even
though this never bothered me with other people. I think it helped
that I knew he wasn't the type to tell me I was traumatized and
needed a therapist, as Apple had done when I told her my mother
had abandoned our family without warning, and that because I
was the last one to see her, my father sometimes casually wondered
aloud if it was something I'd done or said that had made her leave.
He didn't mean to hurt me, it was just the way he was.

So I told Hoang about my mother: her breakdowns, her illness,
her spite, her cruelty, her disappearance, the years of radio silence,
wondering if she was even still alive, and, now, finding out from
my father that she apparently was.

"Sorry if this is a dumb question, but when you say she went
off her meds—she was bipolar?" Hoang said.

"Yeah. And yeah, she took them sometimes. She was fine
when I was growing up, but my father has since told me that she
was really bad about it before I was born. She said they blunted
her creativity, and she thought she did her best work in the beginning stages of the manic episodes. It's fucked up but it's probably
true. But she was convinced she could control it, and she couldn't.
She would push herself, and go too far, and when you're that
deep in it you don't believe the things you believed at first, you
think you're like, a god, of course you're not going to think you
need medication. But she was taking them consistently until I
was like, eleven? I think she got bored. But even before that, she
was always very cold. She was a cold person. She never treated me
like a kid, even when I was really little. I would try to make her
laugh at something I was doing and she would give me this look
that was like, I know you want me to laugh and I'm not going
to do that for you because I don't think it's funny. But of course
I still loved her. I admired her. She was like this beautiful person

who lived in the house with us, who I got to talk to whenever I wanted. I didn't even know she was bipolar until I was a teenager, way after she was gone, and my dad finally told me all this stuff he had kept from me, and only because I asked so many times. It's very Chinese, just straight up not telling your children about huge parts of your life—their life—because you've deemed it unnecessary for them to know. So I didn't know she was ever on medication, or that she stopped taking it. Which made a lot of stuff make more sense. Like later on, when she wouldn't shower, and then wouldn't talk, and my father took all the knives in the kitchen to his studio and brought her takeaway food to eat in her room. Which she didn't eat. It's the two sides, right, and that was the depression. And the other side—"

I stopped speaking. Beneath the silence of the room, I thought I could hear a high-pitched noise. I could feel Hoang listening to me, the pressure of it. I rubbed my eyes.

"I'm sorry, I don't like talking about it. Normally I don't. For a long time, I told myself that every mean thing she said or did to me was because of the illness, but really she was fine, mentally, for most of my childhood. It was just her personality. I can understand that now, but it took a while. It's a lot harder to accept, and it's hard to disentangle one from the other. And then when I was thirteen, she was going through a manic episode—things happened—she left, and she never came back, and, like I said, I thought maybe she was dead. But I don't like talking about it. I find it," I paused, "I find it circular. Going over the past. It never leads to anything new."

"Do you want to see her now?"

"I don't know." I shifted around on the sofa. I felt agitated, and I was trying to figure out why. I had divulged my past to Hoang because I wanted him to know me, but it was not like me to divulge, and so now that I had done it I did not feel like myself.

It was a lie that confessions unburdened you. It seemed to me that they reminded you of the weight you carried, rather than lightening it. For years I hadn't thought about my father hiding the knives, and leaving the meals, and now I was thinking about it, and remembering the smell of all the food she wasn't eating, and the sound of his knuckles on the locked door, soft raps.

"I never talk about her," I said again. I laughed, and it was like the way Hoang had laughed in the kitchen of the Rivebelle earlier in the night. "I feel worse now, having told you."

Hoang said, "Well, I'm glad you did."

"Apple hates that I don't like dwelling on sad stuff. She thinks it's good to dwell."

Hoang nodded. He said, "It's like you're living with a big hole in the middle of your life, you can't fill it ever, so you just skate around it. Or you can chip away at the edges, making it bigger and bigger, but why would you want to do that? Maybe that's what it feels like when you talk about your mom. That's how it felt when I talked about my parents and my sister, for years. It still does sometimes. And it's always hard telling somebody who doesn't know, because you're thinking about what they're going to think, and you know how it's going to make them feel. But you have to tell them some time. Once is usually enough for me. Maybe for you too. But like I said, I'm glad you told me. And I'm glad I told you about me, too."

The conversation meandered on. He was interested in my life in China, so I told him about wearing a little red scarf and a tracksuit, singing the national anthem on the sports field in the dead heat of August, laughing at the children who fainted in the sun and had to be carried off on stretchers. I described the daily routine of cleaning the windows and blackboards, mopping the floors of our classroom and fetching and serving lunch from the kitchen, which we ate on metal trays at our individual desks. While I retained no love for the marching exercises, I had grown to appreciate over time the merits of the group caretaking of our classroom, in which we spent most of our time and which we felt already was ours. Instead of a hamster or rabbit on which to focus our collective feeling, we polished the windows out of which we longingly gazed when lessons recommenced, watching the clouds move across the sky and dreaming of escape and play. At Hoang's high school—a high-ranking magnet school, which he didn't mention, but which I knew because it was famous in Philadelphia for its extremely competitive entry requirements—cockroaches lorded over the hallways, and black mold bloomed on the walls, and the students were taught from decades-old textbooks with missing pages and lewd scrawlings. He said he thought my idea of a universal program of classroom cleaning was a good one, but he wouldn't want it to imperil the jobs of the janitors, who had been cool. I assured him that my school still had janitors. We called the female cleaners ayi, aunties, and one of them once caught my friend smoking a cigarette in the bathroom and whacked it out of her hand with a broom.

"What time do you think it is?" I said at some point.

"Late. It might even be morning soon."

"Do you often stay up late?"

He shook his head. "Not unless I'm working. Do you?"

"I do. But I feel bad. I feel like you're too polite to tell me to leave."

He smiled, which I took as assent.

"How about this," I said. "When you want to go to bed, just make a signal, and I'll go."

"What kind of signal?"

"You could whistle."

"I actually can't whistle."

"Me neither," I said. "Then maybe, maybe you could slap me or something."

"Slap you?"

"Like a light slap?"

He was smiling. "I don't think I want to do that."

"It doesn't have to be—" I could feel my face getting hot. How had I ended up in this conversation? Why did I ever talk at all? "I just meant, like, lightly. As a nonverbal indication. For when you want to go to bed."

"Alright." Hoang said. He reached out and touched the side of my face, a mock-slap. "I want to go to bed." His hand was cool on my cheek, which felt flushed. He kept it there. "Do you want to come get your phone?"

I nodded, and the motion caused his hand to move, as if he was stroking my face. He laughed softly, and thumbed my chin. "Come on," he said.

Mutely, I followed him. My heart was pounding. My throat felt constricted, and I was afraid to speak, lest I unleash some kind of unsexy croak.

His room faced the street. There were books heaped on the floor, some stacked like Jenga tiles and some just scattered around. I saw a slim volume that said *Field Notes*, and a book with a red cover that said *The Sympathizer*, and, facedown on the carpet, *Farewell to the Horse*. Its placement suggested he might have been reading it in bed, the book I had told him to read. There was a large poster with labeled illustrations of different types of fish, eels, crabs, and one octopus. The poster said NORSKEKYSTEN in block letters, and it was right above his headboard. His bedsheets were pale blue, creased from the last time he had slept in them, the bed unmade.

"Here you go," Hoang said. He was holding out my phone.

"Thank you."

"No problem."

We were facing each other now. He took off his glasses and

rubbed the lenses with the thin fabric of his shirt. My phone was in my hand, and I automatically pressed the button to power it on.

"I like your socks, Forest."

We looked at my socks. They were mismatched, one stripey and one patterned with cartoon hamburgers.

"I can never find the same ones."

"You pull it off, though."

I looked up at him. I could see his stubble and smell the detergent on his clothes. The silence was leavening between us. I grasped his wrist, and he grasped mine, and tugged me minutely closer. Under my thumb, I could feel his pulse.

In my other hand, my phone vibrated, and, instinctively, I looked at it.

"Oh my god."

Unthinkingly I hurled my phone at the floor.

"Whoa, Forest, what's wrong?"

An email—it had to be an email, because I had him blocked on everything else—from Paul. I glimpsed one phrase: *in New York if you're around*

"Are you okay?" Hoang said. He picked up my phone and handed it to me. "Is it about your mom?"

I shook my head. "I think I have to go. I'm sorry."

"I'll walk you out," Hoang said, and then hesitated. "Did I do something?"

I shook my head again. My entire body felt cold, shocked out of the heat that had coursed through it just a moment before. I wanted to say more, so he would know that he had done no wrong, but I couldn't speak.

He held the door open for me while I hauled out my bike. I cycled home, mindful of the slick surface of the road, where the snowflakes were already on their way to becoming ice.

EIGHT

As we pulled out of Thirtieth Street Station, the droplets of condensation that had been trembling on the surface of the window began to streak in horizontal lines across the glass, pushed into movement by the acceleration of the train. The paths they left behind them cleared the blanket of vapor that blurred the outside world from view, mapping islands and mud cracks onto the translucent pane. The moving water made the trees and buildings look liquid as they rushed past.

Trains always helped me think, even when I didn't want to. I was thinking about the last time I saw Paul, outside the Gare du Nord in Paris. It was late in the afternoon, and raining, and in the sunlight the falling water looked like snow. I was heading back to Philadelphia, where Paul was supposed to join me later on. We'd just spent a month with his family in France, where we'd retreated because he'd overstayed his visa for the U.S. and if he'd remained there any longer he might have been banned from returning. He was going to look for a job, or apply to grad school—whatever could get him back into the country.

The unfortunate thing about knowing someone better than they know themselves is that sometimes you know they are lying before they do. When Paul told me, that day at the station, that he would see me back in Philly, I believed him, and I lived sweetly in this belief until I turned away, at which point I realized on some level that he was not going to join me, that it was over, that I had lost him again. I flew back and, left to his own devices, inertia set in. He overslept appointments at the consulate; he missed application deadlines; he blamed an inscrutable fatigue. He insisted it had nothing to do with me, but when I suggested marriage as a bureaucratic expediency, he was evasive, persistently so, even as he continued to insist that it had nothing to do with me. We kept going for a few months, but the rot of unmatched expectation had set in, and as it grew and spread, it became impossible to ignore. Now, two years later, he had written me an email, which I pored over, conducting forensic sweeps, learning nothing except that he still had the power to upset me.

Farmland flashed by the window. So much of my memory of Paul was associated with trains. He grew up in Toque-Faubourg, a small town or large village, the distinction escaped me, in the French countryside. His parents lived near the station, and whenever the trains passed, no matter where we were in the house, the sound of them filled the whole room. The summer we lived there, we often took the train to the city because there was nothing much to do in Toque-Faubourg. There was one bakery, open three days a week, and one restaurant, which was always closed. So we went to Paris, sometimes with tickets, sometimes saving ourselves the ten euros and hoping the conductors wouldn't single us out for a spot check, and that Paul would be able to charm them into releasing us if they did. Many times we stayed too late in bars and missed the last train and had to wait until the morning, drifting in and out of sleep on cold metal seats under the cavernous fluorescence of the Gare de Lyon, his head in my lap or mine on his shoulder. The train left Paris near dawn, and on the journey home we watched the sun unfurl over the wheat fields. The carriage windows were kept open, and white fluffs of pollen, identical to the kind that filled the air and the drains and made the world ethereal each spring in Beijing, floated in from one window and out through the other side, like apparitions from my own childhood home, overlaying the present with memories of the past, merging the two in a way that made it hard not to interpret the sight as some kind of portent.

In the evenings when Paul and I were not in Paris, we lounged in the grass of the unkempt garden at Toque-Faubourg, which opened up into the forest where so many Impressionists had wandered with their easels, and where Napoleon met Pope Pius VII, who had to trudge through the mud to reach the emperor. We ate bread and cheese and Paul poured amber beer into squat steins for us to drink, tilting the glasses to leave light wisps of foam. What did it mean to have that kind of experience and then return to your elsewhere life, as I did? What if the email meant he was pining too? That he wanted to come back? That he needed me? The idea that I might be able to access those tactile beauties again, might smell the dew on the grass in the early mornings and watch the pink dawn seep through the copse of oaks, my mind alive with the fevered clarity that jetlag gifts, made me so excited that it almost made me sick, the yearning rising in my chest like bile.

I looked to the other side of the carriage, and through the far window the words flashed by in white letters: TRENTON MAKES

THE WORLD TAKES. Did Trenton still make? The bridge that the slogan spanned was a beautiful green Pennsylvania truss, named after the Pennsylvania Railroad, at one time the largest corporation in the world, responsible for almost twelve thousand miles of rail line. The pedestrian lane had close-up views of the interlocking triangles that formed the structure and the backs of the letters of the famous motto. On the New Jersey side was a black plaque with gold lettering that said George Washington stepped out of a ferry there on April 21, 1789, before the bridge existed, to say hello to happy Trentonites before continuing on to New York to be inaugurated as America's first president. The man in the seat in front of me unscrewed the cap on his bottle of Diet Coke, and the gas hissed like a pierced tire. I allowed my thoughts to move on to the contents of my father's most recent voice messages. He said he had talked to my mother. He sent me the name of the town where she lived, somewhere in New Jersey. It was very nearby. But I wanted to assess Paul's email more than I wanted to think about my mother, or how my father had learned of her whereabouts, and why he had told me like this, and how I should feel about the way he was behaving. I couldn't bring myself to be angry at him, because I knew how much he hated sharing bad or awkward news.

I woke Apple as we pulled into Trenton, where we switched to the light rail, which would take us south along the river to Bordentown. If my father's information was accurate, I was now in the same state as my mother. On the rare occasions I did think of her, I used to imagine she had moved somewhere like Zanzibar or Ushuaia. It is easier to believe you have been abandoned in favor of exotic swashbuckling than it is to hear that the maternal apostate now lives in Maplewood, New Jersey. On the left side of the train were the marshes and on the right, an old US Steel site. I wasn't sure if it was still in operation, but it didn't look like it was. Whenever I saw a physical manifestation of decaying industry, which I often did when I traveled around, I couldn't help but marvel at America. In the richest country in the history of the world, there was so much waste just sitting around, taking up space, contributing nothing to national productivity, and it didn't seem to matter: the wealth still amassed. Would America have gotten as far as it did without so much fertile and resource-rich land? The answer had to be no, but now I wanted to pose it to Paul, who had ready-made opinions about everything. Russia and Canada had their endless frozen expanses that maybe global warming would make arable and inhabitable, which would be interesting. I thought of China, of all the desert and barren mountain land that stumped the best efforts of geoengineering, and of the old dynasties that had hewed to the east and left the steppe, for the most part, alone.

It was a short walk from the station to the seminary. I had only a vague plan of what we were going to do when we got there, but I hoped we would be able to roam the grounds unhindered. I had just finished reading a book about the Spanish Inquisition and I didn't feel like talking to any priests. The seminary was located on the former estate of Napoleon's brother Joseph, who had moved to New Jersey after Waterloo. I tried not to think of my mother: St. Helena, NJ. I'd always wanted to visit the estate, which was called Point Breeze when Joseph lived there, like the neighborhood in Philadelphia. Apple was not keen. She was uninterested in pre-twentieth-century history, saying she didn't "see the point." But she came along anyway to Thirtieth Street Station after a morning of flyering outside the Rivebelle. She'd asked me if I was only volunteering to impress Hoang, and I hadn't replied, not because I didn't know the answer, but because I wasn't sure it mattered: if the action was good, surely the motivation was irrelevant.

As we walked, I told her how Joseph had built a mansion on

the site we were visiting, and when it burned down one night, he built another, bigger mansion, which people said was the second-finest house in the country after the White House. Joseph moved back to Europe and died there, and years later an Englishman bought the property and tore down the beautiful house because he hated the French. It was amusing to imagine him acting out his own anti-Bonapartist revenge drama, destroying something that everyone liked, out of spite. Maybe amusing was the wrong word.

"You know," I said, "he offered to switch places with Napoleon. They'd pretend to be each other, and Joseph would surrender to the British, and then Napoleon could have escaped to America. But Napoleon said no. He wouldn't do it. He turned himself in."

"It's a really weird coincidence," said Apple, "that the famous one has the crazy, like, Beyoncé, Cher type name. Like what if he was just called Jake? No one would be referring to him as Jake. Maybe he wouldn't even have been that famous?"

"Jake Bonaparte."

"See what I mean? Oh my god, Pee, it's like me and Steve. Steve is Joseph. I'm Napoleon!"

I changed the subject and asked about Gus. Apple equivocated. She copped to her deception, but refused to explain why she'd lied or how she felt about it now. The question of how he'd found out didn't interest me; it was easy enough to google her name, which made the fact that he hadn't uncovered her lie earlier only startling in that it seemed to delineate another difference between male and female courtship behavior in the modern era. Scouring the internet for morsels of information about a new romantic interest was the first thing any woman would have done, and Gus clearly hadn't done it. I was trying to pare back within myself a surprising flare of moralistic indignation, both because it was very much a glass house situation in terms of me judging Apple for lying and withholding information, and because I suspected I was just being loyal to Hoang, who I essentially believed had been born with a core of incorruptible honesty, and, as if guided by a spectral version of him from which I took my behavioral cues, I wanted to emulate his good qualities when he was not around. I had never had a problem with telling small lies but he seemed so obviously to be someone not only averse to lies, but unfamiliar with their temptation, that even thinking of lying now stressed me out.

The town was extremely suburban, and before long we were passing large bare trees and houses with gable roofs, red-shuttered windows, and big American flags undulating from clipped grass lawns. Apple grew up amid such scenery and was not fascinated like me. She kept her grumbling to a minimum, even when we had to switch onto a larger road with no pedestrian path and hop over puddles, and keep watch for speeding vehicles.

"Remember when the pope came, and they shut off all the streets, and we took those pictures lying down in the middle of the road?"

"I should've asked my mom for her car."

Since I didn't drive, the idea of procuring a car never occurred to me.

"She wouldn't have minded?"

"It wouldn't have been an issue. Are we almost there?"

"Yeah," I said. I looked up from the map on my phone. "All this on our left is the grounds, we just have to get to the main entrance."

I could tell she wasn't in a good mood, because even when I told her Inno had given up on his "*Eat Pray Love* tour," as she'd once called it, to work at McKinsey, her glee was desultory. Possibly it had become a delicate issue to mock now that her own treachery was on the docket.

We turned onto a wide driveway, fields stretching out on either side of the road and trees clustered at the edges of the property. I could tell it was lovely and verdant in the summer, but now it was December, and everything was taupe.

"Do you think they're watching us? From the inside?" Apple said, pointing to a beige building in the distance.

"Maybe. Should we flip them off?"

"Why would we do that?"

"They're all pedophiles?"

"That's offensive."

"Sorry, some of them just cover for the pedophiles."

Apple stopped walking. We were at a parabolic fork in the road, and at the vertex of the parabola was a sign that said PRIVATE PROPERTY.

"You can't just lump all Christians together and say they're evil."

"I didn't. This is a specific critique of the Catholic clergy."

"My parents go to church every Sunday, are they bad people?"

I looked at her. "You're a Baptist."

"So?"

I shook my head. "I can see one. He's coming over."

A man had emerged from the beige building and was walking in our direction. As he got closer I realized he was Asian, and was ashamed to notice some of my hostility ebbing away, disarmed by the novelty of an Asian man in clerical clothing and perhaps also by some atavistic feeling of racial kinship in a foreign land. Maybe he would turn out to be Japanese.

When he reached us my principled opposition faced another blow: he introduced himself as Father Lin. For a nonsensical moment I imagined that here was my mother, reincarnated as a man, a Catholic priest, atoning ineffectually for her sins.

Father Lin told us he was from Taiwan; the seminary gave room and board to visiting priests from all over the world, he said, and he was spending a year in America. I told him my name was also Lin.

"Where are you from?" Father Lin asked. By now we had switched to Mandarin.

"Beijing," I said.

"I'm from here," Apple said in English. She was definitely not in a good mood.

"Her parents are Taiwanese," I told the priest.

"Where in Taiwan?" he asked Apple. "You live in Bordentown now?"

"No, I'm from Paoli, Pennsylvania."

"Her hometown is named after a famous Corsican revolutionary," I said. "Pasquale Paoli. He inspired Napoleon. We're very interested in Napoleon, that's why we're here. We were hoping to take a look around. This was his brother's estate."

"I know," said the priest, "Joseph. He was ambassador to the Vatican, and he negotiated the Concordat. He was a better man than Napoleon. Can you hear that?"

"Hear what?"

"The birds."

There was a cawing, like a young crow, and chirps from something else.

"*Blue jay,*" said the priest. "And *chickadee.* Nothing makes me more homesick than the sound of foreign birds. I wake up in the morning and I have no idea where I am."

We listened. It was pleasant. Vengefully, Apple broke the human silence.

"Isn't it funny that this is Father Lin, but your own father isn't even father Lin?" Apple turned to the priest. "Her dad is a very famous artist in China."

Apple only referenced my father's profession in slightly mocking terms or in the context of a joke, and she never asked about his work, but sometimes I thought she regarded his being an artist as the most interesting thing about me. Apple's secret, guarded passion was painting. Since she was a child she had produced still lifes of the objects in her house—purple-pink geodes, money trees, meat cleavers—on flattened cardboard boxes, using the enamel paints from Steve's discarded model airplane kits. By the time she was in middle school the paintings were nearly photorealistic; by the end of high school, she had developed a way of depicting light and shadow that looked more real than the thing itself, a Taiwanese American Pieter de Hooch. She kept the paintings in the attic until her parents told her she had to clear them out because they were turning the attic into an office. She took photographs of every painting and then threw them all away, even though she could have just moved them into her room. She explained that although her parents hadn't said so, she knew they wanted her to move on. I didn't know if this was true. I saw the paintings once, when she let me swipe through the photos she still had on her phone, that's how I knew how good they were. She hadn't, as far as I knew, painted since.

"An artist?" said the priest.

"Have you heard of Yukon Zhang?" Apple said.

Father Lin shook his head.

"Zhang Yukang," I said.

"Ah, of course!" He gave me a thumbs up. "Very impressive!"

"Thanks," I said. I was stung by his dismissal of our shared name, his positive outlook on my father, and his contention that Joseph was better than Napoleon. "Can we walk around?"

He said we could, and bade us farewell. "God bless you," he said in English, and then he said goodbye in Chinese.

"I can't believe he said that about Napoleon," I said after the priest left, and we began walking again. "But I guess it makes sense. You know the pope excommunicated him?"

Apple didn't say anything, so I tried another topic. "Remember when we were wondering if there were any Chinese soldiers in the American Civil War? I looked it up. There actually were a few in the Union army, like you said, but there were also these conjoined twins who moved to America from Thailand and made tons of money touring the country and showing off their conjoinedness, and became American citizens, and like, settled down in North Carolina and got married and were slave owners with sons who fought in the Confederate army. Isn't that crazy? Also, that's why people say 'Siamese twins.' These guys are the original conjoined twins from Siam, that's where the name comes from, can you believe that?"

Apple ignored me and began to talk about something else, as if picking up the thread of an earlier conversation we had set aside. "You're just lucky, you know. You have moral luck," she said. I asked her what she was talking about. She said I had been born without ambition, which she and Inno possessed, and which meant they had to make unsavory career choices that I would never have to face—not because I had actively decided it was wrong, but because I was uninterested in making money and impressing peers and strangers; nor did I have to contend with parental pressure the way she and Inno did; nor did I have loans to pay off, like she did. I was quite offended by this, in particular what she said about my lack of ambition, but I tried to let it slide. I interrupted her to say that if I was so unambitious, how come we had traveled here to learn more about Napoleon, the most ambitious man in history? She kept going. She said I couldn't accuse her of "selling out"—I hadn't—because she never claimed to "buy in" in the first place. I started to feel that, just as a hallucinatory Hoang floated around my head, telling me to look at the trees and be honest with other people, a ghostly Gus resided in hers, and was listening, from the stands, to Apple's self-defense.

"Okay," I said, "I have moral luck. Do I still have toska?"

"Yes."

"How?"

"I can just tell."

"Maybe you have toska," I countered.

"Maybe. Daylight savings is getting to me."

"Me too."

We reached the edge of the marshes. Across a body of unmoving water, we could see the train tracks on which we had traveled earlier in the day. I was wondering if the sudden vehemence of my anticlericalism, and my willingness to verbalize it, were relics of Paul's influence. He was a vocal and committed atheist in a way that had gone out of fashion in the U.S., but was still common in continental Europe, and he reserved a special hatred for the Catholic Church, as you'd expect from a worshiper of the French Revolution, or, to be precise, of 1793. I was supposed to be channeling Hoang, but was I now channeling Paul again? Either way, it felt better than when I had no one to channel, when there was only me.

"Is this what you were expecting?" Apple asked me.

"I don't know what I was expecting," I said. On my phone I showed her some paintings of the estate in the days of Joseph Bonaparte. She agreed that it looked beautiful. We continued walking, because there were supposed to be tunnels somewhere on the property.

"So are you ever going to tell me what happened after Inno's party?"

I couldn't tell Apple what had happened, or almost happened, in Hoang's room, because I couldn't tell her about the email from Paul. I knew she would be aghast, and disparage him, and monitor me for signs of a relapse, which she would find, and I wanted to relapse in peace. I listened to the sound of her duck boots crisping over the dry grass and the leftover snow that prickled the ground. Because I knew it would cheer her up, I said, "We went back to his house and had some really nice conversations, and then he walked me to the door and then I went home. Also, we ate snow off a railing. We might have hugged, but I can't remember for sure."

"Mm," she said. "Would you be upset if I burst out laughing?"

"Yes."

"Okay, I won't."

I stared at a clump of snow at my feet, heaped like a bowl of bingsu.

"I think we're just friends."

Right away I wanted to take back the "just." What was so bad about being friends? Why did we consider it better to be some-where else on the continuum of interpersonal relations?

"Friends," Apple repeated.

"Friends," I confirmed, believing it now, thinking of Paul and the promise of his email. "He's probably moving to Antarctica."

"Right. Are you going to hook up before he does?"

"Apple, stop."

"You're so repressed!"

"I'm not repressed. I just think some things should be private."

"Can I be harsh for a second?"

"If I said no, would you not say what you're about to say?"

"I think you avoid new experiences and hold on to old ones because you grew up with hippie artist parents, and your mom was a force of instability in your life, so now you crave stability, and never take risks."

"So what?"

"So you agree?"

"Sure. That wasn't even harsh. How is any of that a bad thing?"

"Because I'm saying you've never gotten over your mom's abandonment, and it's holding you back."

"That's not true."

"Yes, it is!"

"But how can it be true if I never feel it or experience it or think about it?"

"I don't believe you. But if that were the case, it would only be proof that you're repressed."

We were standing in front of a small stone bridge, the arches clad with moss and chipped and worn with age. I could feel the old thought patterns revving up, like a tic. Paul hadn't said why he was visiting, or for how long. What if he was moving to the U.S.? What if he wanted to try again? Would he have reached out if he didn't?

"I actually knew about the Antarctica thing," said Apple. "So weird."

"You did? From Gus?"

"No, from Mohd. Is this one of your tunnels?"

"This is a bridge." I paused, absorbing the rest of what she had said. "The mouse killer?"

"The what?"

"Mohd?"

Apple revealed that she had met him at the party in the koala house, which was of course his house, where he lived with the anonymous koala lover. They'd exchanged numbers, but Apple had just begun seeing Gus, whom she prioritized. In the ensuing weeks, though, the memory of her brief conversation with Mohd had returned to her. I asked her what they had talked about, and she said she couldn't remember. She was impressed that she had forgotten the conversation but still retained such a strong memory of him. She admitted that she herself had told Gus how she had been lying to him about her job, hoping it would cause a rift, and while she recognized it was wrong, everything had worked out for the best, i.e., in her favor.

I thought of Gus and his "break" and his "love." Secondarily I felt unnerved by the level of complexity of the subterfuge, and that she hadn't told me about it. Normally she kept me updated before and as events occurred; why was I only finding out about this now? Why, of all people, had she chosen to date men with connections to Hoang? Wasn't there anyone else? I asked if she would keep coming with me to the flyering, and she said she would think about it.

We barely spoke on the walk back to the station, and I couldn't tell if the tension I felt was something occurring between us or my own projection. But on the light rail Apple startled back to life, perusing her Twitter feed and now and then showing me something on the screen: a joke about unprotected sex, something terrible Trump had said, a video of a polar bear inching across an ice sheet on its belly, a picture of the presidents and their wives in the front pew of the funeral of George H. W. Bush, a joke about wanting a sugar daddy, the discovery of a new planet in another galaxy, the appearance of a Eurasian beaver in Italy after an absence of five hundred years. She fell asleep again on the train back to Philly. The winter sun idled above the sharp tops of the trees. I looked at Apple's sleeping face reflected in the window. I felt a sudden tenderness, hearing her susurrate and watching her eyes revolve under her eyelids. Her hands rested in her lap, one clutching her phone and the other, nearer to me, holding nothing. I wanted to reach out and clasp it in mine. I wanted to tell her about Paul, tell her that he was coming back, that he was coming back for me, that the bouts of toska would end, that I was seeing him tomorrow, that I would be happy again; but I let her sleep.

She roused briefly when the train jerked on the tracks, and I turned to her.

"Remember in sophomore year, when we ordered takeout and I called it 'fake Chinese food,' and you started telling me how in

Asian American Studies you learned that Chinese American food should be considered its own cuisine, because it was invented by guys who moved to San Francisco and New York without their wives and made up dishes based on memory, because their mothers weren't there to tell them how to cook it, and they couldn't find any of the proper ingredients? And then I said that was no excuse for bad food, and you didn't speak to me for like two weeks?"

"I stand by that," Apple said, and went back to sleep.

In Chinatown, the streetlamps were on, and clouds glowed in the blue-black sky. There was a letter waiting for me in the mailbox, a short one, written on the back of a grocery store receipt for green apples and spearmint chewing gum.

Penelope,
I picked up your horse book again. I don't know why but the part where he writes about his mother almost made me cry. Crazy how different America was before the Europeans brought the horses over, I always thought they (horses) were here from the start. Zoo this Sunday, meet at the front entrance, by the lion statue!
Hoang

Xinwei was at the standing table, gazing into a bowl of soup. When she saw me she dashed to the kitchen to get me some before I even said hello. It was her herbal chicken broth with red dates, ginger, and goji berries, a winter classic. She served it to me in the bowl Raymond had given her for her birthday, the one with their faces printed on the outside with cartoon blush spots on their cheeks and artificially widened eyes. There was a matching mug.

"It's damp outside! Eat!" Xinwei ordered. "And don't leave the hongzao like you always do!"

The front door opened. It was the third roommate, who had returned from Munich to spend the Christmas season with his parents. He'd meant to surprise them, but upon arriving at his family home, he had discovered that his parents were on a last-minute cruise vacation to Curaçao and would not return until the new year. So he was back for a few weeks; apparently he had been paying for his room the entire time he was gone.

"My Uber dropped me off at the wrong location," he said morosely. "I had to walk five blocks. I witnessed pickpocketing." That was the kind of thing he said instead of hello. Xinwei did not offer him any soup. He went into his room and I asked her if she had spoken to Raymond since he moved out.

"He's saying he wants to marry me now. He realized what it's like to live alone. Now he knows someone was there all along, ironing his socks and cooking his meals."

"Are you going to marry him?" I asked. People ironed their socks?

"Of course," Xinwei said. "But first I will let him suffer a bit more."

"Why?"

"Because he made me suffer."

Through the thin walls of the apartment I could hear the third roommate practicing German on his app. Even to me, it was clear from the sentences he was being tasked to recite that he had not advanced much during his time in Germany. *Fröhliche Weihnachten! Wo ist das Büro? Wieviel kostet das?*

NINE

Paul and I arranged to meet in Tompkins Square Park, about half an hour's walk from the Chinatown bus stop. Almost against my will I had bought the ticket to Manhattan, and I was enjoying the feeling of being once again borne on currents I could not control. It was a Sunday. I had written to Hoang, telling him I wouldn't be able to meet him at the zoo, and hoped the postal system would come through in time. It was the only day Paul was free. I hadn't told anyone I was meeting him: not Inno, who once gave me a copy of Freud's *Mourning and Melancholia* in an effort to fix the state in which the dissolution of the relationship had left me, nor Apple, who I had reason to believe would have physically restrained me from leaving Philadelphia if she found out where I was going. I knew she was wrong about Paul, but the evidence was stacked against me.

He and I had exchanged only a couple of brief messages since I'd agreed to see him, and in the most recent reply, he'd signed off with an old pet name. It augured well for the outcome of our reunion, which I had now begun to imagine I had expected since the day he waved me off at the Gare du Nord. He remained vague about the purpose and duration of his visit, which was characteristic, and therefore not discouraging. In the morning I woke up having dreamt of him the night before, a dream of the encounter we were about to have, and the memory of the dream patinated the city around me: trees recalled it, the pigeons in the air recalled it. I walked to the park, rehearsing the lines I would deliver if everything went the way I hoped it would.

I was early, which meant I could prepare myself for the meeting in the setting in which it would occur, but which also meant I would have to wait. In the park I observed the circumambulations of joggers, dog-walkers, retirees, tourists, and besuited men on phone calls, gesticulating like conductors: people who were not waiting, people unlike me.

I walked three times around the park, and at the end of the third loop, he was there, sitting on a bench with his legs stretched out in front of him, looking at his phone. He had not had his lobes pierced when I knew him, but now he wore a feather earring in one, a stud in the other. He had a canvas tote bag looped around his shoulder. His hair was different, and he was wearing unfamiliar shoes. He stood up when he saw me, and we hugged. His eyes were still blue.

"Hello," said Paul. "You look very nice."

"Shall we take a walk?" I said. Sitting still seemed to me impossible. I felt his hands on my shoulders like stones.

"Yes," said Paul, "why don't we."

He began to talk about a book he was reading, *Sentimental*

Education. He said the English translation of the title was flawed, but he didn't have any idea how he would improve it. He was reading it in English, he said, because when he had studied the novel in school, his literature teacher had been so obnoxious that Paul had avoided Flaubert for years. Now he was trying again, but he could not bring himself to read the version of the text he had been taught. I remembered that his elementary school was named after Victor Hugo and his secondary school was named after Albert Camus, and how I had envied this. My schools had just been numbers: Beijing No. 9 Primary School, Beijing No. 55 Middle School. The trees in the park had no leaves, and their lonely branches cut into the blue of the sky. I was finding it irritating that even in this getup, he was attractive, as if he had tried and failed to spoil his good looks with a bad haircut. I tried to concentrate on what he was saying. He was describing a scene at the end of the novel, when the main character and his childhood friend, now old men, reminisce about the past.

"You shouldn't be telling me this," I broke in. "What if I decide to read it?"

"Will you?"

"Do you think I would like it?"

"I can't answer that," he said. We walked six paces in silence, and then he said, "Yes, you should read it." He started telling me why I should read it. He said I would enjoy the descriptions of the revolution of 1848, which Flaubert based on his own observations. Of course, he added, the man was a reactionary, but anyway it's not as if you—meaning me—would care about that. "Do you still have your Bonaparte fixation?" he said. I said yes, I did. We made a full circle around the park, and when we arrived back at the bench where he had been sitting, he was still talking. I felt a little bored, which was not an emotion I'd predicted I would have in the situation I was in. I wondered when the moment would arise for me to deliver my speech. Perhaps he was waiting to deliver one too—maybe to tell me that he was moving back to the U.S., that he was sorry, et cetera?

Paul said he had passed a bakery on the walk over, and suggested we go there, because the pastries in the window had looked enticing.

"The walk over from where?"

"From where I came," he said, and left it at that.

I asked for a canelé and Paul ordered an entire loaf of sourdough bread. At the till, I couldn't bear his scrabbling in the tote bag for loose change, so I handed over my card to pay for us both. The man at the cash register, who was around our age, made some joke about the new generation where women paid for things. We laughed politely. For the duration of that exchange I envisioned the scene through the eyes of the cashier, who thought we were a couple. We left the bakery, and the error stopped being true.

We sat at the same bench again to eat. Paul was ripping chunks of bread from the paper bag, chewing with vigor, enthusing about the quality of the crust and the crumb. He was making jokes and laughing at mine, he was speaking at what was for him a rapid clip. He was chipper; it was bewildering. He asked for a bite of the canelé, and raved about that too. I thought about asking to try the sourdough, but decided against it.

"You seem kind of different," I said.

"Different?"

"Chattier? Happier?"

He laughed and touched my knee with one hand, very lightly and very briefly, and my body tensed up.

"Probably because I'm taking antidepressants," he said. "Since earlier this year. Isn't that funny? I really feel much better than I did."

I told him I was happy for him, although I had no idea

whether that was true. I wanted to ask more questions, about fifty more, but I didn't know if I would be able to regulate my emotional responses. I suggested we leave the park and walk to the river, and we did, but as the water came into view the thought of it became oppressive, and I told Paul I'd changed my mind and wanted to return to the park. "Okay," he said, and we began to walk. He always acquiesced, that was the danger of him. He tricked you into believing he was an easygoing person, and you forgot about the roiling sea underneath. But maybe that was gone now too. The park was cast in shadow, the winter sun already dipping away, abandoning the world, or rather the hemisphere. The yellow bulbs of the streetlamps suggested warmth, another ruse of light. I was remembering how Apple used to call Paul the worst kind of people pleaser, a covert one. There was the part of his personality that relished provocation, argument for argument's sake. And then there was the part that slunk away from reckonings, that committed itself to lies to avoid having to deliver uncomfortable truths. Apple used to call it a pathology, by which she meant to warn me that he would never change.

It had been almost an hour, and it felt like we had said nothing to each other in that time. I realized that the ambivalence I felt about him taking antidepressants, and improving as a result, was rooted in a sense of proprietary claim. When we were together, it would have been something we went through together, and I would have observed every day of change. I could accustom myself to the idea that, in my absence, he would change, but not to its materiality. Paul wasn't supposed to change, he was supposed to stay the same, and he was especially not supposed to change in ways that, had they occurred earlier, might have meant we had stayed together instead of breaking up. The sun was setting, and the reflected light in the windows of one building pocked the sanded stone sides of another with rhombuses of pale gold. I was still waiting to be overcome by emotion.

We found a bar in which to shelter as darkness encroached. I got a gin and tonic and Paul dillydallied in his familiar way, and eventually ordered a pastis. They served it to him already mixed with the water, and this time it was I who minded, not him, because I so used to enjoy seeing the color of the liquor change in the glass, going from transparent to opaque, and because I wanted to see him pour it, like I had seen him do so many times before. Once we had something to drink, we became jovial, we were bantering, we were enjoying ourselves, helped on by the artifice of "catching up," while underneath lurked everything too painful to say. He was amused when I told him about volunteering with the union, and I became defensive and exaggerated my involvement in response.

"I'm sorry," he said, when he saw that his reaction had irked me. "It's just not something I'd expect you to be doing."

"Inno said the same thing."

"I miss that man. How is he?"

"He works for McKinsey now. He started this week. But he'll quit when he can."

Paul grimaced. "That's what everybody says."

"Well, he isn't everybody. He said he would quit when he makes enough money to—"

"Ah, but they can never make *enough* money."

"Forget it."

I picked up my drink. I was too annoyed to explain about the deworming charities. Underneath my irritation was an unpleasant self-consciousness. I felt, or felt that Paul would feel, that I was fussier and more assertive than I had been when he knew me. I wanted to ask how he'd gotten the visa to come here, but I worried the answer might make me angry, or sad.

Paul said his parents were doing well, and his younger sister would soon graduate from university. I already knew this, because I still had her on Instagram, plus a couple of cousins. I didn't have the heart to unfollow them. I told him that my mother was not dead as I had once speculated to him, but alive in New Jersey. I told him my father had called me while I was on the bus to New York, and I'd thought we were going to discuss my mother, but all he'd done was recount a long story about his most recent psychedelic experience. He never called me when he was high, because I had told him many times that it made me uncomfortable, but he sometimes phoned me the next day to tell me about his epiphanies. The enumeration of ideas and sensations may have felt revelatory to him, but listening to someone talk about their drug trip was like listening to someone explain the plot of a television show you haven't watched and have no interest in watching. At the end of the phone call, I told Paul, he'd mentioned my mother, but only to say that she had stopped speaking to him again, and that he didn't think I should try to contact her after all. Paul laughed and laughed at the story, joked that he wanted to take drugs with my dad. I looked at him laughing with his straight teeth and his five-o'clock shadow and his atrocious feather earring. I had not commented on the feather earring because I was afraid it might be some kind of lover's token, and more than simple jealousy, I found the idea that he could be seeing someone with such bad taste an affront and a disappointment. If it was his own choice that was one thing, but if he was sporting it on behalf of his feelings for someone else, that was much worse.

"It's not funny," I said suddenly.

"Come on, it is."

"Maybe it is, but I don't like you laughing about it."

"Your dad would be laughing about it, don't you think?"

"I guess," I said. I looked at the vesicles of lime at the bottom of my glass, which had separated from the green rind as they disintegrated. Paul's parents were normal. "Let's talk about something else." I said something true but inane about how I didn't understand how anyone could prefer New York to Philadelphia. Paul provided some arguments in favor of New York, even though he had proclaimed his distaste for it many times in the past. This was typical of him, for whom the temptation of contrarianism always outweighed the camaraderie of shared belief.

"I do miss it sometimes," he said. "Philadelphia."

"Yeah," I said. "Yeah, it's the best."

I had the suspicion that the languor I felt as I sat across from him in the dim and congested bar, which by now was filling up with men and women whose hair frizzled with static as they unwound their wool scarves and shrugged their coats off onto spidery leather booths, the languor as well as the minor agitation for something more to be happening, to be feeling something more, was temporary, and would vanish the moment we parted ways, to be succeeded by melancholy, and a painful desire to recover the happiness I had felt when I was with him. But I had not actually felt it when I was with him, so when had I felt it? I had come close in the bakery, but that had been predicated on a stranger's misunderstanding, had only been effective in the brief window in which I could see myself from the point of view of someone who was not myself, and who had all the details wrong. I remembered my speech, the one where I was going to tell him that I had only broken up with him because he'd forced my hand, because I'd hoped it would shock him into action, that at the time it had seemed like the only way to guarantee we might end up together one day; but that none of it mattered now, because now we were older, and maybe we were ready to try again. Then Paul looked at his phone and said he was meeting a friend for dinner, and would have to go very soon.

"How soon?"

"In about fifteen minutes."

"Why didn't you say so earlier?"

"I didn't realize how late it was. I wasn't sure how long we would spend together."

Fifteen minutes, that was nine hundred seconds. It was nothing, and much too long. It would have been better if he'd left immediately, rather than impose the absurd duration, the ticking clock.

"Paul," I said. "Are you moving back, or are you just visiting?"

"Just visiting for now," he said.

The server came by to see if we wanted more drinks, and I asked for the check. Outside it was dark, and very cold.

"So apparently my mother runs this pottery studio in Queens."

"Yes, you told me earlier."

"Do you want to come with me to check it out?"

"Now?"

"Yeah. We can take the train, I looked up the stops."

"I'll be late for dinner."

"Just say you'll be late then. Or cancel. You always cancel."

He gave a big shrug, elbows out, hands in coat pockets.

"I'm trying not to these days."

We kept walking. At one point, I stepped off the curb before the light changed, not seeing an approaching taxi, and Paul pulled me back. He kept his hand on my arm, and as we crossed the road, he ran his hand up my back and squeezed my shoulder, pulling me in. It was so comforting, and it made me feel so desolate. It was like the bakery again, and, like then, it was a lie, and it was ending. I pulled away.

"Who are you having dinner with?" I asked. I felt as if I were being held at gunpoint to say the words, and now I had said them. I knew before he spoke what the answer was going to be, and I remembered how, in the email, he had written, *I miss you.*

"My girlfriend."

"You said friend just now."

Paul sighed. "I know."

After a short silence, he began to talk excitedly about the gilets jaunes, who had been protesting on the streets of Paris for about a month. Paul never gave a justification for anything he did or failed to do, and you'd only upset yourself if you expected one. We were two blocks from the subway. I was very conscious of the diminishing time. Paul said that he was going to have a cigarette before getting on the train, and offered me one.

"You think I've picked up smoking?"

"Sorry. It's a habit."

He took the unlit cigarette out of his mouth and tapped it against his open palm.

"It's made me very happy to see you today," he said.

I nodded. I had nothing I could say to that. He embraced me, and instinctively I leaned into him, and for a while we held each other on the cold and busy street. Then we broke apart, and it was as if we were making eye contact for the first time all day. We looked at each other and saw each other. I recognized myself in his expression, and saw that he saw himself in mine; I felt certain I knew what he was thinking, and he knew what I was thinking, on and on infinitely knowing, like one mirror set against another, an endless reflection, an immanence. For a moment our separate-ness dissolved, and we were the same person; for a moment no one would ever know another so well. But he had an appointment to keep, and he didn't want to be late. He descended the steps to the station, and his shoulders and the back of his head gave no indication of resistance to their departure; he did not turn around.

I headed to Queens. The carriage was quiet, and I studied the map of the five boroughs tacked to the opposite wall. I dis-embarked at Astoria Boulevard and walked to the address my father had sent. All the lights were off, and a sign on the door, which was secured with two bicycle U-locks, said CLOSED ON SUNDAYS, which I already knew, thanks to helpful Google. I pressed my head against the glass and cupped my hands around my eyes to create the darkness that would enable me to blot out the colorful lights of the LED hookah animation across the road and see inside. There were clay vases, mugs, ashtrays, and Willendorfian female figurines on shelves along the walls. There were rows of stools and pottery wheels on wooden tables. There were aprons slumped on hooks and stacks of plastic tubs. There was a framed poster showing different ceramic glazes: I could see jade, pear, plum, frosted turquoise, ancient copper, june bug, merlot. I had not thought I wanted to see her, but seeing the room where she allegedly spent her Tuesdays through Fridays, teaching other people's children to sculpt clay, made me wonder if I did.

I walked back to the subway station. I was beginning to understand that there would never be a thing called closure when it came to Paul. Even now, when time and distance and antidepressants and a different haircut and a girlfriend and a feather earring had rendered him a stranger, he was still the person I loved. Of course I wanted him to be happy, even if I couldn't manage to say it or feel it. All there was to do was live my life without the hope of reviving something that could not be revived in the way I had envisioned. And what the experience boiled down to, a conclusion that strengthened itself in my mind on the bus ride back to Philly later that night, was Hoang. I was sure of it now, as sure as I had been about Paul when I'd left that same morning. Even at the best times, my love for Paul had been a heaviness, an inward turn. I always believed that if I began to fall in love with someone new it would feel the same, perhaps different in its details but identical in its rhythm, its unfolding, its form. But when I thought of Hoang I felt expansive and light, and when I talked to him it cleared my head.

Paul would never tell me in words that it was over, and if I asked him outright he would equivocate, in order, perhaps unconsciously—though I also had to learn that a lack of intent did not absolve—not to extinguish my hope, even if he had no intention of fulfilling it. What had always kept me going was not a belief that he was serving a secret goal hidden in his heart, but the need to understand why he was doing it, and the belief that there even was a reason, perhaps one he hadn't realized himself. Someone who appears to act without self-interest or self-abnegation can be harder to understand than someone who is obviously spurred by an excess of either. As for myself, I liked answers, I liked knowing why people did things, I believed I could figure these things out even if the people in question did not know themselves, and it was hard to accept that I was wrong, that there were things to which I would never be privy, things that concerned me that I would never know; and that even if I did know them, knowing might make no difference at all.

When I returned to the apartment, Raymond was back, and so was the sofa. He and Xinwei were watching a Cantonese drama on his iPad. I went straight out to the fire escape. The inside of the apartment felt too warm, too quiet, too serene. I was in a similar mood to the ones I would get into now and then as a teenager, when I purposely stood outside on the most polluted winter days in Beijing, tasting the acrid air in my nose and throat. If the pollution was bad enough I would actually get a headache after ten or fifteen minutes. In Philadelphia the air was clear and cool, and deep lungfuls of it felt like mint. I leaned against the railing and looked down into the darkness of the empty lot below. On one stair of the fire escape, about level with the monks' upper floor, was a thin orange cushion, and on the cushion, which one of the monks must have placed there for it, was a possum, curled into a crescent, peacefully asleep.

A few days later, Apple and I sat on the floor of her apartment, chewing gummy bears soaked in vodka. They were slimy and turgid with the cheap alcohol, but the vodka itself was hugely improved by whatever chemical sweeteners the bears exuded as they decomposed. I added pineapple juice to mine, but Apple was still drinking it straight. It was one of her college-era concoctions, for when she wanted to save on mixers and get drunk with efficiency. Now she made good money, but the money had not gotten rid of her cost-effective depravity.

"I am for sure freezing my eggs," she was saying. "And I'm not going to wait till I'm thirty-six to do it. That's the mistake everyone makes. I'm gonna do it, like, next year. You should too."

She explained the process to me. It was hugely invasive, time-consuming, and expensive, and it sounded painful. Apple kept using the word "harvesting." I had always imagined, without stopping to interrogate the plausibility of this vision, that they gave you a pill or something and then you plopped the eggs out, like a platypus, into a tube or jar.

"Seriously?" Apple said. "A jar?"

"Not like a Mason jar. Like the ones you have to pee into when they need a pee sample. A hospital jar."

"You need to be thinking about this way more seriously than you are right now. The conventional route takes years. Finding a partner. Cuffed. Engaged. Married. Pregnant. Think of the timeline."

"I don't want to think of the timeline," I muttered. I reached for the bottle of gummy bear vodka. "What if you get to whatever age it is, and you're still single, and you just have all these eggs in the fridge?"

"Sperm bank."

"Alone?"

"You can babysit."

"Maybe I'll have kids by then."

"Some cute little Dinh-Lins? Holy shit, do your names rhyme?"

"Do not start."

I hadn't told Apple about seeing Paul. Part of me wanted her to know, not because I would find comfort in discussing it, but because I felt guilty for keeping it from her. Another part of me saw it as a way to get even with her for not telling me about Gus and Mohd. Maybe it was childish, maybe I should have just told her. Then again, what was there to say? I hazarded an attempt.

"I'm going to tell Hoang how I feel about him."

Apple peered at me over her glass of discolored vodka. "Which is how?"

"Good, I think. Good."

"Still friendly?"

"Maybe more than friendly."

"Wow."

"I think," I said, "I was still harboring some hope about Paul."

Apple's eyes bulged.

"I thought maybe there was still a chance that—yeah. I guess it was always something to look forward to. But I think it was holding me back. And I don't want it to, anymore."

Apple threw her head back and emitted a small scream. "I almost got a hernia when you said his name, holy shit. Take a shot! Take this! Cheers!"

She launched into a long metaphor about how relationships were like M&A, and my relationship with Paul had been a hos-

tile takeover that I insisted was friendly, and what I needed was
a relationship that resembled a merger rather than an acquisition.

"I've actually thought about this a lot," she said. I told her I
could tell.

"So when are you going to talk to him?"

"Maybe tomorrow."

"Why not now?"

"Now? Do you think I should?"

"Oh my god, just go!"

I left her apartment with the intention of ignoring her and
walking home, tomorrow sounding safer than now, but soon I
was crossing incorrect streets, heading to Spring Garden instead
of Chinatown. As I walked, buoyed by the buzz of the gummy
liquor, to Hoang's house, I thought of how I performed a certain
kind of naïveté when I was with him, a guilelessness, and that
it must be a semiconscious imitation of his manner, except that
when it came to him, there was no performance, and that was his
appeal. I had to stop myself from running down the street. How
many months had passed, with him just a few city blocks away
from me—no distance at all, and still too much for me to traverse?
How could I have wasted so much time? And what for?

I rang the bell, and he opened the door almost immediately.
He was wearing a dark green T-shirt, and he didn't have his
glasses on.

"Forest," he said.

"Hey, what's up? How are you?"

"I'm sort of busy right now."

"Busy with what? Too busy to hang out?"

"I'm actually already . . . hanging out with someone."

"Is it Mohd? I was just with Apple. Did you know about them?
Isn't it weird?"

"No, I'm—"

"Speaking of weird, I'm sorry I ran off last week. I wanted—I wanted to—"

He hadn't opened the door the whole way, but he was doing it now, shifting to the side so that I could see into the living room. There was a girl sitting on the sofa, resting her bare feet on the coffee table, looking at her phone.

"Oh, no. Sorry. I'll go."

He stepped forward at the same time that I stepped away. The door clicked behind him.

"Penelope," he said.

"I'm really sorry for intruding," I said. I backed down the steps, my hand on the snowless banister.

"Where were you the other day?"

I stopped. "What do you mean?"

"The zoo. Did you forget?"

"You didn't get my note?"

"I was waiting around for you. I felt like an idiot."

"I sent you—"

"Hey, look, it's okay. It doesn't matter. I don't want you to be upset. But just—you should have let me know, you know?"

"I know," I said. I apologized again. I had the sensation of being showered with shovelfuls of soil, of curtains being drawn. We stared at each other, each waiting for the other to speak, each on the verge of it ourselves. From inside the house, the girl called his name.

On the walk home, I recalled the long internal conflict I'd had about him, wondering how he felt, how I felt, whether we would ever sleep together, how for months I had flitted back and forth between yes, I must, of course I will, and no, I can't, it'll never happen; now I was thinking, you fool.

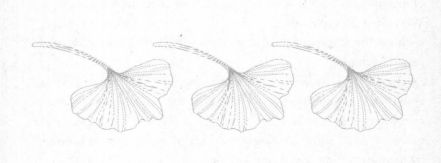

Three

"Penelope," said Dr. Bae, "come in."

Light was streaming through the tall windows of his office, flecking the floor with gold. I sat across from him with my palms on the wooden desk, letting the rays of sunlight make stripes across the backs of my hands. I had just come upstairs from my basement dwelling, and I was envious.

"I would like to discuss the exhibition," he said. "There have been some changes."

"Is this about the Mao quote?" I said. In January we'd argued over the inclusion of a Mao Zedong line about foot binding that I'd suggested we display on one of the walls.

"This is not about the Mao quote," said Dr. Bae. "I thought we resolved that."

"Yes. We did. Oh, the foot?"

His frown deepened. "Foot? What foot?"

"The plaster cast of a foot that I brought here to show you? I shouldn't have taken it out of the storage room. I won't do it again. And we can drop the idea I had about—"

"Penelope, everyone has been very impressed with the initiative you've taken with the Chinese collection."

"Thank you," I said. I turned my hands over on the desk, and the lines of sunlight resettled on my skin, on the life lines, or whatever the psychic had called them, and then used as evidence that I would meet my death in an elevator shaft.

"I want you to know that the new changes have nothing to do with your work," he continued. "There are concerns that the proposed exhibition is not sufficiently inclusive."

"Inclusive of what?"

"We have thousands of other artifacts that, like the shoes, have never been exhibited to the public. Various kimonos, for example . . ."

The museum, Dr. Bae explained, had decided to hold a broader exhibition featuring objects from the Chinese and Japanese collections. The theme would still be women, but there would no longer be a focus on Qing women, or on foot binding. Obviously this meant that I was no longer in charge of anything; I would contribute my small part, and the head curator for the Asian collections—the person who had left the shoes mildewing in the basement for so long—would take over the rest.

Outside, in the courtyard, the ice in the koi pond was melting. I sat cross-legged at the edge of the water and shrugged off my jacket. My relations with Dr. Bae had been frosty for months. I sensed that he didn't trust me anymore, and I worried, beyond the exhibition, what it would mean for my future at the museum. I didn't know how to mend the relationship without addressing the issues that seemed to have derailed it, but I knew bringing them up would not work, because he would perceive any broaching of the topic as an accusation. I felt blurry with defeat.

A bird was making noises in a tree somewhere. I thought of the Taiwanese priest and his contempt for foreign birdsong. Had the birds gone south for winter? Had they already returned? Were they, like me, tricked by the preternaturally balmy February weather?

Soon the cold returned, and people retreated from the parks, and it became harder to disengage Apple and Xinwei from Mohd and Raymond. They were both happy to have me as a third wheel, but I didn't want to be around Mohd in case Hoang came up in conversation, or actually appeared in person, and I didn't want to spend time with Raymond; something about the way he left had soured him for me, notwithstanding the fact that he had returned. Plus, I had gotten used to speaking Mandarin at home with Xinwei, so now it felt like an inconvenience to return to our old trilingual communication style, especially since I had a new urge to exclude Raymond from conversations.

Near the end of the month, Xinwei removed all the Chinese New Year decorations from the doors and walls, because the fifteen days were up. I wanted them to stay, but she was adamant. Once they were gone the apartment seemed gloomier than before, and I found it hard to believe that the days were lengthening, even though I knew that they were. I was demoralized at work after my demotion. When I told my father what had happened he laughed, and said they were doing to me what the Whitney Museum had done to him.

The only part of my life that seemed to have any forward momentum was the volunteer work with the union. It felt a little weird since I hadn't seen Hoang or written to him in weeks, but I also didn't mind, because I realized that it was something I wanted to do regardless of what he thought about it or me.

I wasn't sure when exactly the switch occurred, but it seemed to have happened the way habits form—as a result of repeated action. It felt good to be doing something rather than thinking about it, and to feel tethered to strangers by a commitment I had freely made. Chris started taking me to strategy meetings so I could meet more of the people involved in the campaign and get a better idea of how organizing worked. At the first meeting I attended, we sat at an elliptical conference table and ate fried chicken and iceberg lettuce salad off paper plates, and people went around the room sharing progress updates. The mood was exuberant. The organizing committee of the Rivebelle had gone public with their desire to form a union, and now committee members were wearing union pins and lanyards at work, getting into gleeful confrontations with their managers. They needed to convince more coworkers who were on the fence about unionizing, because there would eventually be a vote to decide. The hotel was trying everything it could to discourage them, giving presentations at mandatory staff meetings about how much better it was to work at a nonunion hotel and referring to the Rivebelle as a "family" that a union would disrupt. The managers were on the lookout for the smallest infractions, which they could use as pretext to fire pro-union employees. One committee member had already been fired for allegedly eating a sandwich outside of his lunch break.

There had been a huge upswing in the number of housekeepers—the largest contingent of workers in the hotel, and thus the most crucial to win over—joining the campaign, after one of them had walked into a vacated guest room to find feces smeared all over the bathroom mirror, bed, chairs, and floor. It was one of the "sustainable stay" rooms. Her manager wouldn't give her extra time or help to clean the mess, even though it was impossible to do so alone in the time allotted by the electronic system, which meant she was penalized when she failed to move on to the next room. Two more penalties would result in an unpaid suspension.

Gus was at the meeting, and I sat next to him. Mariama, one of the housekeepers most involved in the union campaign, was saying that housekeepers had the highest injury rates of all hotel workers.

"So many of us have to take pain medication just to get through the workday," she said. "But there's no medication for dealing with this poop nonsense."

They discussed a coworker who had been fired after a guest complained that some cash was missing from his room, and blamed housekeeping. When the guest checked out a few days later, he mentioned to the front desk that in fact there had been no theft—he'd found the cash when he was packing—but the housekeeper hadn't been notified or compensated, and she didn't get her job back. I found this appalling. I remembered the dentist who, the first time I flyered for the union, handed back the leaflet and said to me, "What do you expect me to do about this?," and how I'd had the same thought myself. It increasingly seemed that the object of the exercise was to convince such people to instead ask, "What can we do about this?"

When Chris was introducing me, he made a joke about how much he had learned about the Napoleonic wars since we met, and everyone laughed. But after the meeting, he said the union needed good researchers, and if I could focus on a topic that wasn't Napoleon or tiny shoes, it was something I should think about. I asked what such a job entailed. He said you had to do a lot of research—on companies, on politicians, on federal and state policy—and write strategy reports and help with press releases. "We could use your crazy brain," Chris said. It was a lovely compliment. I was touched.

Later, I walked my bike to the SEPTA stop with Gus.

"How's that rich guy doing? Still a handmaid of evil?"

"He actually really hates his job. He told me he might quit."

"Tell him his bartender thinks he should too."

We talked about the meeting and the unionization strategy. I asked Gus if he was still an anarchist, and he explained that he was in fact an anarcho-syndicalist.

"If I'm being honest, the union's too top-down for me. I'm not trying to split hairs right now. That's been a big historical mistake. But they're pretty liberal."

"By liberal you mean not left-wing enough?"

"Exactly. They're good people, but it's very hierarchical, and it's entrenched in the status quo. But unionizing is a good start."

"Right," I said. "Are you going to the rally?"

"Of course. The energy is great, and it's important. Good to get everybody together in one place, rehearse for the general strike."

"What general strike?"

"*The* general strike!" Gus said. I had never seen him so animated. "Oh shit, where to begin? Damn it, the bus is here. I gotta get this or I'll be late for work. I'll send you some reading after my shift!"

"Who else is working today?" I shouted after him.

"He's in Colorado!" Gus yelled. I watched the bus lurch away, embarrassed that he had known who I was asking about. Colorado?

I hoped that Gus wouldn't forget to send me his anarcho-syndicalist reading recommendations. Now that Inno barely had time to catch up, let alone read for pleasure and talk to me about it, no one was sending me any interesting books or articles to discuss. I texted Inno, telling him about my conversation with Gus, and asked if he had quit his job yet. He replied with a long voice message explaining that he needed to wait for a while, otherwise he would have to forfeit his signing bonus, which would not be cost-efficient, but that he did plan to quit, and then beg the Potato Park for forgiveness and a second chance. "Please give me good warning if you turn into some kind of anarchist, and I will try to look past your refusal to countenance the *much* more rational philosophy of effective altruism," Inno said in the message. "I must go, but I would like you to know that I am sitting by the pool with my laptop and a perfectly chilled glass of Chablis, carrying out my menial labor, and I miss you very much. Come visit."

That evening, my father WeChatted me my mother's home address, which I had asked him for. Then he announced that he would be off the grid for the next week to take LSD in the Gobi Desert. He said he had hit a wall artistically and needed to rejuvenate his consciousness. In the last voice message he sent before he left, he told me not to tell my mother that he said hello, as in, he wanted me to tell her that he had declined to pass on a greeting. I tried to talk to him on the phone, so that I could accuse him of timing his trip to be out of touch when I went to see her, but he said he had to leave for an appointment with his acupuncturist, and we could talk when he came back.

I read *Sentimental Education* on the train to Maplewood. In the morning I had been too nervous to eat, but now I had spent two hours on the bus to Manhattan and then forty minutes on the train into New Jersey, and I realized as I stepped onto the platform that I was starving. I worried that there wouldn't be anything within walking distance, because it was the suburbs, but there was a pizzeria close by, in a pretty brick building on a corner lot, between a juice bar and a bank.

It was a quarter to twelve and there was no one in the restaurant besides the waiter, a man in his fifties wearing a white shirt with a starched collar and, on the breast pocket, a small pin of an Italian flag. I ordered a dish of spicy rigatoni and thought of my friends as I shook parmesan cheese over the pasta. Recently I had come across a news article about the unseemly things that McKinsey was doing in China and Saudi Arabia and other places. How could it be morally impermissible to eat certain foods, but, as Inno argued, a moral imperative to take a job with such a company in order to donate some of your earnings to charity? Was I naïve for being made uneasy by utilitarian rationale? Was it better to do something sort of shady that you enjoyed and make a lot of money and keep it, like Apple, or do something even shadier that you hated and make more money and give a lot of it away, like Inno? Or was it better to do something neutral but impactless, and make not that much money, and keep it, like me? Was Apple right that I had moral luck? Was it better to say you believed in something and then let yourself and others down, or say nothing, do nothing, believe in nothing? What was it, really, that Inno believed in? Perhaps I should have challenged him more. The waiter came by to check if everything was alright, and I asked him if he knew a woman named Rose Lin, a resident of Maplewood. He said he didn't.

"Rose Williams?" I tried.

"I know a Rose Zhang. She made that."

He pointed at the small white bowl that held the grated cheese. When he left, I picked it up and studied it. The bowl had fine ridges all around its lower half, and the rest was smooth, tapering into a dainty lip. I checked the underside: *r.z.* in childish blue letters, a loose oval around the initials. The oval was imperfect. I could see where she had tried to join the end of one line to the other to complete the shape, and missed. It was this detail I found most upsetting of all. As with some of the embroidery on the shoes I cataloged at work, it was the imperfection that made you realize there was a person behind the artifact. I put the bowl down. Why was she using my father's name? Her legal surname, until she changed it in her twenties, was Williams, the name of her adoptive parents; she had not taken my father's name when they married, believing it antiquated and unfeminist to do so. Rose Lin was how she made sure to introduce herself to the parents of my school friends. That way people knew she had given me her own name, saw in it a matrilineal revolt. Now she had left me with it. What was "Rose Zhang"? Witness protection? Performance art? An elaborate joke? An admission of defeat?

After the pasta, I ordered a panna cotta, and then an espresso. When, on my second coffee, I realized I was procrastinating, I disciplined myself and paid the bill. The house was only a few minutes away from the restaurant. Now and then a minivan slid by, silent on the freshly laid asphalt, but apart from that the streets were empty. I crossed to the other side of the road so that I wouldn't end up directly opposite the house and would be able to sidle up to it at an angle. I already knew from online that it was big and butter yellow, fringed with white. In the version I had seen, there was a yard sign saying REFUGEES WELCOME. I wasn't sure if that was my mother or the previous tenants. The house was still yellow, but the sign was gone, and ceramic flowerpots, reminiscent of the cheese bowl at the restaurant, lined the stairs to the porch. Some were filled with soil and some were not, but nothing grew inside.

I sprinted back to the restaurant, feeling absurd. The waiter was clearing the table. He asked if I'd forgotten my umbrella.

"You know Rose," I said. I was out of breath.

He said that he did.

"What does she . . . what does she get?"

"I'm sorry?"

"What does she order? When she comes here?"

He eyed me. "Are you a friend? A relative?"

I nodded, unwilling to answer that question in words.

"She likes our pizzas. Sometimes she'll get the rigatoni that you had."

"She comes a lot?"

"Yes, I'd say so. She very kindly made us our parmesan pots, and for free, too."

"Kids?"

"I'm sorry?"

"Does she have any kids?"

"No, I don't think so."

He picked up the tray on which he had placed my coffee cup and saucer, my glass of water, and the sugar packet I had torn open but not used. I followed him to the kitchen doors. He told me I couldn't come in any farther, so I waited for him in the dining room.

"Husband? Boyfriend? Girlfriend?" I said when he returned.

"May I ask why you're asking?"

"I'm her—" I stopped. Why was it so hard to say daughter? "She's my mother."

He studied me. "Rose is your mother?"

"Yes."

"She's never mentioned a daughter."

"Yes, I know, you said."

"And you're here to visit her?"

I nodded. The waiter took off his glasses, wiped the lenses on his apron, and put them back on. It made me think of Hoang. What was he doing in Colorado?

"But you know that she's not here," he said.

"She's not?"

"She's in California, I think for an arts festival."

"I didn't know that," I said eventually. How did he know so much? Was this a particularly friendly town, or was my mother a particularly friendly person? Had she, like Paul, become a better version of herself after leaving me?

"The truth is, I was adopted," I said. "She's my, my biological mother. I was coming here to surprise her. That's why I don't know anything about where she is."

It was a lie, but it felt metaphysically true. My mother was adopted, and she abandoned me. All the constituent parts were there. All I had done was jumble them around.

"Oh," said the waiter. "Oh, I see. I'm so sorry. What a shame."

He asked me if I wanted to leave a phone number or an email address, and I told him it was fine. He looked like he was about to insist, but he stopped himself. He asked if he should tell her I had come. To say no would be to deny myself something I wanted very badly, but to say yes risked knowing, if I did not hear from her, that she did not care about me. I told him I would leave it to him to decide.

I thought I would head back to the train station but found myself walking again in the direction of the yellow house. When I came within sight of it, it had all the dimensions and aura of a normal house, indistinguishable from its gray and white neighbors. Now that I knew it was empty, it had lost the creepy magnetism it had earlier possessed. I walked up the porch steps and stood on the bristly welcome mat, and then I pressed the electric doorbell. "Für Elise" pealed through the house. The first-floor curtains were drawn, but gauzy, and through their film I could make out living room furniture in neutral colors. On the coffee table was a copy of the *New York Times*, open to the crossword page, a white bowl filled with coins, and a bamboo hairbrush. The very last time I saw my mother, she was standing in the bathroom of our apartment in Beijing, shaving her head with my father's electric razor. This was right before the release of the paparazzi photos of Britney Spears shaving her own head, and when that happened everyone at school was laughing about it, and no one could understand why I became so upset whenever the subject came up.

That day, I got home from school and found her in the bathroom, naked, her long hair dripping wet. She sometimes listened to xiangsheng to practice her comprehension of Chinese, and it was blaring so loudly that I heard it in the hallway before opening the front door. She was aping everything the comedians were saying, high pitched for one man and low for the other, but shouting, like she was trying to drown them out, and speaking directly into the mirror. She saw me in the reflection and asked me to fetch some scissors. When I didn't move right away, she banged her hands on the sink and said, "Now! We can't waste any time! They'll come for you, too!"

I stood in the kitchen for a long time, unsure of what to do. I opened a drawer and stared at forks, spoons, and chopsticks. My father had removed the knives months earlier. I opened another drawer and found the blunt kitchen scissors, wrapped in a dishcloth, perhaps as a disguise. Eventually she came in, after she had called my name and gotten no response. She said, "Why are you crying?" I shrugged. She told me to stop crying. She said, "Great things are coming, but not if you act the way you always act." She spotted the scissors, which I was holding to my chest. She said, "Oh, good, you found them." She took them from me and walked back to the bathroom. I followed her. Again I looked at her looking at herself, and marveled at how alien she seemed, how easy it was for someone you loved to shut themselves off from you, as easy as closing a door. I could tell she wanted me to say something in protest, like she was daring me, and if I spoke it would render her triumphant somehow. She crackled with a malicious, frightening energy. She seized her wet hair in one fist and moved it into the mouth of the scissors. She paused for a moment, measuring the violence, and then lopped it off. When she was done, she turned and offered the scissors to me, blade first. "Will you help me even out the back?" I shook my head, and she said, "I told you not to act the way you always act. But I knew you would." That was when she spotted the electric razor and decided to forgo the bob. If not for the bamboo hairbrush on her coffee table, a banal object in an assortment of banality, I would not have wondered, standing on the porch of her empty home, what her hair looked like now. I thought of my conversation with the waiter. *I'm her daughter.* A sentence I hadn't been able to say, because I did not feel like I was hers.

The liquefied natural gas plant bloomed into view. After we passed it, the Meadowlands: tiny lakes moated by reeds and brush, and the Hackensack River, a thick gray ribbon. From the upper level of the bus, at a certain angle, the road became invisible, and it looked like we were coasting on the water. Suddenly I felt warmth, and I could hear murmurs from the other passengers over the voice of the narrator of my Napoleon podcast. On the opposite lane of the highway, now only a few feet ahead, a large truck was stationary in the middle of the road, and it was on fire. We zipped past, and my face burned. The flames were a virile orange, wet and opaque, and the air around them was glassy with heat. We left the burning truck behind. The drivers of the cars closest to it were filming on their phones. Behind them, more vehicles slowed and stopped, joining the jam. In *Sentimental Education*, Arnoux, short on cash, opened a pottery factory, but he couldn't replicate "the copper-red of the Chinese"—the color vanished from the surface of his pots when they went into the kiln. The bus sped on. I wondered if my mother and Paul were in cahoots, except I could not guess their collective aim, besides making pottery an unbearable subject. When I thought about them together like this, as an abstract collective, it all made very little sense to me—why were there people I loved so much, whose approximate locations I knew, but who were not in my life? Sunlight flicked through the bare trees. If, the next day, I bought a plane ticket to Beijing, sat for thirteen hours, disembarked, pressed my thumbs into the scanner, queued at immigration with all the foreigners and my American passport, hailed a taxi, and gave my father's address, I would see an identical scene from the window of the cab—the skeletal husks of the poplars in winter and the weak sunlight whisking between them, racing like a horse alongside the cars, slowing as we slowed. Outside the air would smell wonderfully of coal and inside the taxi it would smell of cigarettes and sweat.

The trees made me think of Hoang, of his misleading tattoo. I tore a blank page from the end of the book. Gus had clarified, in between reminders to read the links he sent to Emma Goldman, Lucy Parsons, and Bakunin, that Hoang had taken some time off work and not, as I feared, moved to Colorado. I traced the "H" of his name over and over with my pen as I thought about what to write. I wanted to apologize again. I dreaded that he was vacationing with the girl from his living room and struggled not to imagine them on a romantic road trip together, camping under the stars, observing beautiful sunsets, touching each other, and so on. I was failing in my struggle not to imagine it. In the end, I made no reference to our last meeting.

Hoang,

Gus told me you're in Colorado, I hope you're enjoying it there. I don't know when you're back, but tell me when you are. I'm writing this on a bus. I just tried to go see my mom, but she wasn't home. I haven't seen her since I was thirteen. Maybe it was good she wasn't there. I think I wanted mostly to see her expression when she saw me. I've been trying

to conjure it, the expression more than the face, if that makes sense. I
have an outdated idea of her face, but I wanted to see emotion on it.
I wanted her to be stricken. Now that I'm writing it out, I remember
feeling that way as a kid. She said smiling and frowning would give her
wrinkles. I remember specific occasions when I made her smile, that's
how rare it was. I always just wanted her to react to something with her
face . . . which sounds weird but I don't know how else to put it. I guess
I was thinking that seeing me today could have been surprising enough
to make her

I stopped. It was like I had forgotten I was addressing Hoang
and started to write a diary entry. I tore out another page, copied
down the first two lines of the letter to send to him, then shoved
the first piece of paper to the bottom of my bag.

The scenery became uninteresting on I-95. We passed a long
single-story white building. PREFERRED N SERVICES, it said. We
passed some kind of business park with dark brown windows and
Toyotas and Mitsubishis parked out front. Next to the cars was an
area of grass, and a very small pond. We passed a long gray building. AMAZON FULFILLMENT CENTER, it said, and then up ahead
I saw four deer grazing on the side of the highway, clustering
around the tufts of weeds that sprang up between the road and
the chain-link fence. We passed the deer. I looked at my hands,
prone in my lap, and then up at the window again, where now
there were no more deer. I concentrated on the trees flickering
against the road and the flat fields beyond them and tried a difficult mental exercise I attempted sometimes. I tried to imagine
what the land had looked like before it looked like this. I looked
until I could make myself see what it might have been like before
the highway, before the parking lots and storage facilities and the
land cut up into invisible parcels of ownership. There would have
been hills and forests and streams and there would not have been

boundaries, and the deer would not have had to avoid the cars on the road to get to the grass they wanted to eat, or to roam, and there would have been many more of them, and they could have raced to the other side of the continent if they liked, no highways or cities or toll booths blocking their way, or they could have stayed right here, and right here would not have been called New Jersey.

"Siri, what's my phone battery?" the man next to me said to his phone.

"Fifty-six percent," said the female voice. Unbidden I thought: I have heard the voice of this software more than I've heard the voice of my own mother. I didn't know if that was true now but I knew at some point it would tick over into being so.

Maybe what I had to accept was that sometimes you loved someone and there was no reconciliation. Sometimes you loved someone but there would never be a place for them in your life, or for you in theirs, and that was that. Of course, because you loved them, it seemed as if there had to be some magical solution to this problem of not fitting in each other's lives, but there wasn't. You loved them and the love didn't end, and maybe they even loved you back, and, notwithstanding those details, you were bound to remain apart.

Near the state border, crossing back into Pennsylvania, we passed a cemetery where all the headstones were embedded flat into the ground, and vases of bright flowers stood upright. A man driving what must have been a mower, but looked like a quad bike, bumped up the slope between the graves, and the wheels kicked up dirt and grass. I couldn't see how he avoided running over the headstones and the flowers; maybe that was an unavoidable corollary. Four lanes across, behind a tall fence, schoolboys played lacrosse in neon vests. Small brown birds whirled in the air, making shapes out of nothing, and then alighted on the telephone wires in perfect rows. Their flight paths and landing spots seemed predestined, like guided missiles. I wondered how they knew where their place was on the wire and if they ever got it wrong and landed on another bird, or missed, or stepped on one another's toes. I wondered if it was right to call them toes. It was always a relief to see the Philadelphia skyline come into view, even if I never spent any time in those tall buildings. As we crossed the Benjamin Franklin Bridge, I craned my neck and tried to count the sky-blue suspension tines.

Back in Chinatown, the soothing smells of wet-market water, vegetables and fish, street grime, and dried conch. In the vestibule, the scent of cloves. Xinwei was grading papers on the couch. I asked her if there was any mail for me, and she said there wasn't. I asked for the key.

"Postman comes once a day," she said.

"I know, but can I have it anyway?"

"Are you waiting for something?"

"No."

"Then why are you always checking?"

Raymond was elsewhere, so we spoke in Mandarin.

"There's someone I talk to, but he doesn't have a phone, so he sends me letters," I said.

"Boyfriend?"

I shook my head.

"Then?"

I decided to give her an abridged version of events. It was possible that because of my mood, I painted myself as the victim of the story, but unconvincingly, because when I finished telling it, Xinwei was unimpressed.

"I don't think you've considered how he might be experiencing this situation," she said.

"What do you mean? That's all I consider!"

"You wonder whether he likes you back, how he feels about you, but you're not really thinking of how he sees things."

"I don't understand."

"You're trying to guess what he thinks, but from your perspective, not someone else's."

I was astonished, because this was how I characterized Apple's way of thinking about other people. Was I only as self-aware as Apple? It was an alarming thought. Xinwei was still speaking.

"You say it's hard to understand how he feels, but to me, he seems clear, while you're giving mixed signals. Wouldn't that make him more cautious?"

"I don't—"

"You feel your feelings and then wonder what's correct based on that. But men do the opposite. They try to understand the situation and then they decide how to feel. You want him to be overwhelmed by emotion for you, but he won't act until he has the emotion. Maybe he likes you, but he won't think about it until he understands the situation. Or he liked you, and you rejected him, so now he's moving on. And you should have gone to the zoo. It's disrespectful to change plans without warning."

Later, on the fire escape, I looked through the photos I'd taken at work. One object that was no longer appearing in the exhibition was a shadow puppet of a girl with bound feet from around 1900, one of the ones I'd hoped to use for an interactive performance. I thought it was funny that the rods were attached to the arms of the body of the puppet, and the legs didn't move, because it meant they were purely ornamental, like bound feet themselves, which sacrificed function—the ability to walk—in order to signify beauty. According to the slip of paper attached to the puppet, a man named Walter Barr donated it to the museum in 1932. The typed description didn't even mention the bound feet, I suppose because they were a given. It read:

shadow puppet of a girl from a respectable family. Black hair in braided bun. Black chemise with orange lotus flower pattern. Red pants. Teeth.

An email popped up on my phone: it was from Paul. He wanted to tell me, again, that it had made him happy to see me, and he wanted me to know that he would be back in New York in the summer if I wanted to "see one another again." Regarding our last meeting, he conceded nothing. He never spoke frankly, only in abstractions. "I sensed a desire to relitigate trials and perhaps selfishly evaded its fulfillment" was a sentence he had written. What? He also included a link to an article about the gilets jaunes that he wanted me to read. This was why I'd had to block him on everything—not because he had done anything especially egregious, but because if I let him, we would just keep talking, and it would go on and on, and it would never stop meaning something to me, and what it meant to him would always be a mystery. I looked at the email for a while. There was a time in my life when I was incapable of leaving Paul unanswered, when the very thought of doing so caused me distress. What a pleasure it was to betray one's past self, I thought, and then I pressed delete.

The next day, I allowed myself some time to recover from my stressful and unfruitful excursion to New Jersey. Raymond and Xinwei were visiting relatives, so I had the apartment to myself. In the morning, as she and Raymond were preparing to leave,

Xinwei asked me if I had slept well, "Because your skin looks very gray." I told her I had slept fine, which wasn't true, and she said she knew that I hadn't eaten dinner or, it appeared, breakfast, and that this was the cause of my gray skin. She instructed me to eat; I placated her with promises that I would.

When the doorbell rang around two in the afternoon, I was sitting on the floor, resting my head against the seat of the sofa and staring at the ceiling, listening to the 1981 recording of the *Goldberg Variations*. Through the peephole I saw Apple, frowning in her Canada Goose parka, her eyes obscured by the thick coyote fur trim of the hood. I let her in and then returned to my position on the floor, hoping to reenter the semi-meditative state into which I had lulled myself. Apple stood over me, coat still on, eyebrows raised, inspecting.

"Are you on drugs?"

"No."

"Pining for mouse boy?"

"No!"

I turned off the music and remained on the floor. I was weighing whether or not to tell Apple about my mother, imagining how she might react, what she might say. I decided I didn't have the energy for such a conversation.

"Have you eaten?"

I shook my head.

"Were you planning on it?"

I shrugged.

"I can make you something. And by something I mean like tinned sardines and rice. Maybe a fried egg if you're lucky."

I nodded, looking into Apple's familiar face, the pursed lips, the perpetual arched brow, the thin chin and cute plump cheeks that she hated to have pinched.

"Pee, are you okay?"

"Yes," I said. "All good."

I hauled myself off the floor to demonstrate that all was good, only to be engulfed by lethargy and flop onto the sofa.

"Dude," Apple said. "Toska."

She shrugged off her jacket and went into the kitchen. I listened to the fridge door open and close, the clatter of the loose-hinged cabinet doors, the click of the stove spark and the whoosh of the gas. I wondered whether Apple had inherited her brisk caretaking from her mother, through blood or experience. I remembered at Thanksgiving when Apple's mother had cut a pineapple after dinner and, finding it slightly unripe, brought out salt and told us to sprinkle it over the fruit so that it would be sweeter, and would not singe our tongues.

"Did Xinwei tell you to come here?" I called over the kitchen noise.

"Can't hear you!" Apple shouted.

After some more sputtering and cursing, she set a plate on my lap. Rice, sardines, and a fried egg, as promised. She handed me a pair of chopsticks.

"Thank you," I said. "Looks great."

She scrolled her phone while I ate. After a while she said, "Xinwei did tell me to come over. She even told me to heat up the leftover rice. I didn't know she had my number. I had no idea who was calling, so I didn't pick up the first few times. She has a very abrasive voice."

"She's just unselfconscious."

Without looking up from her phone, Apple said, "Do you think she's like a replacement mother figure for you?"

I stopped chewing. "Why the hell would you say that?"

"What? You're the one who's always going on about how you feel comforted when she scolds you for drinking the wrong soup or whatever."

"My mother was never like that."

"But that's what I'm *saying*, she's—"

Apple broke off, perhaps seeing the look on my face.

I read what Gus sent about the general strike. I was skeptical, but it was rousing. I read more of *Sentimental Education*. The protagonist's cynicism about revolutionary change, his emotional detachment from the political passions of others, felt very much like reactions I understood, but they also made him seem a little sad, and this made me wonder about myself. My father returned from the Gobi Desert, repentant, and called me in the middle of a weekend morning. I told him what had happened.

"Do you want me to tell her you went?" he said.

"I thought you weren't speaking to her anymore."

"I'm not. I can get Fei to tell her."

"Don't worry about it," I said. I was lying on the floor of my bedroom, balancing the phone on my forehead, staring at the ceiling.

"It's probably just as well," he said, "I don't think she's changed."

"What do you mean? She's still . . . ?"

"Hm. No. She's taking lots of medications. But she's not," here my father paused, "remorseful. She has no explanation for it. She definitely has no apology. And that's what you want, right?"

I said, "I don't know."

He cleared his throat. "With her condition, and the medicines she was taking, it can affect the memory."

"So?"

"That *incident*." He was referring to the last time I saw her; he had always referred to it in this way, with the English word, as if to distance himself from it. "I don't know if she remembers. I could be wrong."

I closed my eyes, and the ringed ceiling bulb transformed into a hazy green lozenge, multiplying in the blackness, and studded with other, imperceptible colors, like amoebas under a microscope slide.

"Why did you have to tell me about her?" I whispered. "Why did you have to tell me she was here?"

"You always told me I shouldn't keep things from you. Now I'm telling you things and you're unhappy?"

"Don't you see? Now I know that she knows I'm here. I can't pretend she's in the desert, or on the moon, or dead. She's so close, and she knows how close I am to her, and she doesn't want to see me. She's fine without me, and now I have to know that, forever."

"I'm sorry, Niuniu," my father said, using my childhood nickname. I could feel liquid tickling my ears. I wiped my face and sat up, suddenly furious. The phone dropped into my lap. I stared at it, waiting for my father to say more, but the other end was silent.

"I have to go," I shouted at the phone. "Goodnight, goodnight, goodnight."

At the union office I helped glue hundreds of posters to hundreds of sticks of wood for people to hold up at the rally. As we glued, I asked Mariama about the woman who had found the poop in the room, and how she was doing.

"She is fine. That day, she came to me and said, 'I cannot do this, because I know who I am.' Good for her. It wasn't even her section."

Then Mariama began to tell me, after I prodded, more about herself. She said she used to take night classes at the community college because the U.S. didn't recognize the accounting degree she had from Mali. But her housekeeping shifts never ended on time—she would be scheduled to work until half past four, but most days she didn't finish until eight or nine in the evening—so she kept missing classes. If she missed a certain amount, she would lose her financial aid scholarship, but she couldn't leave work early, because then she would lose her job. So she dropped out. She had teenage twins, she said, a girl and a boy.

"Do you think I should talk to my daughter about all that?" Mariama said.

"About what? The union?"

Mariama laughed. "No. You know. All *that*. How did your mother talk to you?"

"Oh," I hesitated. "She wasn't much of a talker."

Mariama nodded. "Chinese culture is quite conservative."

"Yes." I patted a poster dry and set it aside. "Exactly."

"My mother would always be direct with us. It was rare. To be honest, I liked it. Maybe I was a bit embarrassed, but I loved her for talking to us as adults, not as children." Mariama started to laugh again. "And now I do even more, being a mother and feeling how hard it is to do the same!"

She asked me if I had any advice on parenting a teenage girl. I worried she thought I myself was a teenager, and could help because of this. I told her I couldn't think of anything specific but from the way she described her daughter, I was sure everything would work out.

"What you say is too good to be true," Mariama said gravely. "Any daughter of mine is bound to be a handful. I remember how I was at her age, hence why I worry."

I asked her if she thought mothers and daughters emulated one another at different stages of life, and she said yes, they undoubtedly did. She said when her daughter was a toddler, Mariama's mother was constantly telling Mariama how similarly she had behaved at the same age.

"And you?" Mariama said. "Did you act the same as your mother?"

"Oh, I don't know," I said. "I hope not."

"How come?"

"I just mean, I don't really know what she was like. When she was younger."

Or now, I thought, or ever, but it didn't seem worth bringing up. Mariama asked me if I had a boyfriend, if I wanted children. I said no, and yes, one day.

When I got home, Xinwei told me something had arrived for me in the mail.

"It's something that will make you happy," she said, and stuck out her tongue.

I found the postcard on my bed. The picture showed sand dunes, and snow-capped mountain peaks rising in the background behind them. On the other side, it said,

Penelope,
Finally got my license so I figured I had to drive somewhere far. I'm in a tent in Colorado, flashlight in my teeth writing this. It's so cold & the stars are all over the place. I should be back in March. Thought of you this morning when I jumped into a freezing lake, the water was like fire, I never felt so alive.
Hoang

ELEVEN

The union was finalizing plans for the big rally. There had been a last-minute change of location from Boston to Philly, and getting all the right permits in time had been difficult, but now there was a laid-out route, and people who worked at Bonaventure-owned hotels all across the East Coast were going to attend. The national president of the union was going to make a speech, as well as hotel workers who were on strike, and maybe even the mayor. When I arrived at the office I asked if Mariama was around, but Chris said she was at work. I had a box of longjing tea I'd promised to bring her.

"I'll get it to her," Chris said. He opened the lid of the tin. "Smells like grass."

"Nice, right?"

"I guess," he said, looking dubious. "Hey, since you're here, you wanna help me with something?"

"Flyering?"

"No, not flyering. You seen the *Inquirer* today?"

He showed it to me. He actually had a physical copy of the newspaper. Taking up a third of the front page was a story about Bonaventure, something about a credit union. I took the paper to read it properly.

"You can study up later," Chris said. "We gotta stock some shelves."

He told me, as he drove us somewhere in his car, the backseat of which was filled with newspapers still trussed in their pre-dispersal twine, that the *Inquirer* had just published an investigative report on Bonaventure's "predatory lending practices." For the past two years, the article said, the company had aggressively flogged a credit union to its employees, telling them they would save money and gain access to better mortgage interest rates and car payment plans. Many workers had signed up, only to be charged an alarming number of fees: monthly fees, transaction fees, penalty fees for a low-balance account or an inactive account or overdrafted account. Overdraft protection fees, to avoid the overdraft penalty fees. The credit union also offered loans, and many people had taken them, including many at the Rivebelle, because after Bonaventure bought the hotel, the new managers were erratic about scheduling shifts, which meant people ended up making less money than they had before and needed extra cash. The loans had pretty steep application fees—$50 for a $400 loan, for instance—but not everyone felt they had much of a choice.

"They say the credit union is independent, but every single person on the board is a Bonaventure executive," said Chris. The *Inquirer* article laid all of this out, comparing the Bonaventure credit union fees to those of credit unions all over the country, showing that they were substantially higher, even compared to other hotel groups. It listed those in Bonaventure's upper management who had gotten multi-million-dollar mortgages from the credit union, and used that to illustrate the informal two-tiered structure that existed, where wealthier executives benefited from favorable policies while poorer employees were bogged down by charges and penalties and driven further into debts they could not pay. The journalists had spoken to Rivebelle employees who, under condition of anonymity, because they feared reprisal at work ("You know some of them," Chris stage-whispered in the car), had described feeling trapped by the lending program they'd hoped would pull them out of dire financial straits; worst of all (from the perspective of hotel management), the article ended with a quote from one anonymous employee who compared the system Bonaventure had established with the credit union to the practice of sharecropping.

"They're mad as fuck over that line," said Chris. He was pulling into a parking space about fifty yards from the entrance of the Rivebelle.

"Wait, why are we here?" I said.

"This morning I had a hunch. An inkling. So I checked. And I was right."

"About what?"

"They emptied out every 7-Eleven, every Wawa, every newsstand in a five-block radius. They must have known it was coming and sent people out at the crack of dawn to buy the papers up or something. So I started restocking. When I got hold of all these, I was walking into stores like I'm on a paper route and dropping them off. Easy. Except," he crouched low in his seat, "then I learn from everybody that's on shift today that all the daily papers for the hotel arrived as usual, *New York Times*, *Wall Street Journal*, and what have you. Except no *Inquirer*. Not in the lobby, or the lounge, or the rooms. And that is where you come in, Napoleon. I need you to go in there and plant these truth bombs."

"Me? Alone? Why can't you come with me?"

"I'm a suspicious character," Chris said. He pointed at his face to indicate his skin color, and then, which also seemed pertinent, at his bright red T-shirt, emblazoned with the name of the union and a cartoon fist raised in the air above the word: STRIKE!

"And I'm not?"

"No. You're incognito."

"I am?"

"You are. And now it's time to go behind enemy lines."

I allowed myself a couple extra spins in the revolving doors before walking into the hotel. It was afternoon, and check-in time was over, so the lobby was quiet. I carried two plastic bags, a bundle of newspapers in each one, and more papers in my backpack. The handles of the plastic bags were slipping back and forth in my hands because I was sweating so much from the stress. I felt like I was trying to rob a bank, with Chris waiting outside, engine ready, and me inside, about to have a panic attack.

The lobby was easy. I spotted the newspaper rack right away, tucked between empty sofas, far from the reception desk. I slipped a bunch of *Inquirers* into the empty shelf where they were supposed to be and then stuffed some more behind the other papers and magazines. But Chris had said the lobby wouldn't cut it. He wanted me to go to the executive lounge, which was on the thirtieth floor of the hotel. To postpone the terrifying task I went to the bar, where I knew Gus would be on shift, getting ready to open for the evening.

"Lychee martini?" he said when he saw me. I was tempted, but I shook my head. I explained the situation to him, and his eyes lit up. He told me to put one newspaper on every table, and asked for some extra to keep behind the bar, "just in case."

"Chris is a legend," he said.

"Do you think I still need to go to the lounge then, since you're gonna have them here?" I said. "Probably not, right?"

"Oh, definitely. That's important. That's where all the VIP motherfuckers hang out."

As the elevator doors dinged open on the thirtieth floor, I received a text from Chris:

u need a key card to get in the lounge chill for a sec n crystal will come get u

Waiting for Crystal was torturous. I tried to reassure myself that there was no way I could go to jail for this. But couldn't I?

Finally Crystal arrived. She cackled when she saw me.

"I knew there must be something hot in that paper!" she shrieked.

She said she was the one who normally stocked the executive lounge, and when she'd asked her manager where the *Inquirer* was that morning, because some guests said their deliveries hadn't come, he'd told her he didn't know what she was talking about and then ran away, "like a dog."

"After you, madam," she giggled as she pressed her key card in. "Good luck!"

The lounge had floor-to-ceiling windows and a sweeping view of downtown Philadelphia. There was no one inside. I flung newspapers onto tables and bar tops, stuffed them into Taschen shelf fillers, slipped them between copies of the *Economist, Town & Country*, and *Philadelphia Magazine*. The door beeped. I whirled around, praying it was Crystal. It was not. It was a man in a suit. I had no idea whether he was a guest or the general manager.

"Hello," I said.

"Hello," the man said, after some hesitation.

"Welcome to the lounge?" I tried.

Curtly, he nodded, and moved toward the refreshments. He poured himself an iced cucumber water and picked up a mango parfait in a shot glass: a guest.

I scuttled out of the room with my empty plastic bags. As the elevator closed I could see, through the glass door of the lounge, the man in the suit settle into a leather armchair, straighten out a copy of the *Inquirer*, and begin to read.

At work, we were preparing a booklet for the exhibition. I was to contribute a short essay on foot binding, and I submitted a draft I was pleased with. When the head curator sent it back to me, he had rewritten it to such an extent that at first I assumed it was someone else's work. He had also removed a section of which I'd been especially proud, which explained that not only did women bind their own feet, but very often it was older sisters doing it to younger sisters, mothers doing it to daughters, mothers-in-law doing it to daughters-in-law. Why were mothers mutilating their daughters? And why did those daughters grow up and do the same? Who was making them do it? Why, I had written, did mothers choose, over and over, to cause their daughters pain? I intended the questions to be rhetorical, to help visitors think about the abstraction of social control, but the curator said the language was too emphatic and might be upsetting. I tried to talk to Dr. Bae about it but he claimed he was too busy to meet. We had once gotten along so well, back when he told me about his days observing waterfowl. It annoyed me that I couldn't correct what I considered to be a misunderstanding between us, but more and more I thought that the fault lay in his behavior, not mine, and began to feel retroactively defensive of the failed and future unions he thought I had been championing, and suspicious of the museum's commitment to the wretched "underserved" and its institutional judgment in general. Maybe they had been rash to let me lead the exhibition, but they had also been wrong when they struck me from it. It was something I could do, I knew that, and I would have done it well.

Between the demotion and Dr. Bae antagonizing me, I found I was caring less and less about my job performance and the impression I made at work. I began behaving in ways that, for me, were tantamount to acts of open rebellion: I came in late, left at five on the dot, and idled as long as fifteen minutes past my allotted lunch hour. One day, as I indulged in this latter activity in the museum cafeteria, slathering a bagel in cream cheese and eavesdropping on the physical anthropologists at the next table as they lamented the sexual aggression of male baboons, I noticed a sniffling sound. I turned to see what it was; it was Annalisa, sitting alone at the table behind me. We made eye contact, which meant that it was too late to go back to my bagel and pretend I had not noticed her. I asked if she was okay.

"Louise and I broke up."

"Who's Louise?"

"Luis, Luis! My Uruguayan boyfriend!"

I told her I was sorry. Our conversation at the base of the sphinx came back to me: the dirty frat house, his mother's perfume, the sense that it was meant to be.

"Wait, are *you* crying?" Annalisa said in a tear-muffled yet still disdainful tone.

"Am I?" I rubbed my eyes. "Sorry. It's just sad. What happened?"

She told me they had gotten into an argument about whether or not Luis was white (she said he wasn't, he said he was, or maybe the other way around), which then spiraled into a bigger argument about their compatibility and their future together. He said some hurtful things about her inability to speak Spanish and she stormed out of his luxury student housing. It was a difficult story to follow. I didn't really understand why they had been arguing about whether he was white, or how this had led to their breakup. Mostly I was glad that I was no longer in college. By the end of her story, it transpired that they were probably going to get back together, and had been sending each other semi-detente texts throughout the day.

"I thought I was going to have to get back on fucking Tinder," Annalisa said. "Can you imagine?"

"I'm glad you're okay," I said.

"Yeah." Annalisa narrowed her eyes. "Are you?"

"Me? Of course."

"You're acting weird."

"I don't know what to tell you," I said. I finished my bagel and went back to the basement to catalog some more shoes.

After work, I finished reading *Sentimental Education* on the fire escape of the apartment, because the third roommate, who seemed to have returned for good, was eating McDonald's again. At the end of the book, the protagonist, Frédéric, after spending his whole life chasing a married woman and half-assing various jobs, is sitting with his childhood friend Deslauriers, and they are recounting their shared past. They linger on one incident from their adolescence, when they try going to a brothel for the first time. Frédéric is nervous, and the girls in the brothel laugh, and he runs away. He and Deslauriers agree that the best time they ever had, their fondest shared memory, was this: one in which they had not even achieved what they had set out to do. It was the scene Paul had started to describe the day I met him in New York.

I wondered what he had wanted to say about it, but not enough to reach out and ask. I went back inside and placed the book on my shelf, next to the Frank O'Hara anthology and the concise guide to North American trees. I picked up the poetry volume and opened it to the random page in which I'd slipped Hoang's most recent postcard. Could he be in that tent in Colorado with the girl who was in his house? Would he have written such a message if he was? The poem under the postcard was *To the Harbormaster.* I began to read it.

I wanted to be sure to reach you;

It continued. When I came to the last lines, I flung the book across the room. Seconds later, there was a knock on my door. It was the third roommate.

"Hello?" he asked me, as if I had called him.

"Hello," I said.

"I heard a noise."

"And?"

"I've never told you this, but sometimes you can be quite disruptive."

"Sorry?"

"When that loud friend of yours comes over and tells her stories on the fire escape, I can hear—"

I slammed the door without saying anything. I retrieved the book and returned it to the shelf, patting its cover by way of apology. A moment later, my phone buzzed. A new text from an unknown number:

clark park at 9?

The trolley exited the underground station into a world of darkness and snow. I got off at the corner of the park and found Hoang on a bench, reading a book under a large leafless elm, squinting to make out the words in the dim light of the streetlamp and the moon. The snow had quickened its pace, and close to an inch of it laminated the ground.

"Forest!"

He dog-eared his book, and I saw that it was *Great Expectations*.

"You have a phone now?"

"I had to, it was getting impossible to schedule my shifts. My manager would always be texting Gus or Danny, and they were all getting really annoyed at me."

"Why didn't you say anything?"

"I kind of liked the thing we were doing."

He took the phone out of his pocket so I could see. It was an old Nokia he had found in a drawer in his grandmother's house in North Philly.

"I think I used to play Snake on one of those," I said.

"I got Snake!"

He let me play for a little bit, but I kept eating my own tail or smashing into the wall.

"I swear I used to be good at this."

"You've been living like a prince with your touchscreen. No calluses."

We started to walk farther into the park.

"Wait, but how did you get my number?"

Hoang laughed. "I asked Gus if he had it after a union meeting and like five people offered to send it to me. I'm like the only person at work who didn't have your number. Mariama loves you, by the way."

I asked him why he was reading *Great Expectations*, and he said he had made a promise to an old man he met on a mountain in Colorado.

"He was talking about Dickens and I told him I've never read any Dickens, and he made me take this, he told me it was his only copy and he was expecting it back. He wrote his address inside so I could mail it to him with a review of what I thought, because then that way he said he'd know I actually read it."

He showed me the address. It was for a Bernard who lived in Penzance. Hoang said they started talking because he saw Bernard wandering the hiking trail, looking lost, and asked if he needed help. Bernard said he was an amateur geologist and was searching for a specific type of rock that he'd never seen before. Hoang spent a few hours helping him look for the rock, and when they found it, Bernard embraced him and shook his hand.

"He didn't take the rock—I mean you're not supposed to— but he didn't even take a picture of it or anything. He just looked at it, and it made him so happy. And then he went home. Isn't that great?"

We reached the edge of the bowl. The bowl had once been a pond. Now it was a shallow crater in the middle of the park, grassy in the summer and snowy now. From a certain distance away, in the daytime, its curves had a distorting effect, akin to an optical illusion, or, from what I gathered through my father's exhaustive accounts, like taking a low dose of a psychedelic drug, just enough for things to shimmer and move.

"I wish we had a sled," said Hoang.

"Me too."

"You know this is where I used to release all the mice."

"I remember," I said. I began to walk down the slope, using small steps so I wouldn't lose my footing, and Hoang followed. We stopped when we reached the center.

"When I lived here I liked coming to the park and lying down in this exact spot, because you can't see any buildings from that angle, just the sky and the trees. And if you tried really hard you could pretend you were in a field in the middle of nowhere."

I hadn't planned on telling him that, because it was something I used to do with Paul, but once I said it, I realized I didn't care. I kicked the ground. Snow spurted and fell.

"We should do it," Hoang said. So we lay on our backs and looked up at the ceiling of the sky, watching our breath condense into fog in the air above us. The tree trunks were dark against the clouds, which were suffused with the light of the city, but all of their branches, from the boughs to the tiniest twigs, were white with snow. They looked like icicles, like glass crystals you could take a bat to and smash in one swing. With some of the thicker branches, the wood was still visible, pencil-thin, vein-like. I thought of the embroidery on the bound-feet socks in the museum, the ones that looked so immaculate and so heartbreakingly homemade, that so arrested me because I thought I sensed the presence of their maker.

I told Hoang that Philadelphia was the first place in the country to build a pneumatic tube system for sending mail, and the object they chose to test out the tube was a Bible wrapped in an American flag. The mail traveled so fast it was almost like instant messaging, and that was more than a hundred years ago. The network of tubes was still underground today, but nobody used it anymore. Hoang said if they brought it back he would throw away the Nokia phone, and I said I'd throw my phone away too.

"You do love throwing your phone," he said.

"Yes. So. Why did you go to Colorado?"

"I've never seen the desert."

"You went alone?"

"I went alone."

"Why so suddenly, though?"

"I told you how I'm trying to go to Antarctica, right? It's because I want to see the ice and the southern lights, you know, the aurora, down there it's called aurora australis. But I've also always wanted to see the desert, and I thought I should see it before I went to Antarctica. I got worried if I didn't then I wouldn't appreciate all the ice as much because I'd still have this older wish to see the sand. I don't know. Does that make sense?"

"I guess," I said. "Actually, not really."

"I just didn't want to leave it unfulfilled."

"Don't you think some desires are better left unfulfilled?"

"No, definitely not. Do you think that?"

"Kind of, yeah. Like, maybe it gives you some forward momentum? And sometimes things are better in your head than they turn out to be in real life?"

"Maybe," he said. "But real life is pretty great."

I told Hoang I wanted to quit my job, and he asked me what I wanted to do instead. I said I didn't know, but I wasn't worrying about it, and he said he thought that was a good way to look at it. I was too shy to admit I wanted to work for the union, too self-conscious of his "truer" connection to it than mine. We lapsed into silence. I was enjoying the snowflakes arriving and dissolving on my nose and forehead and cheeks. Again I had the feeling I'd had many times before with him: an urge to share more, or a wish that he already knew more. I wanted him to know about my narcissistic father and my invisible mother and my distant friends, and I wanted him to tell me about his feud with Mohd and his grandmother in North Philly and his childhood grief. I wanted to know what he did with all the hours of the day he wasn't bartending at the Rivebelle or camping in the wild in Colorado or talking to me.

"Look," Hoang said. He pointed to a ragged cloud floating above us. "Five fingers. Like a hand. And look." He gestured to a bright dot in a gap between two of the cloud fingers. "Do you see that? It's moving. Maybe it's a shooting star."

"I think it's a plane."

"Let's just say it's a shooting star."

I looked for the plane and saw it in the same spot as a moment before, and realized I was wrong and he was right. It was a star, though not a shooting star. It was the cloud that was moving. We watched it slip across the sky, watched as it dimmed the moon, obscured it, then revealed it again, slowly, the light spilling out bit by bit until it returned.

"Eclipse," I said. We were so close that the fabric of his coat rustled against mine as he breathed. Turning to look at him felt like something that required a gargantuan will. My arms and legs felt jittery and weak. I sat up quickly.

Hoang raised himself on his elbows, watching me. I felt over-charged with energy. I looked away.

"Hey, I forgot," he said, after a moment. "I brought you something."

"You did?"

"Yeah. Bread."

"Bread?"

"From the restaurant. Danny gives me the extra after service sometimes. It's really good."

He sat up and reached for his bag. There was snow on his back, and I leaned forward to brush it off. "Thanks," he said, smiling over his shoulder. He held a small baton of bread in his hands. He tore it in half and handed me the larger piece. I took a bite, but my mouth was so dry that it was hard to chew.

"Let's walk around," I said, barely getting the words out.

I felt weak, almost dizzy. We walked back up the slope. I saw a lamppost and moved toward it, mesmerized. The cone of illumination made by the light was alive with motes of snow, falling diagonally in the air, appearing out of nowhere and then vanishing as they passed the boundary into darkness. I leaned against the post and looked at Hoang. He had a new look on his face, a look I liked. He moved closer to me, into the warm ring of light, his brown eyes incandescent in the tungsten.

"You're like, looming," I blurted out.

He stopped, moved back.

"I'm looming?"

"Not looming. Sorry, I didn't mean, like," I swallowed. "Looming. I don't know what I'm saying."

I wanted to kick myself. The tension had become unbearable, but now it was gone, all the energy was gone.

Finally he said, "You confuse me."

"I confuse you?"

"You're confusing."

"I'm sorry."

"It's alright."

I felt trapped. We had established, over the course of our interactions, a way of communicating that seemed to preclude other, more conventional, perhaps more direct ways, and now that we had established it, I didn't know how to revert to convention. And I couldn't get the image of the girl at his house out of my head.

"We should probably head back," he said.

"Yeah," I said, even though hearing him say it made me feel, ridiculously, like crying. I warded off the impulse. I almost never cried, but recently it felt like that was all I was doing.

I looked out into the street, in the homeward direction, east. It wasn't that late, but the weather had kept people indoors, and Baltimore Avenue was quiet, the trees weighted with snow, the trolley tracks wet and glinting on the dark road. A squirrel sat on a fence, holding its hands to its chest, watching us through its huge blank eyes.

"You don't want to keep hanging out?" I ventured.

"I don't know." Hoang said. "Penelope, do you?"

"Of course I do. I love hanging out with you."

He opened his mouth to speak, and then closed it. He gave me a look that could have been described as beseeching, or exasperated. He walked in a tight circle around me, taking big strides. He walked to the lamppost and put his hand on it. I followed him. I put my hand on the lamppost as well, just below his. He looked at my hand and then looked at me, and then he removed his hand from the lamppost, and I removed mine too.

"Okay," he said. "Can I say something that's true, but that might be weird to say? Sorry, that's a weird way to start. Okay, okay. There have been moments when we're together where I felt—where I felt like I should kiss you. Like just now. And, I don't know, it seemed like you wanted me to kiss you too, but then it seemed like you didn't, so, yeah. I don't know. And you, like, show up at my house really late at night, asking if I want to hang out. Normally that means—I mean, you know what it means. I'm not annoyed, I'm not. I'm really glad we're friends. I'm not saying, like, yeah. It's just been getting kind of confusing, you know?"

"Hoang," I said, "I—"

"What? What is it?"

I had stopped speaking, and I was staring beyond him. I shushed him and pointed. "Can you see that? Am I imagining it?"

Peeking out from the bushes, its black eyes twinkling, was a very small mouse. There was something attached to its ear.

"Holy shit, that's my boy," Hoang said. He started to laugh, and I did too. I realized that some small cynical part of me had reserved judgment on the mouse story, had wondered whether it could really be true. Because it seemed too good to be true. When we looked again, the mouse was gone, scared off by our noise. But we had seen it. It was true.

We walked down Baltimore Avenue. I recognized that it was now my turn to speak, that I had not yet responded to him, that every second of delay might be damaging. But I could not think of what to say. Of course he had been about to kiss me; I had known it up to the moment I ruined it. It was like my brain had short-circuited and made me think there was no way it could really be happening, no way that Hoang of all people would want to kiss me. But I was also almost afraid of it happening—afraid it would break the spell, that the lead-up would always be better, that there would be a feeling of deflation. I'd felt that before with other people, even with Paul, and I didn't want to feel it with Hoang.

I remembered the night he told me about his family, and weighed this fact against the Hoang I knew, or at least the one I'd observed; his warmth and humor and lightness, his unforced optimism. I wondered if it was something he often talked about, if it was something that preoccupied him when he was alone. I began to understand Apple's frustration whenever I declined to talk about my mother. Maybe he tortured himself about what had happened; maybe he was at peace with it, and never thought about it; maybe, like me, he was somewhere in between. Was there a way to ask? Now wasn't the right moment; if I continued my silence, there wouldn't be one again.

We walked past the museum, and then started over the South Street Bridge. At its middle point, I stopped walking, and said, "I didn't mean to be confusing."

He didn't say anything, so I continued to talk.

"I just finished this book where this guy is remembering how when he was younger he went to a brothel with his friend, but then he feels like all the prostitutes are laughing at him, so he chickens out and runs away. But then at the end of his life, thinking back, he says it's like, his happiest memory. Even though the only thing that happened is that he didn't do the thing he wanted to do. I guess because he was scared."

Hoang ran a hand through his hair and gave me an incredulous look.

"Am I the prostitutes in this story?"

"No! Kind of? Honestly I don't even know if I understood the book correctly, it's pretty dense, and it was an old translation . . ."

"Penelope," he said again, instead of Forest. "Why do I feel like I'm torturing you? I just—like I said, I'm glad we're friends. I don't know if I understand what you want from me, but I don't want to feel like I'm torturing you. I really don't like how that feels. I'll see you at the rally, okay?"

I looked over the side of the bridge. Snow was falling into the river and disappearing into its eddies.

"Yeah," I said. "See you there."

TWELVE

On the day of the rally, the sky was blue. It had rained the night before, and the morning air was bracing and cool. When the sun came out it was balmy, but when the wind and the clouds picked up the cold came back quickly. We kept pulling off our sweatshirts and then pulling them on again, shivering and sweating in five-minute turns. Cherry trees were bursting into flower all over the city, their pink and white petals drifting earthward, where treading feet crushed them into a mulch that lined the sidewalks in pale dirty hills.

When I found Gus and Chris in the crowd of red-shirted people that filled Independence Square, I saw that Apple was with them, holding hands with Gus. When he left to talk to a coworker, I asked her what had happened to Mohd. Even she, for once, looked a little sheepish.

"He's cool," said Apple, "I just think I'm too basic for him. You know he doesn't vote?"

The mood in the square was lively. They were blasting the Rolling Stones and people were dancing as they waited for the first speaker to go on stage. Someone threw me a red T-shirt, and I put it on. The plan was to march up to Rittenhouse Square, then make a loop back to where we started, passing City Hall on the way. There were thousands of people, and they had come from Pennsylvania, from Boston, from Delaware, from Ohio, from New York. I said hi to Chris, and told him I was skipping a party at the museum, a quarterly fundraising drive that my boss had told me I needed to attend.

"It's happening now?"

"Yeah."

"Like right now?"

"As we speak."

"Then why aren't you there?"

"I don't know. I don't like big events."

Chris laughed. "You're at one."

I spotted Hoang a few meters away, talking to Mariama and Danny. I waved, and he waved back, and I was shot through with a current of pleasurable pain. The president of the national chapter of the union made a speech, and then a city council member made a speech, and then Crystal, who was emcee for the day, introduced a group of workers from the unionized hotel in Boston, who were also going to speak. This was exciting, because they had just ended a sixty-day strike after management acceded to their demands, so they were very much the ideal of what the Rivebelle workers could achieve.

A young Latina woman made the first speech, and she spoke in Spanish. After a few seconds, Gus started translating for us under his breath. I was shocked by his apparent fluency.

"She says they get triple pay for overtime now, because of the strike. Wow. She's talking about what it was like during the strike." Gus hooted. "Oh, fuck yeah. So she's a housekeeper, and apparently when they were on strike the managers had to clean all the rooms themselves, and were like running between the different hotels in Boston trying to get everything done. She's making fun of them because they took like four hours to clean a single room, when the housekeepers do eight or nine rooms in the same amount of time. Oh man, they had to bartend too!"

She finished her speech, and an old Asian woman toddled onto the podium. She wore a bucket hat over her perm and the red union bandana tied around her neck like a scarf. Someone lowered the mic for her, and she wrapped her hands around it, coughed, and began to shout in Cantonese. I looked around. It was a very multiracial crowd, but there were comparatively few people who looked like they could understand Cantonese. It didn't seem to matter. She spoke with force, and whenever she paused, everyone took it as a cue to shout and cheer. Apple started filming on her phone, saying that we could find someone to translate for us later, which gave me an idea. I texted Xinwei, and when she responded, I called her and put her on loudspeaker, holding my phone up to my ear and motioning for Chris and Gus and Apple to crowd around.

"It's so loud!" Xinwei said. Then she started to translate.

"I've been working at this hotel for thirty years and they treat me like I'm . . ."

"Dude," Gus interrupted, as the crowd cheered, "we can't speak Chinese."

"That's the whole point of this exercise," said Apple.

"Oh, wait, right," I said, "she's translating into Mandarin."

We decided that I would listen to Xinwei and then translate what she was saying into English for everyone else. I had to press my phone against my ear to hear anything.

". . . My husband is eighty-four years old. [cheers] I'm seventy-one this year. [cheers] He needs more than ten different medicines, and we don't have secure health benefits. [uncertain cheers] How can Bonaventure treat us like this? [cheers] Thirty years in one job, and they can't even give us this?"

Here we paused, because she had paused, and the crowd, sensing the indignation in her last few sentences, and recognizing the word "Bonaventure" amid the foreign sounds, was roaring louder than ever.

"We were resolute. [cheers] We didn't give up. [cheers] We said we would keep striking until we succeeded, and we did! We won! [cheers] We won, and you here in Philadelphia can do the same! [cheers] So don't give up! [cheers] We won! [cheers] We won!"

"Gus," I said, "how come your Spanish is so good?"

"Gotta be able to talk to los camaradas, dude."

Apple rolled her eyes. "My god," she said, but she couldn't suppress her smile.

After the speeches we headed to Market Street and then turned west. The outdoor tables of restaurants and cafés were jammed with people. They watched as we came past. Some took videos on their phones, and one or two whooped or clapped, but mostly they just looked. We passed two Asian girls around the same age as me and Apple, clinking mimosa flutes with two guys. Apple nudged me in the ribs.

"See that crew of Kevins and Vivians brunching over there?"

"For someone who claims to want a normal name, you make a lot of fun of people who have them."

"Yeah, yeah, see the girl in the Ray-Bans? The one vaping? We went to school together. She's the one who made everyone call me Scrapple."

"But you love scrapple."

"I know, that's why it was so traumatizing. They turned it against me."

It was a huge crowd, and we were chanting, and in between the chanting, inside the swell of people that swept down the car-less avenue, we were talking to the people beside us, introducing ourselves to strangers, shaking hands as we walked. And everyone was doing the same thing. I understood a little more of what Hoang had meant about community, about already being something, and how that made success seem inevitable. I could hear Gus telling Apple about the theory of the general strike. I could see Mariama's bobbing head and what looked like her two teenagers on either side of her, linking arms with their mother. I caught up with Chris for a moment, and he told me again that the union was hiring campaign researchers. I promised him I would apply. I had no idea where within the thousands of participants we were located, no idea where Hoang might be. We must have been near the middle, because I couldn't see where the procession began, nor its end. Someone had a trumpet, and its raucous blare sounded in short happy bursts. When we passed City Hall, I shook Apple's shoulder, and she said, "I know, I know, it was the tallest building in the world, taller than all the churches, so tall, so crazy . . ."

I said, "Tallest *habitable* building. You have to specify, because of the Eiffel Tower."

After the march ended, Apple and Gus disappeared somewhere

together. Everyone else dispersed quickly too; the workers who had come in from other cities had long bus rides ahead of them, and most of those from Philly had to go straight back to work. I spotted Hoang in the thinning crowd. His black hair glinted in the sun. He was wearing basketball shorts, and I noticed that he had beautiful calves. I ran up to him and touched his shoulder. I was worried he might be standoffish after the last time we saw each other, but his face relaxed into its usual smile.

"Look," I said. "Listen—"

No words were coming into my head, but he was looking at me, listening, like I'd told him to. It was enough of a sign. I put my hand on his chest, and stood on my toes, and kissed him. The spell didn't break. When I stepped back I was smiling, and so was he.

"It just felt too perfect," I said. "The other night. I know that sounds insane."

"It doesn't sound insane."

"Really?"

He pulled me in and kissed me again, his arms around me, pressing me closer.

"I mean," he said, "maybe a little."

We walked without aim, past rowhouses, gas stations, fast-food outlets, construction sites, blossom-strewn streets. Everything was luminous. The puddles on the street looked brighter, like disks that each contained their own sun. We passed a huge empty lot where a woman was walking a terrier in a blue coat, and a few kids were throwing a basketball around.

"This used to be a chocolate factory," Hoang said.

"Really?"

"Since like, the eighteen hundreds. My best friend in elementary school lived around here. I loved visiting him because the air smelled so good."

"When did they tear it down?"

"Pretty recently, I think. It's kind of sad. Chocolate air for a hundred and fifty years, and now it's going to be a bunch of fancy apartments." He shrugged, and we stopped to consider the empty space, which smelled, now, of nothing in particular. "At least they're letting people use it before they start construction."

We stood there for a while, watching the kids play basketball.

"So," said Hoang, "I got that job in Antarctica. They emailed me last night. It doesn't start for a few months, it's winter there, but I think I might spend the summer—the normal summer, our summer—in Vietnam, since I have this passport now."

"When would you leave?" I said.

"Maybe August, or July? I want to see this through first. The union. I mean I don't know where it'll be at by then, but I'll be back eventually either way."

I nodded, and tried not to dwell on the fact that July was very soon, and eventually was far away.

"Do you want to head to the river?" I said.

"Let's do it."

We started walking north, parallel to the Schuylkill, searching for a good point to cut in. As we waited at a stoplight, I realized that because of the rally we were wearing the same shirt, like those Chinese couples who only ever went around in matching outfits. When the light turned green, we stepped across the road, and Hoang put his arm around my shoulders. He was humming.

"Are you excited about Antarctica?"

"I am, I am. I'm excited about everything. I'm excited to fly on a plane."

His excitement was contagious. It was strange: the despair I had anticipated I would feel upon receiving this news, which I had sensed was coming, had not arrived. Being around Hoang, I had somehow integrated his worldview into my own, and his was this: everything

is great, and everything will be okay. Maybe that was an oversimpli-
fication. But it seemed to me that it was what you had to tell yourself,
what you really had to believe, if you wanted it to be true, or become
true one day.

We reached the banks of the Schuylkill, where there was a thin
strip of park and a running trail, and huge boulders on which
people sunned themselves with their eyes closed and their T-shirts
balled up as pillows. The new towers and their attendant cranes
hulked over the water on the other side of the river.

"Philly and Antarctica are kinda far apart," Hoang said.

"Everywhere and Antarctica are far apart."

"I'll send you postcards from there. And from Vietnam. How
cool will that be?"

We sat in the grass. A swallowtail landed on a pebble very near
us. Its wings were pale yellow.

"Sometimes you look at a butterfly and you just know he used
to be a caterpillar," Hoang said, and I laughed out loud. I thought
of all the things I hadn't known half a year ago—the way he held
himself, the way his face opened up when he was talking to a
stranger, his eyes bright and trusting because he was never suspicious of anybody; the way he hummed or sang under his breath,
but never whistled; the way he made me hopeful, and a little
more brave.

"That night you showed up at my house," Hoang said, "I was
like, whoa."

"You must have thought I was so weird."

"A little," he said. He was smiling. "But not like, 'Oh, she's
weird.' Like, 'Oh . . . she's *weird*.'"

"I can't believe you're leaving," I said. I was thinking that one
year might as well be one hundred, it seemed so long. At the same
time, though, I felt certain everything was great, and everything
would be okay.

He tucked a loose strand of hair behind my ear, and I turned to face him, surprised by the gesture.

"I still have a little while," he said.

We lay down in the grass. It was soft, and it smelled like spring, fresh and clean in the warm sun. All around us, the park bristled with life. I could hear the newly leafed branches of the trees moving in the wind, making their whooshing sound. Black cherry, box elder, birch.

Acknowledgments

Special thanks to Iwalani Kim, Drew Weitman, Nneoma Amadi-obi, Janet McDonald, Delaney Adams, Rebecca Munro, Chris Welch, Ingsu Liu, Elizabeth Riley, Lara Drzik, Daniel Finkel, Colin Lodewick, Michelle Fang, Stephanie Zou, Jessica Zuo, Cressida McKay Frith, Navya Dasari, Michelle Mao, Mike Bird, and my family.

There was a partial eclipse over Philadelphia in 2017, not 2018. I know, I'm sorry—I wanted an eclipse!